The Last Whippoorwill

"I dreamed I heard that Whippoorwill sing.
She sang my song and called me by name. . . ."

Lyrics by Blackberry Smoke

You almost never see them, the whippoorwills. They rest on old autumn leaves for camouflage, blending so perfectly that the only evidence of their existence is their haunting cry on bright, moonlit nights. It is said that they coax in the new season and then urge away the summer with their last call, which promises a new spring in the coming year.

To my great-grandmother, Lucretia Etherton Amos

To my grandmother, Ethel Cora Amos Martin

The Last Whippoorwill

Mary Bryan Stafford

ISBN-10: 1507736606
ISBN-13: 978-1-7321682-0-6

Published High River Ranch Press

Library of Congress Control Number: 2015901532

This is a work of fiction. Although some characters and incidents are based on historical records, the work as a whole is a product of the author's imagination.

Acknowledgements

To Cindy Antolik, Robert Holt, Myra McIlvain and David Wilde of The Novelcrafters, my critique group, along with Paula Rogers who encouraged and needled me into making the book better. To my daughters Elizabeth and Rachel who read and reread, vetting the pages to keep me on track and accurate. To my great-grandmother Lucretia who with relentless determination struck out for East Texas and my grandmother Cora who told me the story, except all the parts I made up.

Chapter One

Mama and I always had our differences. My brothers maintained that we were too much alike—an assessment I found ludicrous. I would be a grown woman before I came to understand how accurate their perception was. We *could* agree, however, that she bulldozed through our lives and never more so than that August of 1900 when I had just turned eight, and Papa lay barely cold in the grave.

Those last months of summer, Mama seemed even more upset than when Papa died. It lurked in the tone of her voice, the twisting of her hands and the impatience that colored every demand she made of us children.

To illustrate her perversity, one evening she fixed Sunday dinner on a Friday night and made peach pie, but then turned around and sent Annie Laurie, Nannie Bee and me straight to bed after we ate. Oh, she promised a surprise the next day, but I alone seemed to find the whole situation suspect.

Later that night, when the delicate snores of my sisters began, I rose and touched my hand to Amazing Grace, the border collie who had shadowed me day and night for as long as I could remember. Bunching my nightgown into a wad, I slipped to the bottom of the stairs and crouched in the shadows watching Mama unfold and smooth a paper flat on the kitchen table.

Before she told us girls anything, she always told Ben and Joe. They were nineteen and sixteen, respectively, and considered themselves men. "Cousin Frank sent me this letter," she said to them. "There's a small farm near his place down in Ladonia, Texas. He sent a map." She leaned forward and jabbed at the paper with her finger. "It's black soil, he says—a good living."

Those words and the soft scraping sound the paper made as she slid the letter across the table are what I remember most. That and the long silence with nothing but the smell of fried chicken lingering in the air. All else muted except the rasp and tick of the clock's pendulum. Such a simple phrase—*Cousin Frank sent me this letter*—but it changed everything.

Then her voice took on that certain tone. "It's been nothin' but heartbreak here in Missouri."

"I know, Mama," said Joe, "but it won't always be this way. Will it, Ben? We just didn't work hard enough. Give us a chance."

It must be terrible if Joe felt so upset. Joe who always believed that there was one good bite left somewhere in a rotten apple.

Before my brothers pieced together the fragments of the riddle she put before them, she said, "My grandmother was a wealthy woman. She gave each of us a fair amount of money—to put aside in secret for emergencies. This is my emergency. So I've bought that land in East Texas. It's good cotton farming, and we're the ones going to be doing it."

For a second there was dead silence. Then Ben stood, and his chair crashed to the floor. He wrenched away from her outstretched hand. "You have not thought this through, Mama. This is crazy. You can't—"

"You overstep, son. I can and I have. A wagon train leaves from Springfield the second week in September. And we'll be joining it."

Joe sat there, his mouth open. "Why, Mama? Why would you give up on everything Papa ever dreamed of?"

She stormed through the front door, the screen banging behind her. When she charged back into the kitchen, she slammed a rock against the fireplace. "I will not spend my life with blisters on my hands and my shoulder to a plow that turns up nothing but rocks. And neither will you if you're smart. It's my decision and it's in the best interest of this family." Mama stared at my brothers whose lips were pressed in tight, bitter lines. She turned to the fireplace and picked up the rock she had thrown against it. Placing it in the center of the table, she said, "Remember this rock. Take it with you if you like. Plant seeds on it. Shed your tears on it. Pray for it. But it will never change. What it *will* do is remind you of what we left behind when that first cotton crop comes in from the black soil of East Texas."

A look of defeat passed between my brothers. Of course, they would do what she wanted. Even they could be intimidated by her and her cast iron will.

Mama folded the letter, smoothing each turn until it formed the size of a seed packet. "It's the start of a new century. Times are changing. Women are changing, too. I'm doing what I think is right. And you are coming with me."

I had worried about Mama, that she'd go crazy when Papa died, and that was exactly where she had gone.

—〰—

Upstairs, a shaft of moonlight streamed through our bedroom window. It gave the only light I had to see by when I placed the mirror before me. Gilded with flower and leaf etchings, the old mirror reflected my image as fogged and run through with striations. Nonetheless, satisfaction swelled in my chest as I laid the shears against my scalp and closed the blades around each lock of hair. The curls floated to the floor like a blackbird's plumage might—one feather at a time. And with each, I whispered, "Papa."

I felt victorious punishing my mother this way. She used to love to brush my hair, never pushing off the task to Nannie Bee or Annie Laurie. As she brushed, she always sang. "Black is the color of my true love's hair."

But that was before.

—〰—

The next morning, a shriek we always attributed to Annie Laurie woke Nannie Bee and me. Annie dropped to her knees on the pallet where I lay and scoured my head to find remnants of the dark locks. "Darling Cora, your hair!"

"Well now, you've outdone yourself," said Nannie Bee, "It'll grow out. Won't take more than six months or so. Question is, how's Mama going to take this?"

Annie Laurie glared at Nannie and put her arm around me. "We'll fix it, honey. Why, after our period of mourning is over, we'll make you a pretty straw hat with silk roses and a satin bow. You don't want to look like a boy."

"I can look like a boy if I want to. I can look like any old stupid boy!"

Annie Laurie stepped back, hands to her lips. "Well, I declare, Cora. Of course, you *can*, but one day you might change your mind. Ladies do that, you know. We're allowed."

"I ain't no lady. I ain't never gonna be no lady."

Mama rushed through the doorway. "What's wrong?" The fear on her face made me think she'd be relieved that I had only cut my hair, but that proved not to be the case.

"Cora Allen! All your beautiful curls? How could you cut—"

I fingered the butchered tufts. "I don't care."

She took me by the shoulders and shook me. A rag doll in my mother's hands, I made no effort to resist.

Mama's eyes flashed, but somehow, she must have dug deep to find some degree of control. "I know you hurt." Her voice broke. "We all hurt." She brushed her hand across my forehead and flicked away the last few tendrils. "But you can't make it worse than it already is."

True. I knew that much, but I wanted to bear a scar, some ugly sign to show what my heart might look like if they cut me open and peered inside.

Mama turned toward Annie Laurie and Nannie Bee who watched from the doorway. "Put a curl in a locket. It will remind her that self-mutilation won't assuage grief."

My sisters looked at each other like they always did when they felt superior, but they backed away and began whispering as they followed Mama downstairs.

I stood at the railing and yelled down at them. "She ain't even told y'all yet! Boy, are y'all in for a surprise!"

They hesitated before stepping into the parlor, and moments later I heard Annie Laurie sobbing.

The boys out in the barn could've heard Nan. "Mother!" Her voice ricocheted off the walls. "I am not going. I will marry Albert. He'll ask me when he hears you're uprooting us. And even if he doesn't, I'll ask *him.*" The door slammed behind her as she came charging out of the sitting room.

The knob still quivered when I leaned over the railing and called, "Wanna borrow my scissors?"

From the parlor came strains of "Requiem" Mama didn't cry, but she played that piano with a vengeance. While Papa lay dying, she sat at the piano and asked of it the miracle she wanted from God. First came a prayerful offering as she played the delicate runs, but by the time she reached the second transition, the forté became a demand. That morning she assaulted the keys again.

I realized one thing then and there. While we might be leaving Nan in Missouri, we would be taking the piano.

I refused a scarf. I refused a bonnet. I decided to wear Papa's field hat to shut them up. When I marched into the kitchen later that morning wearing one of Annie Laurie's outgrown pinafores and the hat, Joe started to laugh, but then glanced at Mama and shut up. Ben looked from Mama to me and back again and asked, "What on earth happened here?"

"I know y'all are faking all that worry about me because Mama's staring at you but wait until you hear what you're gonna have to load on that old wagon." I paused for effect. "The piano, that's what!" I waited for the impact of my words to hit home.

Ben turned toward Mama, his eyes asking for contradiction.

Joe stopped at the door and turned. "Four mules can't handle that!"

I snagged a biscuit and ran to the mulberry tree to review the beauty of my revenge. The row carried well into the treetop. "Pianos were moved from St. Louis to Salt Lake City!" and "They were found buried in sand along the Platte, too!"

In clipped and measured words, Mama said, "My father brought that piano from Kentucky in the very same wagon and if he could do it, *we* can do it. If I have to leave all my mother's Wedgewood china and my books, I will, but we are taking my piano. Get some help from town." Then, nothing but silence.

Dismal best described supper that night—nearly as bad as the day we buried Papa. Mama sat stiff as a wickerwork mannequin. Only Annie Laurie's soft sniffs broke the quiet. She got up once and left the kitchen to sob briefly against the parlor sofa before regaining some control and returning to sit with her napkin to her mouth and her eyes red and brimming.

The boys excused themselves claiming to have chores in the barn. I wanted to say that it made no never mind. It didn't matter anymore.

Nan stood and in a manner of fact tone said, "If you plan to leave so soon, I think Annie Laurie and Cora need to start packing." She took us by the hand and led us up the stairs, leaving Mama sitting alone.

Annie threw herself back across the bed and pounded the mattress with her heels. When she wasn't having a hissy fit, she stood tall and buxom for her fourteen years. Like Mama with her black hair and shockingly blue eyes, she looked as beautiful as the models in *Harper's Bazaar*. Proud would have been an accurate description, but she had the saving grace of fawning over the smallest animals—a fledgling fallen from its nest or a baby rabbit she rescued from a circling hawk.

Smaller and rounder than Annie Laurie, Nan had reached the marriageable age of seventeen. She had prospects. Well, one prospect. He'd only come courting twice in the last month and even though he wasn't "a dreamboat" as Annie Laurie had so remarked, he promised to be a safe bet—a hard worker. Such a hard worker that he seldom found time for Nan, but he had come courting just the same. It made sense that she refused to go off to Texas. Not prone to tears and foot stomping, Mama's decision still left her reeling. I admired her willingness to stand up to one as formidable as our mother. I lamented not being older. I could have married and stayed right here in Douglas County, Missouri.

Annie Laurie sat twisting her hands instead of braiding her hair. "Now, Nan, who knows what nice men you might find in Texas?"

"Aren't cowboys always gone on cattle drives?" Nan folded my bloomers and tucked them into the trunk Annie Laurie and I would have to share.

"It might not be much worse than your beau," Annie Laurie said. "He's off in the fields all the time like Papa used to be, trying to grow corn from rocks."

"You are saying that because you're too young to have a beau and—"

Annie grasped Nan's hands. "Oh, I'm sorry. If you love Albert, I want you to have Albert. But I cannot believe you will desert all of us."

"I am not the deserter. I am the only one with the courage and determination to stay."

Annie couldn't hold back tears. "Then it will be all up to me to take care of Cora."

My sisters carried on as if I weren't there. "I don't need taking care of!"

"Well, I think you do." Annie Laurie didn't miss a beat. "What do you think, Nannie Bee?"

"Oh for goodness sake, what do I think about what?" Nan had begun to systematically wind her hair into braids and hated to be interrupted at any task she'd begun.

"About Cora, of course. I don't know how to help her. She won't let me pet her or distract her. She won't wear a bonnet. I don't know how long it will take her hair to grow out." Annie Laurie began untying her own ribbons. "I saved these lavender ones for you, Cora." She wound them around her fingers in a figure eight. "Now it may be years until you'll need them." And then to Nan, she cried, "What in the world can I do with her hair when it's barely past her ears? She'll look like—"

"Cora's hair will be as long as a cat's tail by the time next summer rolls around. Meanwhile, keep a bonnet on her."

"Papa's hat, you mean. Do you think Cousin Frank will be shocked?"

Nan let her hands drop to her lap and looked over her shoulder at Annie Laurie. "Oh my, from what I hear about Texans, nothing much drops their jaw. You've got to quit stewing over this. There's nothing you can do. If there's anyone to worry about, it's Mama. She's beyond reason." She unwound a badly plaited braid and began brushing her hair again. She winced as the brush snagged on a tangle. "There's more to this story than we are privy to."

"I don't know. Mama's always been headstrong."

"Sister dear, you are naïve." Nan stopped and looked Annie Laurie straight in the eye. "Something's behind this, all right. I've got one thought, but it's too audacious to say."

"Whatever do you mean? You're always so suspicious."

"I've got two years on you, sister dear. I know far more than you when it comes to examining feminine motives."

"Oh, how you go on." Annie Laurie blew out her candle. "I am not listening to another word."

I didn't need to listen to another word. I knew something didn't feel right. Mama had more reasons than she let on—more than rocks, more than the promise of blackland farming in Texas.

And then I remembered.

It had been dusk last May when the knock came at the back door. Mama was fixing supper. The dog never barked and the tap came so soft, we almost didn't hear it. She didn't call one of the boys to answer like usual. Instead, she told us to finish up, that she'd be back soon. Disregarding our surprised looks, she quietly stepped into the twilight. Moments later, I slipped out behind her.

"Lucretia," I heard Nathan say. He didn't take Mama's arm. Didn't move close to her. He looked straight ahead and walked. She walked with him—knowing Papa had only just died. Knowing her sister Harriet lay dying from consumption as well. But Nathan Cage was married to Aunt Harriet, and maybe he had something important to say.

He didn't look at Mama until they were beyond the creek that divided our properties. Wood smoke drifted about, and I hid close enough to smell a waft of the bay rum aftershave he always wore.

Something else suffused the air, something I didn't understand. Crickets heated up the night with their pulsing, and the way spring winds worried through the trees frightened me.

A night bird called—a whippoorwill.

I turned back to the house and ran.

Chapter Two

The course had been determined, and Mama went full throttle. I remembered Casey Jones and imagined the force generated by the freight train when he called for more coal. It had only been six months since he had gone full throttle to make up time. By the time he heard the warnings, it was too late. He plowed into a passenger train. Songs were written about him and his ambition and the terrible train wreck. Mama's behavior wouldn't merit a ballad, but similarities existed.

I tried to stay out of her way, but sometimes I studied her surreptitiously while she packed. She picked up the silver hand mirror and stared at her reflection. I stood over her shoulder, shocked at the anguish I saw there. I watched as she placed the mirror and matching silver brush into the prettiest box in the house and called for Nan to deliver it to Harriet.

"Well, I'm not doing it!" Nan shoved the box back into Mama's arms. "It's bad enough you're leaving everything and everybody we've ever known like they don't count for anything. And you want *me* to say your goodbyes? Deliver this to Harriet? To your sister lying on her death bed?" She turned to go out the door but stopped and looked over her shoulder. "I won't do it, Mama!" She slammed the door behind her and yelled from the other side. "And Annie Laurie won't either if that's what you're planning. I'll see to that!"

Mama turned and pushed away the lock of hair that had fallen into her eyes. "The boys might." she said. "Well, Joe would." She sat down on the bed. "No, I'll do it. I'll just have to do it." Then she turned to me. "But you'll have to come with me."

I was quick to voice my objections, but they were nipped in the bud. I realized I would be her shield, taken along to keep the conversation light between her and Harriet.

Mama talked constantly on the way over to their house. "I've made up my mind not to speak about how sick Harriet is. And don't you look shocked if she looks bad." She glanced down at me. "She might look real bad." Mama stared ahead as though she were talking to herself and said, "I think it's better to say goodbye, smile and kiss her—wait, better not kiss her—just promise to write. Can you remember that, Cora?"

Nathan met us at the gate to his homestead and took the box from Mama to carry into the house. They walked side by side and never said a word. "Harriet?" he called from the doorway. "Your sister's here."

"Amanda?" Harriet's voice sounded so much huskier than it had the last time I had seen her. But that was before Papa died.

"No, it's me—Lucretia." She tapped on her sister's bedroom door. "And Cora. Cora's with me."

Silence.

Mama lifted her chin and stepped into her sister's room. "I—" Her hand over her mouth, she turned to face Nathan, but he looked away and set the box on the dresser. She faced Harriet. "I've not been to see you and I'm sorry. I guess Nathan has told you about Frank's letter. You remember Cousin Frank? He—"

"I remember Cousin Frank, Lucretia." A cough rumbled in her throat. She pressed a cloth to her lips but couldn't stop it. When she could breathe again, she said, "I'm sure Nathan will help you. You always could count on Nathan, couldn't you."

"Yes, Harriet. Drury and I both. And I would have been more help to you if Drury hadn't been so sick. You understand—"

"I understand." Her lips twisted ever so slightly. "What *did* you come here for?"

"Why, Grandmother's silver brush and hand mirror. The one she had monogrammed. I wanted you to have it." Mama took my hand and stepped closer to the bed, but Harriet kept her eyes on me and refused to look at her sister.

"Nice to see you, Cora, but y'all best get on back. You've got lots to do to get on the road. I'm sure Nathan will keep track of you."

Turning her head on the pillow away from Mama, she spoke, her voice small and sullen. "Won't you, Nathan?"

He leaned one hand against the wall and looked out the window.

Mama whispered her last words to her sister. "I'm sorry. God bless." She closed the door softly behind us and we walked away. Nathan didn't follow.

Chapter Three

Mama often remarked that Cousin Jimmy played marionette to my strings. I chose to believe that he merely wanted to please me, and so I'd instructed him to bring a pair of britches and a shirt and meet me down by the barn.

When he took one look at the prickly little sprigs that tufted out from my papa's hat he said, "Want me to get a doily from Mama's dressing table? We can—" He started to laugh, but I sent him a blazing look that shut him up.

"You can keep your opinion to yourself." I pulled the crown of the hat down to my ears. "I came here to make a trade and since I'm soon long gone, it'd behoove you to cooperate." I opened one finger at a time to reveal an agate marble cupped in the palm of my hand. "Want it?"

"Well, of course, I want it. Where'd you get it?"

"Found it. When Mama made me pull weeds in her garden. Dug it up. Pretty, ain't it?"

"What do you want?" He narrowed his eyes. "You're known to be a conniver, Cora Allen."

"I'm choosing to ignore that and I am going to go easy on you. Just that stuff I told you to bring. That's all. And maybe one more thing." I cleared my throat and went on. "Anyway, this is practically a going-away gift from me to you. Here, you can hold it." As I held out my hand, palm up, the blue swirls caught the sunlight. "I even cleaned it up for you."

Jimmy lifted the treasure and held it up higher to the light. With reverence he whispered, "It's beautiful."

"Thought you'd like it. Now!" I slapped my hands together. "I'll need those nice leather boots you've practically outgrown and that there pair of pants and shirt, of course." I met his eyes with a hard stare. "Close your mouth. That's my deal."

"Daddy'll—" But he stopped.

"Tell him I cried, and you didn't want me to go off to Texas without satisfactory clothes." I squinted my eyes. "There's rattlesnakes there, you know."

His fingers slid over the polished stone. "You know I'll be minus the good pair of britches I own. Them boots pinch a little, and I never liked that shirt much, but I ain't got but a few." He sighed. "You're gonna have to pull them hard to get them off me. Here, grab the heel." He sat and stuck his boot up for me to take hold. It took me only moments to remove them both. "Lordy, girl, you ain't wastin' no time!"

I had already pushed my feet into the boots. "They fit good enough. Deal?"

"Deal." As an afterthought, he added, "Might not want to wear them until you get down the road a piece. Your mama'll know where they came from and make you bring them back. I bet she will."

"Probably right. But after we're on the way, I don't think anything will turn her around. You know how she is." I hesitated. "Guess this is so long. Keep an eye out for that old calico cat. If she ever shows up again, you can have her."

"Well, write, maybe."

I turned with a half wave and trudged back to the house, my dog at my heels and Jimmy's clothes wrapped in newspaper. I only paused once to take a quick swipe at my eyes.

—⁂—

Katydids had yet to relinquish the night, but their chirps had slowed to occasional squawks in the earliest hours of dawn. I sat on the porch steps and tried to impede the final process of packing.

My deluded sense of power knew few boundaries. "I am not going anywhere." I crossed my arms. Ben and Joe stepped over me as they loaded the ham and preserves, sacks of flour and coffee into the wagon.

Ben nudged me with his boot. "You better move yourself over, little girl. We might squash you like a bug."

"You won't squash me like a bug. Loading that piano last night nearly squashed you and Joe like roly-polies." I planted my fanny even more firmly on the steps. I stuck out my tongue at him and said, "It took you the best part of an hour and a smashed hand to boot, and y'all not wantin' to go any more than me."

Ben only shrugged, but on his way back into the house, he rubbed my head. When I swung at him, he grabbed me up and pinned my arms at my sides. Nose to nose he held me, but I clenched my eyes shut. "You ain't gonna make me go nowhere."

Being the eldest put him under pressure to be the bravest. With his hazel eyes and blond hair, Ben looked something like Papa did in an old photograph. Ben had been my first hero but giving in so easily to Mama put him squarely in the realm of suspicion.

"You don't need to be a worrying about anything," he said. Then he gave me that crooked smile. "Except your grammar."

"Well, I *ain't!*"

"You know what, baby sister? We're gonna be all right. Papa would've wanted us to strike out for new land." Ben blinked. And I saw right through his bravado. "Imagine! The turn of the century! Texas! Cowboys and Indians. We'll have a grand old time."

"You're lying again, Ben. Lyin' like a dog!" I ducked my head, but he kissed my nose anyway and set me on the edge of the porch where I'd be out of the way.

Mama called me to come help take the last items out to the wagon, but I slipped along the side of the house to the rose bush Mama called "First Love." What a stupid name for a rose. I saw no sense in naming flowers. But I couldn't escape my mother. Her face took on the color of those faded roses as she tracked me down and dispatched me without ceremony. I trudged back to my chores.

When at last we were loaded, and the boys on their mounts, Mama ran back to the climbing rose and cut a section. She wrapped it in a wet handkerchief and put it in the back with Annie Laurie who sat with her face in her hands.

Nan stood holding her own valise. "I don't know why you want to take a piece of that old rose bush. It's got the worst thorns I've ever seen."

In almost a whisper, Mama said, "Since you're staying with your grandmother, how could this make the slightest difference to you?" She stood, stared at Nan and cleared her throat.

The throat clearing almost disguised the heartbreak. It hurt Mama that Nan refused to come. Not that she would ever admit it. She would pretend no loss. And Nan would pretend no loss. What good did it do to pretend when something was killing you?

"Goodbye, Nannie Bee," called Annie Laurie, but then she jumped down and ran to grab Nan by the shoulders. "Come with us," she whispered. "Please, come with us! I don't think I can stand it if you don't—"

"It'll be all right, Annie. I'll write. I'll write lots of letters."

I stood beside them holding Nan's fingertips. "I bet there'll be some nice cowboys there. Or get Albert to come along. The boys could use some help. We can stop in town for a preacher. I bet we can find a preacher right quick. Can't we, Mama?"

"I believe Nan's made her choice, girls. You heard her. She'll write." Mama started back toward the wagon. "Are you walking or riding?"

"I'll ride," said Annie Laurie. She squeezed Nan's hand and climbed into the seat.

I stood behind the wagon. "I'm not going!" I stiffened my arms and clenched my fists. "I want my papa!"

Mama turned slowly. Her bottom lip trembled even as she tried to draw her mouth in a hard line. Her thumb bit into my collarbone. "Your papa's gone to heaven," she said. "And *we* are goin' to Texas."

—⁊⁊—

As the sun rose, I shuffled backwards behind the wagon keeping my eyes on the small white frame house as we began the trek up the hill. Even if the eye-like windows couldn't fill with tears or the empty rooms ache for the sound of girls' laughter, I imagined it so. Over the house, the mulberry tree cast long shade in the early morning light. I would miss that tree and its mulberries that stained my hands and clothes. How many summer days had I stood before Mama with my purple mouth and fingers, unrepentant even with the lectures and the soapings and scrubbings? The secret hours I spent perched among the cool leaves provided a world where I fancied myself a chameleon hidden in shadow and sunlight.

I followed behind the prairie schooner, its great white sail ballooning before me. I slowed and finally stood immobile to let the wagon go on without me. Then I was running home, my feet pounding the rocky ground, my breath surging in my ears. Tears streamed down my face, and the terrain around me became unclear. By my side, Amazing Grace herded and barked, blocking my path. I stumbled and pushed my arms out to keep from skinning my face but tumbled anyway, sliding on my cheek. Sobbing, I picked up my papa's hat and ran on.

Almost back to the porch, I heard the hoof beats. Ben's arm scooped me up and plopped me in front of him on the saddle. I kicked at the horse's neck and beat my brother's thighs with my fists. "You let me alone!"

He laid his cheek on my head. "Shh, it's gonna be all right. You'll see. But don't kick Blackjack, honey."

I gave up, but tears stung my cheeks as I sobbed all the way back to the wagon. The border collie trotted at the side of the horse and nipped at its hocks. Mama had pulled the mules to a stop. I thought she wanted to wait for Ben to catch up, but she stared at the fence line between Nathan's property and what had once been ours. He stood there in the mists of dawn and raised one hand in goodbye. When Ben lifted me over to sit between her and Annie Laurie, Mama flicked the reins and yelled, "Gee up!" Our heads snapped back, and I grabbed my sister's arm. In that one command, Mama's voice embodied anger and regret. Even I understood that but dared not ask why.

Chapter Four

If Mama talked at all those first days, it was to carry on about making it to Springfield. I refused to speak to her. I barely spoke to anyone except Amazing Grace. Annie Laurie tried to make light of the happenings on the journey, but the monotony left little to remark upon.

"You better look into getting some oxen, Mama, if you intend to travel like this." Ben took off his hat and wiped the sweat from his forehead with the cuff of his shirt. "You're gonna kill old Plato."

"You know oxen can't pull as fast as mules. They're slow creatures. Maybe that stallion of yours would like to spell Plato a bit. Think so?" she asked, a harsh glint in her eye. Ben ceased his suggestions.

For a September evening, it was hot, and the air took on a damp closeness. After we camped, I sat cross-legged studying the sky for a long time. I wished for bad weather—anything to delay our connection with the wagon train. The clouds folded high on themselves and grew dark at their bases. Against the sunset, color diffused into the western horizon with blues settling into aquamarines and pinks blending into golds—an opaline glow as though seen through water.

After sopping up the last bit of stew with their biscuits, Ben and Joe spread their bedrolls and propped their heads against their saddles. The constellation Scorpio scrolled across the southwestern sky. I begged to sleep out under the stars, but Mama refused me. Later that night, Amazing Grace struggled over Annie Laurie to whine and wriggle against me. I woke to the low growl of thunder and saw the lightning rivet across the night sky. Wind slapped the canvas back and forth as Ben and Joe clambered into the wagon.

"Good lord almighty." Joe scrambled behind Ben and tried to tie the flaps that thrashed in the wind.

Ben lunged forward to grab the other side so that between them, they could control the contortion of the canvas. He turned to face us. "All right? Everybody all right?"

"We should be asking you the question," Mama said. "The mules tied?"

"Best we could. Didn't want them jerking on the wagon. Hank is the one likely to set back." Joe pulled me close. "You okay, little girl?"

I pressed my face against his shoulder to hide the flame of hope that blossomed in my heart. I couldn't help thinking there might be a chance we'd give up here knowing we'd likely not make it to Springfield in time. At worst, it would be a wasted trip.

Mama knelt as if in prayer, clutching us to her. She deserved God's punishment. My faith in God restored, I thanked him under my breath; he had already answered *my* plea. The fear of lightning and thunder seemed a small enough sacrifice if we got to turn around and head back home. With the next burst of lightning, the canvas flap belled and opened. A tree some distance from us glowed before it erupted into shards of fire. A bright stream roiled across the shadows revealing landscape as ink-drawn artwork. The animals shrieked. I imagined the whites of their eyes rolling in fear and the pink caves of their nostrils flaring with the acrid smoke of the singed summer growth. It smelled like silk burning.

The wagon rocked with the punch of the storm, and the wind hummed through the wagon wheels. It swelled and sucked the canvas like something gasping and alive inhaling us. Soot collected on the canvas above the lantern and fell on my hands in darkened drops.

The storm moved on at last, its lightning only firefly flickers on the horizon before I finally fell asleep and dreamed of home.

—⁂—

The next day Annie Laurie and I plodded along beside the wagon that lumbered through the mud. Even the hot sun bearing down felt better than the nauseating jerk and bounce in the belly of the wagon. The gumbo sucked at our boots and all the high stepping wore us out, but with each step that sank into the mire, my hopes lifted.

The piano sat upright and with every lurch of the wagon, it objected. Its protests spanned from deep base clef to its treble's pitiful plinks that sounded like glass breaking. So often did Joe and Ben have to stop and dig the wagon out of the mud that we only managed two miles that day. I pinched my lips together to keep from smiling. It was only a matter of time until we had to toss the piano overboard.

Ben called out to Mama, "Let me drive a while. You go back and rest. You didn't get any sleep last night. Joe will spell me."

But true to her nature, she refused, citing her lighter weight would be advantageous to the mules. I knew quite well her real motivation. She suspected the boys would drive too slow and trusted no one who might sabotage her mission.

That night I returned with firewood and quietly stacked the kindling while my brothers talked as they brushed the dried mud from the mules' backs and massaged liniment into their legs and haunches. Joe said, "Do you think Mama's all right? I mean she's got us up and out of the house before Papa's grave has settled."

Ben shook his head and kicked at the dirt. "She's eaten up with this passion to get to Texas. Like she can outrun heartbreak. Annie Laurie will be all right, but I'm not sure about Cora. She's got the same streak as Mama."

Joe gazed at the autumn moon already on the horizon and shrugged.

Ben dropped his voice and chuckled. "Don't you ever tell Cora I said that."

Too late. I sank into the shadows. A screech owl's call put a wavering emphasis to Ben's words. I refused to speak to him after hearing his criticism of me.

—⦚—

The next day we passed a farmhouse, and Mama sent the boys to find out how much farther to Springfield. She kept driving so as not to waste a minute of travel time. Five days we had been on the road. I crossed my fingers. Maybe Springfield lay four days ahead and the wagon train would be long gone. Sun and effort had reddened her face enough that I forgot what our pretty mama had looked like before that hell-bent-for-leather expression took over.

It was hours before the boys got back, but they seemed relaxed and wore smiles of relief. Mama grinned back at them. "What's the word, boys? By your looks, I'd say good."

Their expressions changed to blank masks. "The Browns sent some fresh baked bread for you." Ben stretched out his arm with the loaf wrapped in a dishtowel. "It's real good."

She dropped the reins and sat back. "What did they say, Ben?" Her face erased any sign of optimism. She looked from one to the other. "Spit it out!"

"Three and a half days, Mama. Maybe three, if we're lucky."

I stared at my hands as I turned my thumbs around each other and hid the smile that I could feel sneaking up at the corners of my lips. I cleared my throat and frowned at the pattern on my smock.

"Then, we'll travel all day and some of the night too. That should get us there. I'll drive until dark. You boys can spell me while I sleep. When we take turns, you'll hitch your horses up and let them do their share of the work. You can sleep in the day." Mama turned and pointed. "Girls, your jobs are water hauling and fixing something for the boys to eat that won't need cooking."

Ben spoke up. "Mama, I can't let you kill the mules just to get us to Springfield. We'd still need them to travel with the train." With a quick glance at Joe, he continued. "There is one thing that will pretty much guarantee you getting there on time, but you won't like it."

"No, I won't. You dump the books and the china. I can live without those things. I cannot and will not give up my Steinway. I'll buy new animals in Springfield if I need to. Something that can pull better than four mules."

My brothers set the boxes of Shakespeare and Wordsworth and Hawthorne off to the side of the road. They set our grandmother's boxes of Wedgewood with its delicate designs under an oak tree.

"Too bad we didn't know this before we went to the Brown's farm," said Ben. "They would've got a superior education and fine dining to go along with that good bread. Maybe they'll come across it. I hope so. Nice people."

"I figured we lightened the load by two hundred pounds. Maybe this won't kill the mules if the girls walk the rest of the way." Joe stretched his back.

Mama flicked the reins. The mules shouldered into the traces, and I heard her whisper, "Don't look back, don't look back."

I spent the evening thinking of how to stop Mama. Getting snake bit seemed unlikely. I doubted even breaking my leg would slow her down. All I had to rely on were my hopes and prayers that we would still not make Springfield in time. And I prayed day and night.

During the long day as I walked alongside the wagon, I schemed. Our arrival depended on the mules. Not that I would injure a mule, but I could damage the rigging. With the wagon in almost constant motion, it might not be possible, but I couldn't give up. When we stopped for water, I planned to fill the buckets and then stand by Hank's head and cut into the strap that hitched him to the reins. I could use a butcher knife. With no time to cook meat, no one would notice the missing knife. In that brief hour before sunset when we stopped to feed the animals and rest, I planned to quietly run the knife back and forth across the strap of the breastplate. Like he did every night, Ben would be massaging Pfeiffer's Heat Rub into Blackjack's legs. Sometimes he seemed to care more about that stallion than me.

Hank was a roan draft mule, bred to pull. His head bent low over the bucket, and his nostrils flared as he sucked. He closed his eyes, never lifting his muzzle from the creek water. I leaned against his neck and slipped the knife under the smallest piece of leather attached to the breastplate. I hummed a pretty little song and stopped occasionally to pat Hank's sweaty neck. The shadows of the evening fell long across the fields, fragmenting into vague folds of dark.

Only when Ben's form blocked the fading light across Hank's shoulder, did I cease my attempt to sever the leather binding. I kept humming as I slid the knife behind the breastplate to hide it and scratched Hank's head with my other hand. I prayed Ben hadn't seen, that he just wanted to say hello or check on me. But he grasped my wrist. Very gently he unfolded my fingers. Paralyzed, I clamped my eyes shut, refusing to look up into the accusation I knew I would see in his eyes.

"What am I supposed to say to you, Cora? That if the strap had snapped, Hank would have lunged forward and fallen, taking Plato with him? Likely splintering their canon bones. And then Ornery and

Socrates. You could have killed everybody riding the wagon. Is that what you wanted? To sacrifice *us* for what *you* want?"

"That's what Mama's doing!" I wheeled, turned my back on my brother and marched away. I refused to consider the consequences of my behavior. In my repertoire of self-defense, I enumerated a weak line of justifications. Somebody had to stop Mama. I had only been able to nick the edge of the strap anyway, and Ben acted like a serious old worrywart. Then I did imagine what might have happened—Hank straining against the weakened strap as he tried to pull the wagon, his knees buckling with no breastplate to support him, his front legs snapping under the forward force of the wagon and Plato, then Ornery and Socrates falling with them. I dropped to my hands and knees. Deep down in my belly, guilt roiled and funneled to my throat. It scalded its way to my mouth, and I vomited among the trees. I swiped at the dark foam with my palms, pressing it into the leaves that only recently cluttered the ground.

Chapter Five

Two mornings later, we drew onto South Street toward the square in Springfield and asked for the wagon train heading to El Paso. We were directed to a poster nailed to the bulletin board of a general store that gave directions to Brookline Corner, southwest of town where a Captain Richards took applications for the journey.

I went smug at the news that the trip could have been cut short by half a day. Since Mama had only heard the meeting would be in Springfield, we traveled through the entire town and down the main street instead of cutting across the southern portion to Brookline. She whipped the mules ahead. Hank stumbled, but the traces caught him, and he picked up his gait despite the back hock that hitched after it hit the ground.

I walked behind the wagon and stared with sullen surprise at the breadth of the streets and the elaborate architecture of the buildings. We turned west on Walnut Street. Compared to the simplicity of our home, the Queen Anne structures looked like mansions with wide verandas, porch skirts of latticework and second story balconies that circled the front corner of the houses. The finely planed lumber accentuated the trims of green paint or red, sometimes brown. The rooflines climbing to steeply pitched gables signaled wealth that I could not imagine. Weather vanes of flying horses, doors with stained-glass panes, and roof shingles laid in detailed patterns were so different from the small white farmhouse that Papa had built by hand.

I heard it coming as if it weren't going to stop at all. But at last, the air brakes screamed against the iron tracks and with a great exhale, the train blocked the road, hissed and rested at the depot. The racket assaulted me. I held my hands over my ears and stared at the back of the wagon.

It came to me then that this might be the time to don the new wardrobe I had requisitioned from Cousin Jimmy. Mama's reaction might be enough to slow her down and miss the wagon train. As we waited to cross the train tracks, I climbed over the tailgate and pulled out the hidden flour sack where I had stuffed Jimmy's clothes and boots.

While the rest of them were stupefied by the clamor of the city, I wriggled into the pants, buttoned the shirt and slipped my feet into the boots. Pleased that the boots were a fraction too large, I practiced the strut they helped me achieve before falling with the sway of the wagon as we started up again. I'd have given anything for a looking glass. Not a soul in the world would think me a sissy girl. I adjusted the hat on my head. I could hardly wait until Mama got to the wagon train and saw my new attire.

—⁂—

The barking of dogs and squeals of children came from thirty-plus wagons beside the road in Brookline. Mama pushed the team up to the end of the line and descended from the driving seat. "See to the mules," she said to the boys.

Ben and Joe exchanged glances, but just "Yes, ma'am" slipped from their lips. Mama never looked back as she headed for the front of the train. They caught up with her before she passed the wagon ahead of us. "Mama, wait," Ben called. He made his voice deeper, portraying the man of the family. She stared at him a minute and then nodded for them to come on. So engaged with their mission, they failed to notice that I swaggered behind them plotting a severe case of yellow fever.

Nobody could miss the captain. His suspenders barely held up his britches, but he talked louder than anybody else to assert his leadership. Not that I cared. I never doubted I could fool an old man with tobacco stains on his beard.

"Ma'am," Captain Richards explained, "we've done voted to leave first thing in the morning. I'll be happy to inspect your wagon and mules, but I expect it will be darn close to a miracle for you and your team to be able to move out at that time."

"I assure you, sir, that my mules are fresh and recently shod," said Mama. "Our gear is in order, and I can promptly agree to any stipulation you find prudent."

Ben and Joe's eyes met over Mama's head.

"For starters, ma'am, I see from here that you've got four mules hanging on their harnesses. They ain't gonna last, I'm telling you." He removed his hat and twisted it in his hands. "I don't think them mules could pull a two-wheel sulky, not to mention no covered wagon. I can't accept the responsibility."

"I am prepared to do what is necessary. We've made it thus far with what we've got by spelling the mules." Mama breathed deep, arching her posture to its five-foot, seven-inch height—tall as Captain Richards.

I stood looking from the captain to Mama before I tugged on her dress. "Mama."

"What in the world, Cora? What are you doing here? Mother of God! What have you got on?" She looked accusingly at Ben. "Did you let—"

Ben lifted his shoulders but before he could defend his innocence, I promptly collapsed to the ground.

"Goldurnit," said the captain. "I ain't got time to deal with this. What's the matter with him?"

"I do believe there is nothing the matter with this child."

I flickered my lashes long enough to see Mama's eyes narrowing alarmingly close to my face.

"Take her back, Ben."

"Now ma'am, this confounds the whole situation. I cannot knowingly take on a sick child. I cannot allow a wagon I ain't inspected to join us and I can't let no foot weary and bedraggled mules pull a wagon." Captain Richards spoke as though he were addressing a case of dementia. "You got to understand the problems this could cause for the folks who got here on time and voted and signed up to obey the martial law I've set forth." In an attempt at gallantry, he swept off his hat and said, "There'll be another train come spring. Forgive me, ma'am, it is the law."

I fought to suppress the smile that teased my lips as Ben lifted me and began the walk back to our wagon.

"You're not foolin' me, missy, and I doubt you fooled Mama." He sucked the next words under his breath. "Not that it'll do us any good."

I pressed my lips in a tight line and tried to draw my eyebrows together in a painful frown that I hoped represented cholera or smallpox. Mama followed on the graveled road behind us, the stones crunching hard under her footsteps, suggesting there would be hell to pay. Hell seemed a preferable alternative to Texas.

"I'm going looking for an oxen team." Mama snapped her gloves on. "Take care of Cora, if you really think it's a necessity. And get her a change of clothes."

"Ma—" Ben said as she marched away. He jerked his head at Joe to delegate the responsibility of my care, turned and strode after her.

Joe parked me in the wagon and advised me to get over myself. The blankets smelled of mildew and human sweat, but I dug my face into the squares of quilting. I did not request water for a while. I slept, letting my face grow warm in the covers. When the last light of the day came through the flaps of the wagon, I let my eyes roll to the right and strangled out the word "water." Then in a weak and trembling voice, as if indeed I had no strength for words, I called, "Annie, Annie Laurie!" And she appeared with a ladle of water brimming at my lips. I smacked in appreciation and then let myself lapse into an overheated sleep.

Well after sunset, Mama and Ben returned. Fluttering my eyelids in what I hoped appeared a good imitation of fevered tremors, I watched them from the corners of my eyes. She had made a deal for four oxen but admitted it cost her far more than if she'd bought them back home.

"We may not be allowed to join the train, but we'll follow as close as we can." Mama peeled her gloves from her fingers.

Annie Laurie's eyes lingered too long on Mama's bare right hand before searching her face for the answer. "You didn't! You promised me Grandmother's ring. How could—"

Ben pulled her away. "Hush. It didn't belong to you yet."

"You don't care." Annie pushed him. "You weren't going to get it." Then she turned back to Mama. "I declare, Mama, you have become obsessed."

Mama covered her hand with the other. "There'll not be another word about it. We have four fine Holstein steers that have been matched to the yoke. Captain Richards can hardly find fault with them. And the poor mules can only be glad I traded them as part of the bargain."

Ben locked eyes with Joe and drew a line across his throat with his finger. Joe's mouth dropped open, and he took a step back before he could recover his composure.

Before any more discussion ensued, Mama began giving orders. "We'll give Cora plenty of time to recuperate. Poor thing. I want her to stay in bed until we get ready to leave. We can't take chances with our precious cargo."

Which meant, as I well knew, that they would not let me leave the wagon under any circumstances. I would be held prisoner until Mama got us well on our way, but what a small price to pay if I had kept us from joining the wagon train.

"Let's all get a good night's sleep," Mama said as she unrolled her quilt. "So much to be done tomorrow and the next day if we're to stay half a mile behind Captain Richards." She used her "busy" voice, the one I recognized as laced with energy that would drive us all until she got what she wanted.

Chapter Six

A hangnail moon still hung low in the sky when Annie Laurie said, "Cora, honey, you feelin' better?" She stroked my back.

"It's not even daylight." I turned over and yawned. "We can't go yet."

"We'll eat a biscuit on the way." She pulled back the canvas flaps. "Look! You can see Pegasus." She pointed toward the sky. No hint of dawn, no twitter of birds to announce the beginning of another day, but there in the dark before sunrise spread a myriad of stars, so thick and bright that they could have been handfuls of glitter cast across the heavens. "Isn't it beautiful?" she said. "I think it must be a sign that this is going to be a good journey."

I looked but sank back against the covers. "I'm too sick to see." To me, the stars were a thousand glittering warnings, a thousand reasons why we should turn around and head back to Douglas County. I covered my head with the quilt and kicked my legs as hard as I could. "Murder, Murder, Murder!" I could have been dying, and Mama would have planned the gravesite in Texas.

When Annie laced her shoes and moved up front with Mama, Amazing Grace lay her head across me and whimpered. I sat up, cradled my dog's head in my hands, looked into the brown eyes and said, "Mama's gonna make us go to Texas, and the devil take the hindmost!" What a reckless thing to say, I thought, but I had said it, even though the devil had nothing to do with it. At least, I didn't think so. Where had I heard those words? I knew, of course. They had come straight from my mama's mouth.

Curiosity was my undoing. How far behind the train were we? Dawn brightened the shadows, and I slipped from the back of the wagon and followed along. Mama talked in her lecture voice to Ben and Joe. "We'll be coming up on Wilson Creek before nightfall. Your grandfather nearly died there back in '61. Fought with the Missouri State Guard and Captain Ben McCulloch and his Texas bunch. They won, but barely. Kept Missouri part Confederate and part Union for the duration." Mama shook her head. "Bunch of hotheads. Don't know why men feel like they've got to go out and do or die, but they do. An ugly thing that war." She slapped the reins on the oxen's backs. "I hope you boys know better than that." If Mama thought about what she said, she would have realized that she provided a perfect example of "do or die."

With Amazing Grace at my side, I intended to judge the rate of travel and count the creeks we crossed. According to Cousin Frank's map, they had names like Little Skin Bayou and Big Sugar. The land rose and fell in swells of autumn grasses like pictures of the ocean I had seen. And if Mama lost sight or trail of Captain Richards' train, maybe we'd just get lost.

I already felt lost in the monotony of walking day after day and hill after hill. Hedge parsley burrs covered the hem of my pants' legs and stuck to Grace's legs and belly. Pollen from broomweed and goldenrod sifted through to my knees and colored them yellow. And to make it lonelier, the call of coyotes filled the night. Even though I sat with the family to eat beans and cornbread, and even though I ceased complaining about chores and the travel, I maintained a dogged disapproval of my mama's decision to take us away from everything we had ever known.

If I found small pleasures, I concealed them. I collected bouquets to make flower people, the center disks for faces and petals for bonnets. I twirled them between my fingers like small characters, moving them back and forth in imitation of a square dance circle I'd seen once. I sang "Skip to my Lou, my darlin" under my breath and ceased if anyone came near. There would be no doubt about my suffering. If I couldn't change their minds, I hoped to make them sick with guilt.

—w—

Nearly two weeks out, Mama sent Ben to confer with Captain Richards. "We couldn't have too much farther to Fort Smith. Maybe three days? You ask him."

"I want to go, too!" I appeared from the folds of the wagon flaps. "Ben lets me ride behind him sometimes, and I can entertain him a little bit, you know." I pinched my cheeks into the smile that revealed my dimples. "Really, I'll be good."

"Surely you cannot mean it, Cora!" Mama appeared to be truly amazed. "After your swooning stunt, do you think Captain Richards wants to see you again?"

"I'll show him I am cured, and maybe he'll let us catch up since we've come this far." I wondered at myself. The day after day humdrum made me reckless about maintaining my depression.

Mama hesitated, and I saw my chance. "Please, Mama? Let me make it up to you." I ducked my chin and looked up at her with my best expression of reconciliation.

I ignored the quick look of amusement on Ben's face before he could turn Blackjack away from the wagon, but when he came back around, he said, "It'll get her out of your hair for a while, Mama. Who knows what she might accomplish."

"Well, that is exactly my point, son, but if you want to put up with her then you go right on ahead."

Ben grinned at me. "Well, little girl, c'mon then."

Instead of climbing to the seat where Ben could reach me, I darted inside the wagon and reappeared, wearing a smock and a bonnet instead of Papa's hat. "In case Captain Richards thinks I've got mange on my head!"

I reached for Ben's arm and he swung me up behind him. He urged Blackjack into an easy trot. I situated myself with my arms around Ben and whispered in his ear. "I knew the bonnet would make Mama happy."

"You've always got an angle, don't you, missy."

We trotted along at a happy pace. So much better than the drudgery of the wagon. For the first time in a long while, I felt like laughing. The breeze lifted my bonnet and it bounced behind my shoulders. When I looked at my shadow, I saw a little gnome of a child seated behind Ben. No locks flowed in the wind. I clamped my eyes shut. When I opened them again, I looked straight ahead and for the first time, I regretted cutting off my long hair that would have streamed behind me like Rapunzel's. But I would never admit that aloud.

In no time at all, we saw the humps of the prairie schooners lumbering up the hills ahead. I set about planning how good I would be. Maybe there were other children I could play with if Captain Richards let us join up. I began to think that maybe I had been hasty in sabotaging joining the wagon train, although it had seemed worth it at the time. I settled the bonnet back on my head and tightened the strings. Didn't need it to fly off and expose the spears of hair that were just growing back.

Ben rode to the front of the train. "Captain Richards! Sir!"

"What you need, boy? Ride along with me. Ain't got time to stop and chat." Richards settled his hat firmly on his head and looked forward with great purpose. "I knew y'all was still back there. You must need to get to Texas in a bad way."

"Yes, sir. My mama is a hard woman to stop."

"Well, what do you want now? That boy cured of whatever ailed him?" Without waiting for an answer, he added, "And who is this pretty little thing?" He arched an eyebrow and nodded toward me.

"It's a long story, Captain."

Obviously, Ben didn't intend on going into further detail, so I slid off Blackjack and sashayed alongside Richards.

"Why, yes sir, thank you for asking. I am ever so much better. And as for the disguise, well actually, sir, I had a thought that if we ran into injuns, it might be better if they thought I was a boy. And my cousin Jimmy recommended I take his garments along."

"So that's where you. . . ." Ben took off his hat and stared at me.

With a quick curtsy, I flexed my dimple muscles. "Turned out it wasn't much of a fever. Mama sends her regards and hopes that we might draw close, sir."

Ben failed to stifle a chuckle.

"I hardly thought I needed the pretense of being a boy while you considered the possibility of our joining your train." I pressed my hands together at my waist and waited for Captain Richards' approval. "You understand."

By the look on his face, he did not understand in the least, but I went on. "I've been seeing berries along the way. I believe I could pick you a bucketful." I smiled with all I had and put my blue eyes to work.

Ben trotted up close to Richards. "Mama needed to find out how much farther to Fort Smith. She figured maybe three days."

"I reckon that's pretty close, barrin' no nasty weather." Heaving a sigh of resignation, Captain Richards said, "Aw, y'all can come on and catch up with us, seeing you made it this far. Can't do no harm. But we got rules here. Even for three days. No alkihol. No preachin' or politickin'. Keep your guns handy, but no firin' unless it's life or death. Got that, son?"

After setting Ben straight, he changed his tone completely as he spoke to me. "Berries, huh?" He winked at me. "Sounds good to me. That-a-ways I guess I can forgive the sign-up fee."

Sensing my conquest, I grinned even bigger. "Think there's any other children who might like to give me a hand?" I hesitated. "If there are, we could pick even more berries!"

"Well, there might be another young'un or two around here. Why looky there! I do believe I see one comin' along now."

A brown-haired girl followed the next wagon in line. She hung her head as she walked past.

I called out, "See you soon!"

The girl didn't look up right away, but as she passed by, she turned and smiled quick as a butterfly's wing.

For the first time in weeks, my heart felt lighter. A friend! A friend on the way to Texas! I wondered if the little girl felt like I did—pulled up by the roots.

—∿∿—

Mama sat listening as I took the lion's share of credit for joining the train. "I promised him berry picking so he'd let us join up. And wouldn't it be better to go into Fort Smith as part of the train? The people would think we'd been with Captain Richards all along." I paused to think. "And I bet they'd be nicer to us."

"He's letting us join up?" Mama pulled the oxen to a stop. "Why that old codger! Now that we're almost there! I don't see how we need his help being only three days out from Fort Smith."

Ben swung me off the back of his horse. "You let me talk to Mama awhile."

I did let them talk. I hung back behind the wagon flaps, peeked through and listened.

Mama squinted up at Ben. "If you want to talk to me, son, you better tie that horse behind the wagon and sit here with me. That evening sun is blinding me."

Ben did as she told him and climbed up to the wagon seat. "It's more than berry picking. You should have seen the look in Cora's eyes when she noticed another little girl about her age. She's lonesome, Mama. And she might be right about our getting a better welcome if we ride in with the train." He took her hand. "It's been hard on that child. It may get harder. Let's give her a few days with a friend. Richards will be heading off toward El Paso instead of toward East Texas, and that'll be the end of that."

"Oh, all right." Mama snapped the reins on the backs of the oxen and yelled, "You critters get a move on."

"It'll make her happy."

"I said all right. Don't get carried away. I believe we can make up the distance if we travel a little longer this evening." Mama popped the reins again, but I heard the smallest of smiles in her voice. The oxen team picked up its pace, and even the afternoon breeze felt fresher. It lifted the strands of hair that stuck to my mama's neck.

Annie Laurie moved forward to sit by her while I stuffed a blanket against a piano leg and closed my eyes.

"Where's Cora?" Mama looked around behind her.

"Napping," Annie Laurie lied. "I can't believe she can sleep so much. Maybe she's bored." She turned and gave me a wink.

"I rather imagine she's faking that nap. She's had a big day hoodwinking Captain Richards."

I opened both eyes at that remark.

Annie Laurie reached for the reins. "You go on back and rest yourself. You've been at the helm too long."

Mama elbowed her away. "We've got to keep going like this to catch up with old man Richards." She shrugged. "I know you mean well, but we have to keep pushing."

"I can push as well as you can, Mama." Annie Laurie pulled her skirt around her and jumped to the ground, but I saw the quick flash of resentment in her eyes.

Mama' shoulders sagged. "I'm sorry, Annie Laurie. Come on back up. Perhaps I do need a little rest. I'll go on back with Cora for a bit. You carry on." She handed the reins over and quietly moved to the back and settled next to me.

I let her lean against me and put her arms around me. It had seemed like such a long, long time.

By dusk, we pulled up behind the train and settled in for the night. Captain Richards spotted us and rode back. "We've only got about three days, but it'll be hilly goin'. Try to keep up." With an uncharacteristic smile, he nodded toward me. "Keep an eye out for elderberries. They should be peakin' about now." He turned to leave but stopped. "I know somebody who might like to give you a hand. Her name is Mildred." And with that, he headed for the front of the wagons.

The sky clouded up that night and stormed so that I could hardly sleep. I thought of the gale a few weeks before. It didn't stop Mama, and this one came too late to make a difference. I scooted to the back of the wagon to watch the lightning display to the south toward Fort Smith.

Chapter Seven

The first one awake the next morning, I watched a glimmer of light hover on the eastern horizon. I thought about meeting a new friend. *Mildred.* The name spoke of suffering somehow, but in my enthusiasm for a new friend, I believed in my power to lift even the saddest spirit. Berry picking would provide the bond, and I felt a surge of kinship to a girl I had not yet met.

Joe and Ben groaned from the pallets. Ben gripped a corner of the wagon and gave it a shake. "Rise and shine, ladies! I hear clanking of skillets up ahead!"

I rushed through chores, scraping the plates and feeding Grace; I rinsed the cups and packed them back in the wagon with a liveliness Annie Laurie remarked upon. Dressed and with a bonnet tied on, I stood primly in front of Mama to ask permission to go find Mildred. "She's in the third wagon. Captain Richards recommended her to me as a friend." I grabbed a bucket. "I'll be sure to pick some berries for you, too. You know I wouldn't forget you." I noticed the arched eyebrow of approval when Mama cast her eyes over the skirt and bonnet I wore instead of Cousin Jimmy's outfit.

"It's only for a few days, Cora. You'll remember that, won't you?"

"Yes, of course I will." I ignored the look of concern Mama directed at me.

"Go on. You be careful. And be back before high noon." Mama had already climbed into the wagon seat. "Keep up with the train and do not get out of sight."

"Yes, ma'am!" I ran off to the other wagons, slinging my pail in my hand, calling, "Grace! Amazing Grace, catch up!"

I found the girl before we reached the next hill. "Tell your mama we have been assigned a berry-picking project by Captain Richards. We've got a powerful dog to protect us. Then grab a bucket." I jiggled my own. "Let's go!"

Head down, the bedraggled child, nodded and whispered, "Howdy." I bet her mother didn't insist on *her* brushing her hair a hundred strokes at night. Didn't look like her mama made her brush her hair at all— tangles stuck out from Mildred's bonnet. Never mind I had eliminated any need to brush my own. At the time it seemed like the perfect revenge, but every so often, no matter how hard I pushed regret away, I lamented my actions when I thought about those black, glossy curls. And never more so when I looked at Mildred's dishwater coloring. Even the girl's eyes were washed out with what appeared to be defeat—a pale color not quite hazel with interesting hues nor a deep, intriguing brown.

Mildred climbed back into her wagon for a bucket and called to her mother, "Ma, Captain said to go pick berries." The gratitude that lit her face broke my heart a little. Here was a kindred soul. In that moment, I imagined the magnanimous gift of friendship I would bestow upon this child. At last, someone who needed me. I would not fail her.

"You're Mildred and I'm Cora, and we are on an adventure!" I took her hand and swung our arms between us. "Where you from anyway? I'm from Douglas County, Missouri, and my mama is making us go to Texas. This here is Amazing Grace. She's the best dog that ever lived. And—"

"I had a dog once," said Mildred. "A coyote got him. Least ways, we think that's what happened." She stumbled over the words, then stopped, let go of my hand and clutched her bucket until her knuckles turned white. "We named him Andy—for Andrew Jackson."

"Maybe you'll find another dog soon. Who knows? Maybe Grace here will have puppies, and I'll give you the pick of the litter! What do you think of that?"

Mildred's smile appeared wistful, but a smile nonetheless.

I picked up her hand again and kept walking and talking. "Grace is with me all the time, and I'm not gonna let any old coyotes get her." I pulled Mildred toward a bush. "I bet those are elderberries. They look like the ones we had at home." I plucked a handful, and we began to fill our buckets.

I studied the color on my fingers, remembering the mulberries. "I had a tree at home." I didn't say anything more for a moment and gazed up at the sky. "But I can't think about that anymore. I just can't."

Mildred set her bucket down very carefully. "There's lots of things we can't think about nowadays." She hugged me tight. "We gotta keep on walkin'."

Our fingers were interlaced with sticky, purple stain that sealed the friendship, not in blood but in bitter elderberry juice. It had the same power. "Friends forever," I said and didn't care if my voice caught.

With no regard for the state of our mouths or hands, we turned and started back toward the wagons. The elderberries were far too sour to eat without sugar, but we had tried enough of them to paint our lips and the corners of our mouths the shade of bruises.

—⁓—

As we neared Fort Smith, I relied on the outward show of berry picking to allow us solitude and companionship. We followed Amazing Grace down deer paths where we were not supposed to go, but when she broke into a tirade of barking, I found her lunging and retreating at a tangle of undergrowth near us on the trail. The vines rustled as a snake struck and recoiled.

I screamed and tried to grab the dog, but she charged relentlessly. Her jaws snapped as she rallied time after time. I dropped my bucket, and berries went flying while I searched for a rock big enough to pound the snake's head into the ground. I found the perfect stone, big as a bread loaf. "You get away from my dog!" With both arms above my head, I hurled the rock at the weaving snake. Its head smashed beneath the stone, it writhed, thrashing the ground. I grabbed Grace around the neck and dragged her away.

Annie Laurie came running. "What's wrong? What's wrong?" She screamed when she saw the snake, seized our hands and pulled us back. "That thing could still bite."

"But my berries! They're for Captain Richards!" I wrenched free, grabbed the handle of my bucket and began scooping the berries back into the pail. "We'll wash them, Mildred. They'll be fine."

But Mildred was undone. Her eyes wide with horror, she clutched her dress with a berry-stained hand. "Mama warned me about snakes. She warned me!" she cried, backing down the path.

Annie Laurie reached around my shoulders. "Let's go on, honey. Bring the berries, but let's get on back."

I grabbed the last handful and allowed myself to be tugged toward the wagons. "Amazing Grace saved us, you know."

—◇◇◇—

Mildred refused to go berry picking after that and insisted on staying within yards of the wagons. But she did talk more. And talked. And talked. "Mama and Papa are headed to El Paso. We couldn't take the train from home but when we get to El Paso, Papa said we could sell the horses and get tickets all the way to California. We're gonna be rich!"

"Well, we're won't be rich. We'll be stuck on some old farm in Texas where there's nothing but cactus and rattlesnakes." I kicked at a rock and sent it spinning. "My papa died."

"Ooh." Mildred patted my shoulder. "I would hate it if my papa died."

"You have no idea." I looked away at the hills, so she wouldn't see the tears flooding my eyes. I thought of Alice when she stood in Wonderland saying, *I could tell you my adventures—beginning from this morning, but it's no use going back to yesterday because I was a different person then.*

Thankfully, Mildred changed the subject. "I've been meaning to ask you. What happened to your hair? You look like an Indian scalped you!" She collapsed in a flurry of giggles.

"Actually, I barely escaped. In our part of Missouri, there are some dangerous tribes. You probably don't know, but there are, and I barely escaped. Maybe that's why Mama thought we ought to leave. She got real upset when she saw all my hair sheared off. I can tell you that." I cut my eyes over to check Mildred's response. "Didn't bother me none. I just picked up a stick and beat up that redskin."

"In a pig's ear!"

"Yes, I did. Like I took care of that snake. You saw that with your own eyes. I don't tolerate snakes and injuns." I smacked my hands together. "No sir-ee, Bob."

Mildred sniffed, but a new look of respect crept into her eyes. "You don't suppose we'll have to whup any Indians in Oklahoma, do you? I hear there's still some ornery ones around there."

"Nah, Mama wouldn't let us travel alone if she thought Indians were around." I grabbed a pebble off the ground and tossed it from hand to hand. "All the same, I could handle them."

Mildred studied my eyes for any trace of lies. "I'm glad we've got Captain Richards to protect us. I'd be real nervous about traveling in a lone wagon."

"Well, I ain't scared. Besides we got Ben and Joe. They are about the strongest boys you ever saw. And don't forget Amazing Grace here. Y'all got to go clear across Texas. Us? We're heading to the east part." I hesitated. "Why don't you talk to your daddy about coming with us? You'd get there quicker, that's for sure. And—" I clasped her hands in mine. "We could be friends forever."

Mildred ducked her head. "I don't think Daddy will change his mind. When he said we were going to California, Mama cried for three days. Three days!" She held up three fingers. "And that didn't work." She shook her head. "Nope, don't think anything will change his mind."

"Nothing changed my mama's either. She's about as stubborn a woman as I have ever seen. Nobody else wanted to go to Texas. Just Mama. And she's hell-bent." I checked Mildred's reaction to my use of "hell." For emphasis, I said it again and louder this time. "Hell-bent, I tell you."

This time Mildred covered a smile with her fingertips. "Cora, you are very daring."

I didn't bother to hide my own upturned lips.

Chapter Eight

The wagon train pulled into Fort Smith. The sound of hammers competed with the rattle of the wheels on the wooden bridge that crossed the Arkansas River. A cemetery with newly mounded graves lay under broken trees. I nudged Mildred with my elbow. "Why, this is not what I expected at all. I thought these people would help us get on our way. Don't look like they have time for anything but picking up and putting back."

Mama frowned into the late afternoon's sun. "Joe, ride on up to the front and find out what's happened here."

Joe had already started forward and moved his horse into a canter.

I ventured a wave at some children who stood by the roadside, but they stared as the wagon train pulled by. Shoulders slumped, the people barely looked up from their work.

Joe returned with word from the captain. "Twister hit not two days ago. Must have been that storm we saw on the horizon that night. Forty folks dead. Captain said to turn around and wait on the outskirts by the river. He'll go in and see what we'd best plan on doing. Looks bad, Mama. Real bad."

Mama caught her breath and called for me to climb up in the wagon. She sent Mildred back to her own family.

Annie Laurie spoke in a whisper. "I've not seen a tornado, but I've heard of them. Not four years ago one went through St. Louis and killed nearly 150 people. More died on the Mississippi River, their bodies never found. The outrage of God's wrath. One afternoon, in less than an hour, homes and people were gone."

"Let's have no more talk of that," said Mama. "No use commenting on the frailty of life. We're headed for a new beginning. Those kinds of words will slow us down."

I felt pretty sure nothing would slow Mama down.

Hours later, Captain Richards returned to our campsite on the other side of the river. He called up all the families and relayed the information he'd gathered. We all stood around while he gave us the details. "Churned right through the middle of town. Took out Isaacson's and Babcock's grocery. Smith's grocery, too. Two churches are piles of kindling. Plumb ruined the town."

I gave Mildred's hand a squeeze. For once I could say nothing.

"Don't know how we're gonna stock up," Richards continued. "Supplies are coming in from around the state. Maybe we can get us enough to get us to Eufaula. We won't have the provisions we'd hoped for. Just have to piecemeal along the way." He moved the wad of tobacco over to the other side of his mouth and spit. "Dang shame."

That evening Captain Richards walked back to our wagon. "Listen, Miz Allen, I hate to add to your troubles, but this here is where we got to go our separate ways. I can't be responsible for y'all while other folks signed up and paid their fee." With the heel of his boot, he dug a hole in the dirt. "We got to head west. You got your boys, and I do believe if you head south from here, you can make your destination in a matter of, oh, a few weeks. I done went to the trouble of drawing out a little map for you. It ain't the straightest shot, but—"

"I assure you that we are perfectly capable of finding our way without your help, Captain Richards." Mama turned to go.

"Mama, don't be reckless. Let the man finish." Ben touched her shoulder. "We don't have anything to lose by listening."

"I ain't got but a few words of advice," Captain Richards continued. "Don't try to cross the Red on your own. Go to Colbert's Ferry. It's your best bet. Won't cost you but four bits. Quicksand's ever'where along that river. I mean ever'where! You'd hafta risk somebody goin' ahead with a stick to check for it. And then there's the snakes. They're treacherous along the Red." He narrowed his eyes at me. "Despite some well-known snake killers in the family, there ain't no point in puttin' your lives at stake. Well, I guess it's all written down here with the map. You can read, can't you?"

That threw Mama over the edge. "Yes, Captain, I can read!" She snatched the paper from his fingers.

"Always suspected you could. My apologies if I have offended you, ma'am." He closed his eyes and shook his head. "Boys, be cautious this side of the river. Some rumors about Choctaw's stirring up a little trouble. Most likely nothin'. Never hurts to be aware. And if you do run into a renegade bunch, don't consider fightin' back. Put up with whatever you got to. They're out for a tussle. Give them a trinket and try not to make them mad." He glanced at the only jewelry Mama had left—her wedding ring. "A few bruises are better than a missing scalp." Captain Richards took his hands out of his pockets and leaned down. "And Miss Cora, it's been a pure pleasure meeting you. Texas probably ain't near as bad as you think. Why, I've been there a time or two and as I—"

"But you promised, Captain!" I had stood and listened until I could stand it no longer. "You promised that Mildred and me could be friends! We picked you elderberries! Don't you remember?" I didn't mean to cry, but the tears began. "Don't you?"

"Aw, now." Captain Richards turned toward Mama and spread his arms. "Help me out here, ma'am. I ain't no good at talking to little girls. At explaining—"

"I'll handle it, Captain." Mama reached around my shoulders, but I swung away. "He's right, girls. Tomorrow we'll head out. Best say goodbye. We'll be gettin' an early start."

"No, Mama! Let's follow along behind like we did before! You wouldn't mind that, would you, sir?" I let go of Mildred's hand and clutched the captain's vest. "We'd be real quiet like we were before. You'd hardly know we were there. Please, Captain. I'll find more berries, I promise. I'll—"

"That's enough, Cora. The man is right. He's not going our way for long. We've imposed enough."

"Aw, ma'am, I don't mean you were any trouble."

Mama grabbed me by the hand and headed to the back of the wagon. "Say goodbye."

I twisted in Mama's grip. "Write me a letter, Mildred. I'll be somewhere in East Texas. The post might could find me. Write!"

Mildred unwrapped the scarf she had always worn. "Take this, Cora. It will help you remember me. You and Amazing Grace saved my life from the rattlesnake." She looped the scarf around my neck. "It'll keep the sun off in summer and the cold away in winter." She waved goodbye with a little flutter of her fingers. "Remember me." Her eyes glazed over, and she tried to smile. She turned and fled to her wagon looking back only once to turn and call. "Don't go beating up any injuns!"

Chapter Nine

We did get an early start. Mama had the boys dousing the fire and harnessing the oxen before sunrise. She and Annie Laurie loaded the wagon with what few provisions we acquired at Fort Smith. With my arm around Amazing Grace, I watched from my pallet.

Annie Laurie shook her head as she folded the last of the blankets. "That little girl hardly gets her heart set on something and seems like it's no time until it's taken away. And look at that hair. It's barely down to her collar."

"If she doesn't take the scissors to it again." Mama touched my head.

I turned over and gathered the quilt over my head. "Let me alone."

"We're heading out, but you stay here in the wagon as long as you want to, Cora." Annie Laurie stroked my back. "We don't mind a bit. You want some leftover bacon? I've got—"

"Let me alone!" I burrowed further into my nest.

Both Annie Laurie and Mama let out those heavy sighs of theirs and climbed down from the back of the wagon. Amazing Grace snuggled closer to me. Trustworthy above all others.

—⚏—

The beauty of eastern Oklahoma provided a distraction that kept us optimistic. The roadbeds were sound in the valleys and creek beds shallow enough for easy crossing. In the distance rose the outlying ridges of the San Bois and Winding Stair Mountains. On the prairies, pale shades of grasses moved like ocean waves and rasped beneath the wagon tongue. The hypnotic effect lulled me into a dreamlike state that let hours drift like deep water current.

We had almost reached the Red River when we met another family traveling in the opposite direction. Even with their heads turned away from me, I heard "renegade" in the whispers. "What does 'renegade' mean?" I asked Annie Laurie.

"You know. Somebody like an outlaw." She produced a fake smile. "But you don't need to worry." She gave me a quick hug. "Let's play 'What Am I Thinking?'"

I sighed. "Oh, all right. But I know you're trying to change the subject."

Annie Laurie put her finger to her chin and gazed at the cover of the wagon. "Hmmm. What am I thinking?"

"Give me a hint."

She contorted her face into a frown.

"Is it crotchety?" I asked.

"Sometimes," said Annie Laurie.

"Oh, you mean all the time. That would be Mama!"

She flushed. "No. No! I did not mean our mother!" But then she couldn't stop the giggle. "I rather had in mind those oxen out there. What did we name them? Babe, Blue, Crusty and Surly. Surly was the one I meant."

"Oh, you did not! We didn't even name them. You thought I'd never get it. I'm not playing anymore. You're making things up." I scooted to the front of the wagon by Mama. "Annie Laurie is a smarty, and one day I'm gonna tell on her."

"Saving it for an important occasion?"

"Well, yes. Yes, I think I will." And I tucked it away for just such a time. "Anyway, I've been meaning to speak to you about something."

Mama looked surprised and then amused. "Go right ahead, dear."

Ignoring her expression, I said, "I heard what the captain said, but I thought the Indians were nice now." Not sure if my words were accurate or wishful thinking, I waited.

Mama put on her patient face. "Sometime back the Choctaws, Chickasaw and Cherokees were driven out of their homes back East. Lots of them died. Others revolted and were forced to live on the Oklahoma land that won't support a corn stalk. Some still carry a grudge."

I understood how they felt.

—⁓—

Along the way, I studied the small changes in Mama's demeanor. Her fists tightened on the reins and bunched the veins across her brown hands. She became even more irritable, short and impatient with all of us.

"From here on," she said to me, "I want you to stay close to the wagon and stop running off to pick flowers or loitering behind like the time you found a box turtle and tried to torture him out of his shell. You hear?"

"Yes ma'am, I hear." But even as I said it, I scanned the wagon's contents for a little entertainment.

The next morning Mama rousted us up earlier than usual. The light from a crescent moon growing paler in the early hours offered the only hint of dawn. I had missed breakfast and refused hardtack, but the barrel filled with cornmeal also contained the last jar of fig preserves. With lips pursed, I set about improving my situation. The figs remained a delicacy to be doled out, but I sat on the tailgate, kicking and singing and clutching the jar between my knees. With my hand small enough to wedge into it, I intended to consume with unrepressed gluttony its entire contents. The figs were soft and sweet, and despite the telltale evidence, I allowed the juice to drip down my chin. I swiped at my face with the back of my hand and wiped it on my britches while throwing a look back over my shoulder to check for witnesses. After I'd had enough to quell the hunger and before sheer nausea set in, I sat in a sugar stupor and thought of home.

The figs brought back the reverie—the hours Mama stood, her face flushed and perspiring, over jars boiling in water and the cloying sweetness of the kitchen steam. But most of all, I relived the amusement of watching the losing game for figs she had played with the cardinals and blue jays. Attempting to scare away the birds, she'd tied strips of white cotton around the branches, but even with the ruckus she created when she hollered and swung her broom, they only scattered momentarily. Their wings fluttering, they attached themselves to the branches and began over again as soon when she stepped back into the house.

Joe rode up along the back of the wagon. "Hey! Share those figs! Toss me one."

"They're too sticky," I said, not wanting to part with the last few.

Moving his horse closer to the wagon, he taunted me. "I bet you can't throw it this far, anyway." He held out his hand. With all my might, I threw like Cousin Jimmy did when we played catch. The fig sailed right at Joe's head, but he reacted quicker than I hoped. He snatched it out of the air, popped it into his mouth and narrowed his eyes. "Why, you little toot."

I squealed and dived back into the wagon. Not in time. I felt a plunk on my rear end. I whirled to find something else to throw at Joe but stopped when his face grew serious and he held up his hand.

His finger went to his lips and he pointed. A large whitetail buck stood at the tree line, his antlers wide and regal. Joe lifted his rifle, took careful aim and fired. The buck disappeared into the woods as if he'd never been there.

"Well, there went a nice venison supper." He jammed the rifle back into the scabbard. "Dang!"

Mama yelled back at him. "What are you doing? You scared us to death. You know Richards said not to fire your guns."

Joe nudged his horse forward to explain.

Pleased with Mama's interruption that allowed me to finish the figs, I resumed my singing and kicking. I swayed from side to side, keeping the rhythm for a few moments even after the wagon lurched to a halt. I never considered any other possibility for stopping other than Joe getting a dressing down.

Amazing Grace's outburst startled me. She scrambled to the front of the wagon, barking. When I scooted forward to get a glimpse, Mama's hand met me head on and shoved me hard behind the bedrolls. Before I could voice my indignation, Annie tumbled in beside me, her eyes wide and lips pale and trembling. "Shhh!"

I inched around Mama's skirt enough to see the two men. As the dust rose around them, the oxen grunted and pawed the ground. Ben offered the barrel of cornmeal, but laughter met his attempt at bargaining, along with a thumping of chest and the gibberish, "*Chahta siahoki*,"

Despite white men's clothes, they wore a bright slash of red across their foreheads. One of them rammed his pony into Ben's horse and dragged him to the ground. He spun a bullwhip above his head. The tip flicked like a snake's tongue before it bit into Ben's leg and then his back as he struggled away. With the next stroke of the whip, Ben's head knocked against the legs of the oxen, and they shied and tried to bolt, their hooves drumming the dirt. It was all Mama could do to hold them.

Joe put his rifle to his hip. But over the dust and chaos, Mama screamed, "No!" She wrestled with the reins but kept her seat.

When the oxen steadied, she sat stern and erect. Her whole body seemed of some starched calico, a patchwork mural blocking my view. She did not turn her head or beg but appeared to stifle quick intakes of breath at each slap of the whip. And with each lash, she twisted the ring on the finger of her left hand.

I thought it a useless thing to do—sit there, turning a ring on her finger while the savages beat Ben bloody.

A Winchester shotgun rested right behind her. I stared at its long barrel with the *WRA Co.* monogrammed on the stock and wished with all my might that she would pick it up. Joe had checked the lever action two days ago, so it was ready to fire. I knew her to be more than capable. I'd seen her level that shotgun at a fox slipping around the chicken coop at home. His hide hung on the fence the next morning.

I turned to Annie Laurie. "What is wrong with her?" I whispered, "I bet if they tried to get her old piano, she'd shoot. Get the gun, and you shoot those redskins." I moved forward to scream for Joe when my sister grabbed me by the straps of my overalls, and disregarding the sound of ripping fabric, pulled me back and covered my mouth with her hand.

"Shhh, be quiet. We can't shoot. It'd only make it worse." Sagging against her, I nodded, and she released me, but I never believed silence would save us.

I inched closer to the gap in the canvas cover and concentrated on the motes of dust that bobbed in the light—tiny particles dancing independently of the outside turmoil. When I finally pressed my eye to the wedge of brightness, I saw Ben slumped against the creek bank as

Mama stood and with one last hard tug, wrenched the wedding ring from her finger and flung it at the man with the bullwhip. "Take it. It's all I've got. Take it!"

I grasped Mama's skirt in both fists and peered around the folds to see moccasined feet shuffling over to the gold wedding band still spinning in the dust. Now as a grown woman, I still remember the image—that last flash of warm brilliance that ricocheted off the ring as the rider squatted and pushed it onto his own finger.

The dark man grunted to his companion, mounted, dug his heels into the flanks of his horse and spun away.

Eyeing the retreating flanks of the pony, Amazing Grace squirmed loose, her fur catching for one quick moment on my buttons. Whining, she struggled against my grip on her hind legs and escaped.

"No, don't! Grace!" I cried out and lunged after her. My boot caught in my pants, tore out part of the hem, and I fell against the seat of the wagon. Amazing Grace scuttled over the wagon wheel and snarled at the feet of the Indian's pony.

His face broad and angular, his full lips almost pursed, the Indian demanded my gaze until he found it and stared at me with a boldness I'd never experienced before in my life. He laughed and in a graceful, athletic motion leaned from his horse to grab Amazing Grace by one leg. Strapping her feet together in one smooth figure eight of latigo, he slung her across the back of the pony. *"Ofi' hohchifo'. Niyah. Himak nittak amofi."*

The rhythm of the words sounded like a child's nursery rhyme, but when I screamed, the men swiveled on their ponies and looked back at me. Their high-pitched yodel mimicked me as they rode away.

They were not going to take my dog. I grappled behind the wagon seat and lifted the shotgun. The 12-gauge didn't seem as heavy as it once had when I had held it. Before Mama could grab it, I lifted it to my shoulder and fired. The shot went high and knocked me backward over the wagon seat and into Annie Laurie's lap. Still sobbing, I cried, "Did I get him?"

"Almost, darling, almost. But we've got to see to Ben," She said as she wiped gunpowder from my face with her skirt hem.

Off his horse and swiping at tears, Joe dropped to Ben's side. I scrambled after Annie Laurie and Mama as they rushed to Ben. He lifted his head, smiled and said, "Them injuns put their rouge in funny places." Then he passed out.

"Please, I can help lift him, too." I sobbed and patted the torn and bloody cotton of his shirt. "Let me, let me," I cried as Mama slipped laudanum into the side of Ben's mouth and bathed the angry welts with water from a canteen. The marks were like lightning bolts across his back. That all this could happen on a beautiful sunny day with no premonition of danger reminded me of another sunny day when I gave up my papa to God. Only then, everyone but me knew it was coming.

I refused to acknowledge what could happen to Amazing Grace at the hands of the Choctaw. I tried to save her, but I had lost my grip. It seemed I had lost my grip on everything in my life, but I made up mind. I wouldn't miss the shot the next time, I told myself. *Not next time.*

"*Ofi' hohchifo'. Niyah. Himak nittak amofi.*" I memorized what I could of the words. I whispered them over and over to myself almost every day—long after we crossed over to Texas. Alternatives to this calamity rumbled around in my head. In each scenario, I created the culprit—my mother, of course. Papa would have never let this happen. If Papa hadn't died, if Mama hadn't been so pigheaded.

—⚅—

That afternoon Mama drove until the oxen stumbled and Joe took the reins away from her. She fought him at first, but then her face clouded over, the veins at her temple throbbing. She got down and walked—a furious stride that somehow seemed to calm her enough to allow Joe to pull up long before dusk. The rage and helplessness in Mama's face confused and frightened me.

She took control of the only thing left to her—caring for Ben. "We need a poultice for Ben's back. Annie Laurie, quick before sundown, mix up some sugar water on a plate. Joe, when the bees start coming around, follow them back to wherever their hive is. Get a good smoking branch of green wood. You remember how. Smoke them to sleep and bring us back the biggest honeycomb. Annie Laurie, start us a fire and boil some strips of your old petticoat. Dry them as quick as you can. Hang them out there on that tree limb. And find that jar of beef suet.

Annie Laurie and Joe stood motionless seeming to try to untangle their thoughts and put them to action.

"I mean, *now!*"

That snapped them into action. I followed Mama as she climbed back to where Ben lay and watched as she pulled out the bottle of Irving's Brandy and the laudanum. "Here. This will help."

"What's that?" Ben opened one eye.

"Brandy." She uncorked the laudanum bottle and counted the drops into the spoonful of brandy she held. She hesitated and added two more drops. "It'll help. You'll feel it when it hits your belly. We're saving the honey for your back."

He winced with the effort but opened his mouth. And winced again. "That's terrible brandy." He laid his head on his arms and closed his eyes.

As Mama turned to repack the bottles, she studied the brandy for a moment before lifting it to her own lips.

"Mama?" I had not been given a task.

She turned and spoke, but her words were flinty. "What? What do you want?"

"I don't know what to do."

"Just stay out of—" But then she took a deep breath and forced a little kindness into her voice. She dropped to her knees and stroked my head like the day I had cut off all my hair. "What I mean is, you can sit here by Ben and sing that little song that goes 'Over the rolling waters.' Something like that."

"The one Papa used to sing to me?"

"Yes, yes. That one."

I wondered if that would do any good, but I wanted to do something, anything, so I sat next to Ben and sang to him between hiccups until his breathing became deep and regular.

Mama walked away from the wagon. I watched her lean against a pine tree and press her face against the bark, watched her breathe in its fragrant scent. But she vomited anyway. "Don't cry. Don't you cry," I heard her say until she collapsed against it and beat the rough bark with her fists until they too, like Ben's back, were bloody.

Chapter Ten

Another family waited with us for the ferry to return to the Oklahoma bank. I watched the ferrymen pole the barge toward us and gazed overhead to the great cable that would guide us across the river. Mama urged the oxen onto the boarding planks to the ferry. The animals balked and seemed to ponder sudden death, but the ferryman maneuvered them onto the barge, blocked the wagon wheels and steadied the oxen until Annie could stand at their traces. Joe braced himself between his horse and Ben's and patted their necks, talking to them quietly. They danced in place but dropped their heads and blew as the ferry steadied into the stream.

I sat close to Ben and prayed this part of the journey would be completed. "You can swim, Ben, but I'm not so good." I touched the back of his head, his hair slicked by sweat. "Getting dunked might make those lash marks feel better, but I'd go down like a stone."

"You could grab Blackjack's tail and he'd be your private ferry across this creek."

"This ain't no creek and you know it."

"Well, it's a big creek, I'll grant you, but there's no denying that Blackjack has a tail."

"Oh, Ben."

"Climb down and take a look. You don't want to miss out on seeing Texas for the first time."

I frowned at the straight line etched across his mouth where his smile was supposed to be. "But, I want to stay with you."

"No, I want to hear firsthand from you what it's like to walk onto Texas soil." He sat up straighter and gave me a little push. "Go on. I'm countin' on it."

I slid off the tailgate, held to the wagon and stared at the towering cottonwood that anchored us to the cable. The excitement I'd hoped for was gone, the starch taken out of crossing the Red River. What should have been a celebration turned out to be more like Moses' people in the Bible, fleeing for their lives across the Red Sea to a land they didn't know. But the Red River? I could have used a little more divine intervention when those redskins beat Ben and stole Amazing Grace.

The barge swayed when a sudden eddy caught its stern, and I grabbed the wheel of the wagon to steady myself. I gazed out over the river. Nothing red about it. Instead, it roiled murky brown, concealing hidden horrors. The sidestepping oxen seemed to intuitively understand the dangers. I remembered Ben saying how people thought oxen were stubborn, but really their obstinacy came from knowing more than humans did. He laughed when he said it, but with the roll of the deck, I tried not to think about what the oxen knew.

The first one to disembark, ahead of Joe and the horses, I felt my heels dig soft burrows into the sand, and above I heard the distant cry of geese headed south. Well, here we are, I thought, in Texas. I hated to tell Ben it looked just like Oklahoma.

—⚏—

Even though it was October, Texas didn't seem to care. She could burn as long as she wanted. The cotton rags Annie Laurie and I knotted across our foreheads didn't stop sweat from dripping into our eyes as we pulled across the last days of our journey. Joe tied Ben's Blackjack behind the wagon. The stallion followed grudgingly as if delegated to the position of a milk cow.

Ben propped himself on his elbows to face backward in the wagon and encouraged Blackjack to keep up, but much of the time he lay with his eyes closed, his jaw tight against the pain. The red streaks on his back festered in the heat, despite the damp compresses we replaced every few hours. He tried to joke, to make us think he didn't hurt as bad as he did, but no one fell for it.

If Ben were trying to fake optimism, surely Mama proved even more false. She insisted on driving even when Joe could have done as good a job, but when she thought no one looked, she took a deep breath and tried to stretch.

"Let me drive for a while," said Annie Laurie. "You've been sitting there twisting side to side for the better part of two days."

"No! You go see to Ben! He needs your help more than I do."

Annie Laurie shrank back from the vehemence in Mama's voice. "Well, Mama, for goodness sake."

"I'm taking care of Ben, anyway," I said. I didn't try to hide the defense in my voice. He had become my possession, my way of not thinking about Amazing Grace. "He told me he'd call if he needed any little thing."

"You know he won't," said Mama. "He'll grit his teeth to keep from asking for help."

"Like you're gritting yours?" I said. "I've been watching you."

"Hush. If you want to be helpful, hand me a couple pieces of hardtack."

"Ain't no more hardtack." I shook out the sack. "You ate the last of it yesterday. Didn't know you thought it to be so tasty."

"I haven't been very hungry for anything else, and the roads are bumpy, that's all. I'm fine."

But as I stepped into the back of the wagon, I heard Mama groan before she yelled at the oxen and slapped the reins against their haunches.

That night Mama excused herself, saying she needed to reflect, needing to have a moment with God. I thought she might need to ask forgiveness for being such a crabby old biddy and this I would have to hear. I followed her into the piney woods.

The wind shifted among the treetops, and I tripped over a downed branch. Mama looked up quickly, but I hunkered down as catatonic as a rabbit in a hawk's stare. I hoped she thought it was an animal. A deer perhaps. Or raccoon.

Mama leaned against a loblolly pine and took a flask and vial from her dress pocket. She tilted her head back. First the laudanum. Then quick the brandy. She clenched her teeth and took another gulp of brandy before she squatted above the pine needles that sponged the dark earth.

It was the mewling sound she made that terrified me.

After a while, she moved to her knees and began to plunge at the earth with a stick and then placed a large stone over the spot. When she rose, she leaned against the tree and finally, limped back to the campsite. I crouched in the pine needles and tried to understand. I crept to the spot where I had seen her set the stone and pushed it aside. The moonlight fell in vague shadows and distorted even the most common woodland features. A rock became a rabbit. A fern became a bird. I hefted the stone away and ran my fingers across the earth. Coagulated and warm, it suggested more than I wanted to know. *Curiosity killed the cat. Curiosity killed the cat.* I ran to camp, never caring that branches scratched my cheek or that I stumbled and fell. Breathless and nauseated, I drove my hands into a bucket of creek water and the water tinted dark in the lantern light.

Mama begged off cooking that night, saying Annie Laurie and I could take over, that she had a mild headache and thought a little rest would do her good. I watched her as she made her own pallet of pine needles and great-grandmother's quilt and curled up into a tight knot. For the time being, I would not explore more than her story. Maybe she could fool Annie Laurie, but I would let it rest for a while in a small corner of my mind.

Later that night, I tucked in beside her. I hated to admit I wanted consolation, but she pulled me close as if she too were in need of comfort. Amazing Grace had always been the one to snuggle close when I felt sad. I cursed the Indians. I cursed them for Amazing Grace. And I cursed them for Ben. "You'll go to hell for this, injuns." I prayed fervently and silently to God. "Vengeance is mine saith the Lord," I whispered. *And mine. And mine.* I tried to think about something else, but the only other thing to think about was Mama. I put my arm around her and took in the vague and sour smell of brandy and something else. But if she didn't tell, I wouldn't tell. It will be our secret—even from each other—to think on.

—⚹—

We stayed another day at our campsite. Mama wanted Ben to rest, she said. Not be jostled by the wagon ride, but I wondered how much rest *she* needed. How nice to sit, even though, the possibility of Choctaw in the area made us edgy. An old red river wouldn't stop them, though I doubted they'd take the ferry. They'd ride across on their painted ponies, and I imagined them floundering in quicksand and sinking up to their necks and trapped there for days while they starved and called for help in their stupid language with no one to hear them. Amazing Grace, being a smart dog, would leap to safety and track me down and jump into my arms as I slept. I played the scene over and over in my mind until I believed it could happen and each night I left a little space in my bedroll for Grace.

We all slept out at night. All except Ben. Joe made his bed at the foot of the wagon, and I liked to listen to them exchange insults. I had seen that Joe had wanted to say something for several days and didn't know where to start. "Ben? Listen, I—" He spoke into the dark night. "I should have never fired at that buck. If I had thought first. Richards warned us not to shoot or otherwise risk Indians. But I did. I did anyway."

"If you're going whine about not meaning to scare up the Indians, I'm not gonna listen. If I'd seen the buck, we'd have had some nice venison steaks. That's for sure. And if *you'd* been the closest to Crazy Horse there, you would of been the one on the ground gettin' whupped. Could've been you, paleface, so quit stewing over it."

"Well, hell, Ben, I hate it. Wish I could've saved you this pain, never mind the mortification and Mama's ring and Cora's dog." His voice broke.

"Don't you worry about it, Brother."

"But how am I gonna make it up to Mama? Losing that ring?"

"You won't. Guess she'd as soon have her boy as a bauble."

"It wasn't just any bauble and you know it. And then Amazing Grace? How can I ever–"

"Another lost cause. But that little girl? She's got grit. She'll find some critter to love. That's the best you can hope for."

Joe felt sorry. Of course, he did, but I would never find some critter to love. I would not.

—⚏—

"What's the matter with Mama?" I asked like I didn't already know more than Annie Laurie did. "The bossy seems to have gone right out of her. Think she's sad about giving up her last ring?"

Annie Laurie never let the threat of Indians keep her from brushing her own long hair. "Ninety-eight, ninety-nine, one hundred!" She set the brush down and checked the mirror before she replaced both in her reticule. "Cora Allen, your lack of intuition leaves me speechless. If you ask me, she's doubting herself—dragging us all on this trek, getting Ben beat to a pulp by savages, least of all losing her rings. She's probably kicking herself for such a foolish, foolish decision."

"Are we talking about *our* mother here?" I fingered the tufts of my own hair. "She never changed her mind in her life."

"You are completely innocent of the ways of mature women, my child."

"What do you know, o woman of the world? You're hardly six years older than me." I stuffed my feet down in the pallet and turned over. "Something's the matter with Mama, and it's more than she's letting on." I sat up again and kicked off the cover. "You're not listening to me and you better! She's bleeding, Annie Laurie. A lot. You should have seen her pallet. She snatched it up before you were awake and hustled it down to the creek. The water turned red—like in the Bible." I covered my lips. "Do you think she's dying?"

"It couldn't have been that bad. Look at her. She's already loaded to move out."

"Yeah, but she let us stay one whole day extra. You see how white she looks and how she hunches over when she walks—not that big walk she's usually got."

"I'll talk to her when we get a minute alone. She does tend to confide in me in such moments."

"But I saw the blood," I said.

"And I shall convey your concerns."

But how Annie Laurie could find a quiet moment with Mama, I had no idea. Ben had to lie in the wagon, and everyone else walked within earshot.

The next afternoon after we'd been on the road for hours, I hinted to Annie Laurie. "Ben's sleeping in there. Maybe I'll take a nap myself." She rolled her eyes but took the hint.

After a while, she began. "You all right, Mama? You don't seem yourself."

"You might as well know."

Annie Laurie took in a breath.

"Women my age can have some unusual. . .well, menses. We are approaching the change, and things become not so predictable. Downright effusive, for lack of a better word."

I listened as she concocted a story about her nearing the change of life and how sometimes these aberrations occurred, the hard cramps and blood. "It's something older women must deal with," she said. "Nothing to trouble yourself about." She patted Annie Laurie's hand.

"But you're not old enough to—"

"I said not to trouble yourself. And don't tell Cora. You know how fanciful she can be." Mama checked back over her shoulder at me, and I pinched my eyes shut. "Go see to your brother. He needs your concerns far more than I."

Later that evening, Annie Laurie told me about the conversation as though I hadn't heard the whole thing. "Well, that's what she said. I didn't even have to ask her outright. So, I guess there's nothing for us to worry about. It's one of those mean little things God plans for women."

"Why, Annie Laurie! Do you think that's true?"

"I'm kidding, silly. We're not to concern ourselves another minute. We've got bigger fish to fry."

If the fish she referred to meant trying to keep Ben from dying and Mama happy, she had a point, so I nodded and stepped to the back of the wagon to offer Ben a ladle of water. Change of life or not, the whole story lay hidden with misdirection and out and out falsehood. I never doubted that. I didn't believe a word Mama said and I couldn't bring myself to tell Annie Laurie what I'd seen that night in the woods.

Chapter Eleven

Despite the milder temperatures of autumn, humidity fevered the days leaving a soft haze of the red oak, sweetgum, and maple trees that lined the road. Annie Laurie tried to draw attention to the beauty surrounding us, but Mama stared straight ahead over the rumps of the oxen as if she wore blinders, her stubbornness the only glue holding her together.

I walked along behind the wagon and collected leaves that had begun to fall. "Look, Ben, this maple leaf is as big as my hand! I think I'll press it in my book."

He tried to smile. "Sure is, honey, sure is." He laid his head back on his arms and spoke louder. "But, you can see way more of the trees from the back of a horse. Get Joe to put you up on Blackjack. He'll get lazy if somebody doesn't ride him."

"I'm not riding Blackjack. He's wild." I'd seen that stallion become unpredictable at unexpected times.

"He's perfectly calm now and tied to the back of the wagon. It's not like you to be so cautious."

"I like walking fine."

Ben propped up on his elbow and called for Joe. "Get this little girl up on Blackjack! She wants to see the view from a higher vantage point."

"I do not! I—"

Joe rode by, grabbed me by the straps of my overalls and hoisted me up on Ben's horse.

"If Mama weren't so mean, and I thought she might kill you, I'd tell."

"Calm down now. You're gonna be fine." Joe patted my leg. Hold on and sit back. He's too tired to do much silly business. I'm right here."

I clutched double handfuls of the coarse black mane and looked up. The trees bent over the road forming a tunnel of color, and if I let go, I could run my hands through the leaves. I felt like Alice in Wonderland. I remembered that Alice had come to a fork in the road and asked the Cheshire cat which path to take. When he asked her where she wanted to go, and she hadn't known, he said, "Then, it doesn't matter." It didn't matter where I wanted to go or what might happen to me. Mama had chosen the path we would all take. "The leaves are pretty," was all I said aloud.

"So maybe there's something to appreciate in Texas?"

"It doesn't matter anymore." I didn't say without Amazing Grace or even grumpy Nannie Bee. Without another word, I let go of Blackjack's mane and reached for the leaves overhead.

—⁂—

The map Mama's cousin sent had blurred with sweat, so she stopped briefly in Paris, Texas and asked directions from an old man standing at the railroad depot.

"Y'all got but forty-five miles down this here road," he said. "It'll take you straight on to Ladonia—four, five more days." The old man wiped his brow with a dirty handkerchief and pointed down the road. "Head south from here toward Honey Grove, then you'll see a sign for Bug Tussle. Bug Tussle! Ain't that a hoot? Some folks say they named it for all the bugs you have to fight off at church picnics. Of course, the young'uns claim the town's so boring that they sit around at night watching the tumblebug races for entertainment. Now if you ask me—"

"The next town, old man. The next town." Mama tapped her foot.

"That'll be Ladonia. Straight shot from there." He slapped his palms together. And without missing a beat, he said, "Woo! Bet you folks is about whupped. Judging from the looks of things." He squinted hard at Ben in the wagon. "You tangle with a wild cat, boy?"

Ben couldn't even attempt a smile. He winced, and I imagined how the sweat must have stung like fire when it dripped onto the raw strips of skin cut by the bullwhip.

"That's all we'll be needing, mister." Mama nodded and snapped the reins. "Still got a ways to go." The oxen lurched into motion.

—⟋⟍—

Three days later, we pulled up at the mercantile store in Honey Grove. Mama penned a letter to her cousin Frank. She paid a rider to deliver it that very day.

Frank,

Expect our arrival at the main general store sometime late tomorrow afternoon. Hope you will be there to meet us.

Lucretia

Mama's fingers shook as she folded a one-dollar bill into the note and handed it to the rider. "I gave you extra there. I want it delivered fast. You hear?"

The young man gawked at the money. "Yes, ma'am, I'm riding out."

I had nothing to say. In fact, I'd said nothing much since crossing the Red River. I felt no elation at being so close to our destination. I had no reason to smile or talk. Amazing Grace had disappeared forever. Tears hardly offered relief, so I seldom cried.

We bedded down that night on the outskirts of Ladonia. A cool breeze kicked up and Ben whispered, "Thank God. I couldn't take any more sweatin'."

"Here," I said, "let me blow on those bad spots. That'll help them cool off faster."

"You got any more of that honey?" I heard a smile in his voice. "I expect that works better than anything else we've tried. Run go get me some."

I hurried to please him and sat at his back and let the honey drip onto the wounds. He had been struck six times. I counted the lacerations again. They had started to pucker with the healing, but parts—the parts that cut deeper—still looked raw. I didn't mean to think of Amazing Grace. I willed myself not to, but the tears began when I remembered that little black and white bundle being whisked away and the laughing Indian with his words, *"Niyah. Himak nittak amofi."*

"Hey there now." Ben sat up and turned around. "Come here. You miss your little dog, don't you?"

I bobbed my head against his shoulder and broke into sobs. "I'm sorry. I'm sorry. I feel worse about you, but at least I've still got you. Those dang injuns! If I ever see one again, I'm gonna find a gun and—"

"Whoa. We can't kill them all for what a couple did. None of us expected this trip to be easy, but tomorrow we'll be in Ladonia, and Cousin Frank will show us our new place. We're a tough bunch, Cora. We'll be fine. You wait and see." He grabbed my fingers and shook them a little. "Think you might try to get a little more honey on those spots up at the top?" He lay back down and seemed to hold his breath as I ceased my tears and let the cooling stickiness drip onto his back.

Chapter Twelve

Mama called me up to sit beside her in the wagon. "We're almost there." She patted my knee. "We'll pick up a few supplies in Ladonia. What do you think? Some flour and sugar and maybe a little molasses? And a few eggs?" She patted my knee again.

I pulled away. "You gonna be happy, Mama? I hope you are real happy."

"I want us all to be happy." She gazed at the sky. "Ever thought of taking charge of the chickens?"

"What chickens?" I shoved my hands into my pants pocket. "I don't see no chickens."

"*Any* chickens."

"What?"

"Never mind. I bet when we get to Ladonia, we might find some chicks. How do you feel about managing settin' hens?"

"I thought settin' hens took care of their eggs, and if we were smart, we stayed clear."

"It's a tricky process. You only allow them to set when you want new babies. For eggs? That's a whole new way of management."

"Didn't Annie Laurie take care of the chickens at home?"

"Yes, but you're old enough to be the one in charge. I need your help."

I cocked one eyebrow at her. "I know what you're doing, you know."

"What do you mean?"

"You're trying to get me to think about something else besides Amazing Grace!" I crossed my arms and scooted as far away from her as I could. "It won't work, you know. It won't work!"

"I understand," said Mama.

"No, you don't!"

"Yes, I do." Her response came in almost a whisper. "Yes, I do." And with her voice too bright, she said, "Would you like to pick out some settin' hens?"

I gave her a slanted glance before staring back down at my hands. "Do you think there might be a Plymouth Rock?" I had always loved the big black and white flecked hens that roamed our yard back home.

"I bet there might be." Mama clicked to the oxen as they made their way down the road, but tears bloomed in her eyes and belied her feigned cheerfulness. I saw it clear as day.

—⁂—

We crossed the railroad tracks past Lyons Lumber Yard and pulled into the square at Ladonia. I had envisioned a town of unpainted, wood-framed buildings, but large stores, a public school, a cottonseed mill, and the Cottonbelt Railway Station lined the square. Even the streets were bricked in. I resented its advantages. I looked for something to hate, and the rancid smell of cottonseed meal provided enough for me to hate Ladonia.

"Looks like we'll find ourselves in the cotton business." Joe pulled up beside Mama.

"Indeed, we will. Frank bragged about its good cotton production." She maintained that false gaiety even when speaking to Joe. "Keep an eye out for the general store and a tall man about your size. That'd be Frank."

Annie Laurie and I elected to walk alongside the wagon through the town. She had dressed as best she could. Her shoes were well worn, her bonnet a little crushed, and her dress needed washing and ironing. I adjusted my cousin's britches and pulled Papa's hat closer to my brows. Although my hair had grown inches in the last few months, it took the shape of a boy's whose mother had not leveled out his bangs or trimmed over his ears.

"Did you see the opera house?" She nudged me. "And the hotel?"

I shrugged and trudged on.

"I also noticed a nice looking young man standing on the steps of the schoolhouse," she said. "Do you suppose he's the schoolmaster?"

"Well, if he is, I imagine you plan to be an A student."

"Whatever do you mean, sister dear?" She collapsed into giggles and then sped up her stroll with pursed lips and blushed cheeks.

"I think you're silly." I drew myself up to my highest stature before running ahead. I stopped and called back in the loudest voice I could muster. "I plan to be the only A student around these parts!"

That caught the young man's attention. He smiled at us and swept his hat from his head in a bow from *The Three Musketeers*.

"Cora," Annie Laurie hissed, "you have mortified us both. And I am telling Mama."

"Mama's gonna get me a chicken and she don't care if I said I'm gonna be an A student. I think she'd be right proud." I raced next to where Mama sat on the wagon.

"Being an A student is a wonderful thing, ain't it, Mama?"

"Why, of course, it is. But you may have to eliminate *ain't* from your vocabulary."

"I don't think a certain gentleman teacher would mind all that much."

She looked down at me. "I see tormenting Annie Laurie is exhilarating."

It had to be him. He had the look of our family about him—blue eyes and a nose better suited to a woman. Mama's family had all been tall and he stood tall, his dark hair showing streaks of silver.

"It is you, isn't it, Cousin?" Mama stretched out her hand to him, and he guided her off the wagon. "Lord, won't it be fine when I don't have to spend the days behind oxen." She smiled up into the man's face and grasped him by the shoulders. "Frank."

"Lucretia. I kept expecting a letter that'd tell me you changed your mind, but here you are. Pretty as ever."

"And I see you are as smooth a talker as ever. And half blind to boot." She looked at us and stopped. "Here are your second cousins. They can introduce themselves to you later, but right now, let's get what I have to get, and get on down the road."

We stepped into the general store. Its dimness, the musty odor of the potato bin, the richness of leather and tobacco and cottonseed oil smelled familiar even though we were hundreds of miles from home.

"I want that one." I pointed at the white frizzle of fluff that stood in its own pen.

The shopkeeper who introduced himself as Mr. Skinner wiped his hand on the bib of his apron leaving what might have been blood stains and said, "Well, young man, that's a right nice one. A Chinaman brought her in two weeks ago to trade for two of our Plymouth Rocks. Called it a Chinese Silky hen. Foreign-like. I'd heard about them, but this was the first I ever saw. I think I got suckered into trading, just the same."

"I want it."

The shopkeeper glanced at Mama for direction, but she had wandered toward the fabric bolts against the wall and touched the cloth with sunburned hands as if her fingers had forgotten the feel of soft cotton.

"I'm told they are kinda a delicate breed, might not be able to stand up for theirselves with others. I'd worry—"

But I had already lifted the chicken and held it close. "Why, you are a pretty little thing, aren't you? I believe I'll take you home with me. What kind of eggs will it lay?" I asked in one last effort to seem reasonable.

"They don't lay a lot of eggs. Probably three or so a week. Tend to be broody, that Chinaman told me. Hearsay is Silkies get settled down, and it's the devil to make them move off the nest. I only got this one, but it ain't laid an egg yet. They take longer than most to get started."

"It sure seems sweet." The Silky had settled right into my arm, ducking its head into the crook of my elbow.

"They're pretty nice little pets, but not what—"

"I'll take her." I stroked the head of the little white chicken with the blue-black beak. "She sure is fancy."

"Well then, Master—"

"*Miss* Allen," I corrected, ignoring the dumbfounded look of the store owner's face.

Mama stepped forward. "Miss *Cora* is fine enough for an eight-year-old. Whatever she wants," she said, while Skinner reappraised the child who stood before him.

I continued. "And I suppose I should choose a few others to go along with her. You know, ones that like to lay a lot of eggs."

"Now you're talking. I've got some nice Plymouth Rocks. They'd get along better than most with that Silky of yours. And they'll lay eggs you can count on. How many you want?" He began to square out a box. "I recommend at least a half-dozen of these here pullets. And that rooster over there. They're young, but ought to get to layin' eggs in a month or two."

Joe came in the store, in time to hear "half dozen." He leaned over my shoulder and whispered "Four. Plus the rooster." His eyes widened. "What is that ball of lint you've got there under your arm? Don't tell me it's a chicken. Looks like a feather duster!"

I stroked the fur-like feathers. "It most certainly is a chicken. Mama said I could pick the ones I wanted. And I want this one. Those others over there are fine, too. Box them up, please, sir." Making purring noises, the Silky burrowed further into the crook of my arm. "I believe I'll carry this one." With that, I marched back to the wagon as though I were toting a fine fur stole.

With supplies and sticks of horehound candy, we followed our cousin Frank down the road out to the east. "It's not but six miles. We'll be there before dark. My wife, Zora, would've come with me, but she wanted to sweep out the floor of your house and tidy up the place before you got there. She'll be right pleased to see y'all."

I hardly cared. Some emptiness inside me began to fill with the sustenance of being needed. Although I wanted to promise that I'd protect my new charge forever, I stopped myself. "I'll feed you and keep you dry and warm. I'll do the best that I can do. That much I can promise." I stroked the feathers that were fine as silk. "But I can't promise anything else. I can't."

—✗✗—

I drifted in and out of a hazy dream when Mama's hand on my shoulder jarred me awake. The sun had gone beyond the dark silhouettes of pine trees and light the color of deep saffron filled the evening. Swallows dived in the sky, their flanks and bellies flushed in the last light of day.

Dominated by heavy stone chimneys at each end with a broad, high porch, the house showed signs of once being painted white and must have been lovely in its prime. Zora stood there, a broom in her hand. "Y'all get down off that wagon and come in this house. I got fried chicken and biscuits waiting. Thought you'd never get here." She brushed the flour from the apron around her ample waist and headed out to meet us.

Mama sat very still. Her fingers gripped the reins, but her hands sagged in her lap. "Pretty evening." Her voice trailed off, losing some of its grit. "I thought it'd never come." Tears crept down the lines of her scowl. "I'm sorry. You must think. . . . I don't know what you'd think." Not making sense, she stopped. The long days' sweat had soaked through her flour sacking dress and darkened the sides of her bodice in half-moon shapes. She sat there a long time.

Zora stepped up to the wagon and laid her hands on Mama's sunburned and roped-blistered fingers. "I know, honey. I know. You're about give out. You come on with me, hear? Come on with me." She took Mama's hands in hers and guided her down from the wagon. She held her close a moment before leading her into the kitchen. "Sit yourself down, and I'll fix you a glass of buttermilk."

I followed. For once, I felt like Mama—too tired to think. We simply followed orders and sat. Mama seemed to find comfort in another woman—one who knew nothing of her past, no judgments, no questions.

Zora sat across from Mama and held forth. "This old house ain't nothin' fancy, but I do believe it's got enough room for your boys, your girls and yourself. These here dogtrot houses got advantages. When summer comes, that space is the coolest spot around and if'n you got a dog—"

"We don't have a dog." Mama cut her off and glanced at me.

"I can see that, but if'n you ever did. . . . Well, never mind. Got this here kitchen and a parlor bigger than most. The whole upstairs is for sleepin'. The privy out back got rebuilt a couple of years ago. And the well. No pump in the kitchen here as yet, but the water's fine. Got that nice barn, some fencing done and if you ever want to expand your acreage, well, there's sure enough land around."

Mama's eyes wandered aimlessly about the kitchen.

"Well, you'll see it all for yourself tomorrow, won't ya?" Zora moved the glass of buttermilk closer to Mama and said, "You know where you are, honey?"

Mama nodded.

"You're at your new home." She patted Mama's hands, cleared her throat and stood. "I'll finish up this supper, and then we'll get you settled for the night." She hollered out the door. "Frank! Get them boys to pasture the horses and oxen. Supper ain't but fifteen minutes off."

"Ma'am, Ben's hurt. Injuns whipped him bad." Cradling the hen, I followed her out to the dogtrot and explained that Ben wouldn't come until he got his horse taken care of. "He's slow on account of his back."

"Why don't nobody tell me nuthin'?" Zora stepped to the porch and belted out, "Frank! Get Ben in this house! Lord have mercy if that don't beat all. You go help that young man!"

"I already tried!" Frank slapped his hat against his leg and settled it back on his head, muttering, "That woman."

For a moment more, I studied Mama through the open door. She *didn't* look like she knew where she was. It annoyed me that she'd dragged us across Oklahoma to sit there like she didn't know where we had got to.

Gazing around me I wondered how the old house would like us barging in, prying its rusty hinges, raking its floors with a stiff broom—its quiet broken with our rowdy laughter and orders from Mama. That is, if she ever got back to being herself.

I watched Joe help Ben from the wagon, but Ben insisted on leading Blackjack around to the gate himself. He leaned against the horse and ran his hands over the shoulders and back. He spoke against the fine head. I couldn't hear, but I understood.

Frank stared at them and then hollered, "I'm gonna unload these here supplies. Joe, unhitch the oxen. There's a field out back where they'll be fine." He stepped behind the prairie schooner. "Good God

Almighty! That ain't a piano in the back, is it?" On the way back to the house he mumbled, "Heard tell Lucretia was always a little teched when it came to playing her music."

He doesn't know the half of it, I thought as I sat on the front porch swing and snuggled the Silky a little closer. Rocking with a soothing rhythm, my toes barely grazing the peeling paint on the porch, I spoke to the chicken. "I do believe I will call you Miss Fancy." I leaned forward to plant a soft kiss on the pullet's head. The other chickens scratched and scrambled in the box, and I tried to figure out what to do with them.

"I got an idea regarding them pullets, Miss Cora." Frank smiled down at me. "We've got a little pen yonder that would do in a pinch for a night or two. Then you might have to sweet-talk them brothers of yours into building you a sturdy coop. I'll help you carry this box out there. It's pret' near too heavy for you, especially with you holding that white one."

I followed him out to the pen and watched as he let the chickens loose. "There's a bucket already drawn from the well and a bushel of corn out in the barn. You gonna be able to let go of that one while you take care of them Plymouth Rocks? Here, let me have her." Frank took the hen and set her down in the pen with the others. "She'll be fine. She needs some water and corn too, you know."

I hung over the pen gate, stroking the Silky.

"'Go, child! Hurry up before it gets any darker. Supper's waiting. Git to running. I'm right behind you."

Supper tasted the best any of us could remember, although after the hell-bent passion of the last months, Mama chewed her food like hard tack instead fried chicken and mashed potatoes. She thanked Frank and Zora for all their help, but her red-rimmed blue eyes were faded almost to gray, and her fingers trembled when she lifted the napkin to her lips. I glanced at Annie Laurie who studied our mother in quick confused glances.

With Zora taking charge, Mama, Annie Laurie and I bedded down on pallets that night, sharing a room. Mama let herself be treated like a sick child by her cousin's wife she'd never met before. She thanked her again and said goodnight in a whisper as Zora left the room.

My eyes closed to slits, I watched Mama lie back against the wedding-ring quilt pattern and run her fingers around the faded circular symmetries. Although the white circle where her wedding ring had tanned over, I wondered again how she felt about the loss of it. I had no idea how binding vows were after the death of a husband. I did know that many women never took up with another man afterward. But Mama had waited no time at all until she went out the door with Nathan. The details were unclear—whether you had to do something or just think about it—but what I had seen proved enough to indict her.

I watched her get up and pace the small room. The bare soles of her feet shuffled across the grit of the pine floor. I remember the waning gibbous moon shining through the window and beginning its slow rise over the tree line. It cast an inconsequential shadow behind Mama. She seemed that way herself—inconsequential, waning.

Chapter Thirteen

Six weeks later, when Mama, Annie Laurie and I sat at the kitchen table, Frank brought the letter in from town. "It came the same time ours did, and I wanted to bring it out myself." He pressed it into Mama's hand. "Want me to stay awhile with you?" he said to her. "Or I'll get Zora."

"No, Frank. Thank you."

"Come over for supper on Sunday then. It ain't but a few miles, and Zora likes to cook enough to have leftovers for the rest of the week." He patted his stomach before touching Mama's arm and stepped away, leaving the door ajar behind him.

Her eyes glittering with the start of tears, Mama stared at the envelope. A wry half-smile twitched across her mouth, and she held up the envelope to show the sender as Mrs. Albert McIntyre. "Nan," she said. She opened the envelope but did not read the letter that Annie Laurie and I knew would say that Harriet had died.

The December sun slanted through old glass window panes leaving skewed rectangles of light on the floor. "I'm tired, just tired," Mama said, "but there is so much to do." She stood to go when a small bird flew through the open door. She sat again, slowly. The wren seemed a companion, a welcome spirit to ease the complexities of life. Its tail posed and spritely, its pale brow slanted above the bright, inquisitive eye, it regarded Mama. It hopped to the window and fluttered at the glass. Finding no escape, it perched for a moment on the sill and cocked its head as if to devise a plan. I wanted to entice the bird to stay but could not think how. It chirped some farewell, bounced toward the open doorway and took flight. Once freed to the sunshine, it called its bold trill.

Freedom. Mama had gained it too, but the wren did not seem so lonely as she. Her face, as inexpressive as it could be when she wanted, revealed more than I wanted to see—a confusion of emotion—like she didn't know what to feel anymore. She folded the letter neatly, perfectly, and handed it to Annie Laurie. She stepped into the parlor to sit at the piano. Woefully out of tune, it remained a wonder that it survived the journey at all. But there it sat, an ornate, bow-legged relic that traveled 450 miles squawking and tinkling its objections to every one of those miles. We should have kept the books instead, knowing how Mama loved to read. She could do that in silence. I knew what she intended to play— that "Requiem" she pounded out when Papa lay dying. Despite Mozart's symbols of *lente, lente*, Mama performed it as *forté, forté, forté.*

—⁓—

The next week when the possum haw holly berries had gone vermilion, I sat on the porch steps and stroked Miss Fancy. I thought to cut a branch for Christmas decoration but wondered if Mama would think it piddling. I wanted to ask her, but she never stopped. Work burned like a fire within her and didn't end with the setting sun. She fueled the rest of us with her energy.

"Don't you ever want to sit down, Mama?" I looked up at her as she headed to the garden, a blur of shadow against the sunset.

"If sitting got done what I want done, well then, it'd be right nice. Go close up the chickens for the night. Ben didn't build that coop for entertainment."

"I wish they'd lay some eggs. I could get more interested in my job if they'd lay an egg every so often."

She called back over her shoulder, "Come spring, you'll have plenty of eggs. Then you'll be complaining about reaching under a settin' hen."

For a brief moment, I saw a smile flicker on her face. It had been a long time since I'd seen it.

Still light-hearted after supper, she sharpened a pencil with a butcher knife and lined us up one at a time along the wall to mark our height. I lined up last and watched as Joe raised his shoulders and took a deep breath to stretch taller than Ben. Annie Laurie inspected her fingernails and smirked at the boys. She had become a willowy creature even taller than Mama, and I felt a sting of envy as I studied the marks on the wall. I would have loved to stand even an eyebrow taller than Mama and offer a patient smile when asked to get the jelly jars down from a high pantry shelf.

The older three had each signed their name by the pencil line that marked their height. When it came to my turn I rolled my eyes. "You know who that line belongs to. I'm the shortest one in the bunch."

"Now, now," Ben said, "we'll check again come spring. I bet you grow like a weed!"

Annie Laurie laughed and patted my head. "You may make it up to here, my little weed." She tapped her shoulder.

"What do *you* know?" In truth, I wondered if I'd ever be as tall as Annie Laurie. It didn't seem possible.

"Well, there's one thing you're tall enough to do." Annie Laurie posed with her forefinger on her lips. "You can help me tote the water buckets in from the well. Four buckets. Three times a day."

"That's what we have brothers for. Joe can do it in half the time. I don't see why—"

"Boys like girls with shapely arms." Annie Laurie put on her prissy look.

"They do not. Do they, Ben?"

"Men like women who can work!" He made his arm muscle bulge.

"Y'all are finagling me!" But I made up my mind to impress them all. I'd do it if it took nine trips a day.

At dawn the next morning, Annie Laurie delivered instructions. "Lower the bucket, Cora. I'll help you draw it up." She leaned over the well and turned the pulley.

"I can do it myself." But my face heated up by the time the bucket got near the top, and she stepped in to finish the job.

"Not quite yet, my dear." Her voice dripped with superiority. "Maybe when you're twelve, you can handle this job. Until then I think you better let me do the hauling up part." She patted me on the head. "I'm teasing, little sister."

I swung at her, but she dodged, laughing.

Only two days later, Annie Laurie taunted me into carrying all four buckets back to the house. "It'll build your muscles so you can manage this job with no help from me."

I had picked up the first two buckets when I heard my sister humming into the well. She liked to hear herself sing with the echo produced in the stone innards and leaned far into the dark hollow and sang.

> My wild Irish Rose,
> The sweetest flow'r that grows,
> You may search ev'rywhere,
> But none can compare
> With my wild Irish Rose.

"We're supposed to be bringing in the water." I stared at the hem of her skirt flouncing over the edge. I was thinking that I would tell Mama when Annie Laurie's almost perfect balance failed her. Her melody merged with a shriek as she slipped past her waist and past her knees, head first over the edge of the well. She stretched her arms wide to brace against the sides, but the stone walls were slick with moss.

I dropped my buckets and grabbed one of her ankles with both hands and held on with all my might. Bracing my feet on the stone, I leaned back and bellowed.

Joe came running, and Mama hurried right behind him. He had Annie Laurie's waist and lifted her out, but I couldn't let go of her ankle. We both collapsed. She sat straddle-legged on the ground, one shoe gone. "You saved me, Cora! I can't believe it. You saved me."

Still gripping Annie Laurie's ankle, I smiled before I broke into tears. I managed only a furious nodding of my head.

Joe, although his face blanched white, couldn't help himself. "It all comes from aspiring to be the next Gibson Girl."

"Why, you!" Annie Laurie regained her lost strength and made a leap for him, but he lunged away.

"Children!" Her arm around Annie Laurie's shoulders, Mama ushered her into the house. "That's quite enough!" But even while she shook her head and looked back at Joe and me, amusement hid behind the frown.

Chapter Fourteen

After an easy winter, spring came much earlier than it had in Missouri. By the first week of March, dogwood trees bloomed with pale and delicate flowers, and the woods were fragrant with redbud. The Plymouth Rocks were laying plenty of large brown eggs, but my favorite had not. It began to be a mild point of contention with the teasing of my brothers about my chicken's lackluster production. At first I'd been disappointed, but as time went on, I began to say that Miss Fancy's destiny should be that of a treasured pet, so anything else hardly mattered. Stroking the Silky's feathers felt as important as Ben spending all that time grooming Blackjack, and I happily noted the chicken's five toes and turquoise earlobes, which clearly excused her from the drudgery of egg-laying.

Meanwhile, in an effort to show maturity, I collected the eggs daily. I tried to encourage egg-laying by naming every hen, calling them by name, even sweet-talking to some of the surly ones. "Mrs. Seville, you let me slip my hand right under here." The hen regarded me with a pinpricked eye as I glided my hand slowly under the warm feathered breast. "You won't be bothered one little bit." Mrs. Seville's eyelid slid shut, then opened. With a nimble twist of her neck, she nailed my wrist and then rose in a flurry of black and white feathers to the top of the roost. Spitting out the snowfall of down that circled my head, I lifted an egg and held it up. "See, Mrs. Seville. I got it anyway. You remember the next time you snap your neck around like that, it may be at the end of my mama's arm. I think I'll tell her you're not producing that well. How'd you like that?" Mrs. Seville cocked her head and blinked a slow wink with her yellow eye.

—◊◊◊—

At dawn, my favorite time of the day before the rush of chores and school, I lay under the covers. I pushed up on one elbow and watched the sun throw spears of light across the fields, casting a blush on the fog that lay in the blackland furrows.

And then it came. Not the robust yodel of the Plymouth Rock rooster, but the buzzing of a kazoo. I piled out of bed and shook Annie Laurie. "Something's the matter with my chicken!" Barefoot and in my nightgown, I ran down the stairs and minced across the yard to the chicken coop.

There among the hens strutted Miss Fancy. And she crowed.

Dumbfounded, I turned to find Ben behind me. At first, he stood with astonishment on his face. Then he began to laugh. Not a little chuckle of amusement, but a downright guffaw that wouldn't stop. Pretty soon the whole family circled the chicken coop, and while the crowing continued, so did the laughter.

"I don't understand," I said. "Miss Fancy? This isn't like you!"

Joe fell to his knees laughing, but Annie Laurie grasped me by the shoulders. "Darlin', life's full of surprises. Fancy will make as fine a rooster as you thought he would a hen. You've got to take it in stride."

I opened the coop door and let the chickens have the run of the yard. Dazed, I padded over to the feedbag and began to scatter the corn to the ground. I bent down and lifted Fancy to carry him to the porch where I sat and held out my palm to feed him by hand. "What a surprise you are, Mister Fancy. No, I think I'll call you Fanciful. It suits you better." I lifted him to my lap, and he ducked his head into the crook of my arm, as he always had.

That night at dinner, Ben squinted his eyes and leaned back in his chair. "You know? I had a revelation considering Miss Fancy becoming Fanciful."

I braced myself. He'd better not be making a joke.

"I think," Ben continued, "that it's an awful good thing that Fanciful turned out to be a boy."

"Why exactly is that?" I asked, squinting back at him.

"These Silkies are little things. It might have been hard on a Silky hen to lay the big eggs with the rooster Mayflower being the daddy. Now? No worries! If those hens lay Fanciful's eggs, they'll probably be downright relieved." He leaned back even more and said, "Consider this a lucky turn of events, little sister!"

—⁂—

Infatuated with his new stature, Fanciful began to swagger about and warble his distinctive crow. He became a ladies' man in no time and lacked the judgment to shut up. Mayflower decided the barnyard had room for only one rooster.

Mayflower made his move. Neck feathers flared, heads thrust forward, the two roosters circled each other, sparring for a chance to make the first attack. Both birds rose in the air, the spurs on their legs slashing at each other.

I rushed to the roosters, hoping to break them up. "Stop them! He'll be killed!" Mayflower flew at me, his wings flogging the air. I screamed, and Ben came running. Despite the furious battering of feathers, he managed to grab the bird around its body and hang him by his feet. Mayflower twisted and squawked, but finally gave in, hanging like a dead rabbit in Ben's grip.

Ben's forehead was streaked with sweat, but he couldn't help grinning. "Looks like he's dinner or a donation."

I didn't know whether to laugh or cry. I approached Fanciful carefully. Still in a state—huffy and unnerved, his feathers ruffled, his eyes wide and dilated—he squawked with high-pitched anxiety. "Come here, darling," I said. "You are saved. Come here." I stroked the ruffled feathers before taking him in my arms. He let out a confused squawk but allowed himself to be cosseted once again. "I bet Cousin Frank would love to have Mayflower. But don't tell me what happens to him. He's been a good rooster."

—⁂—

Later that spring, Ben took me with him when he went to Ladonia. I thought I might see if that Chinaman had come back with a Silky hen—a real hen. Fanciful would like that, and so we stopped off at the feed store. On the boardwalk sat a man surrounded by four puppies—black and white, like Amazing Grace had been. A small man, but because of his color, the shape of his eyes, he could have no scruples, no pity.

I charged him. "Where'd you get those pups, mister? Steal them off some little girl? Grab them and ride off with them tied behind your saddle?"

Ben caught up with me in time to turn me around and begin an apology. The man collected the puppies and watched in silence as I continued my tirade.

I took a swing at Ben. "You know what they did to you. They ripped the skin off your back! How can you tell him *you're* the one who's sorry?" I spun back toward the man. "Maybe this old codger knows! What *do* you red injuns do with dogs? Eat them? Is that what you do? *Amofi himak nittak. Chahta siahokii!* Then I screamed. "What does that mean?" Intent on self-righteous fury, I was appalled when the tears began. I turned to my brother. "Don't you remember, Ben?"

Ben held me before him. He spoke softly. "I remember. How could I forget? But this man had nothing to do with it. You've got to—"

"You let me go!" I twisted in his grip.

"Not until you stand still and stop screaming. He's Caddo. They don't do things like that." He shook me a little. "Can you calm down?"

Not much taller than me, the man came to his feet. He looked to Ben for an explanation and spoke hesitantly. "I do not understand." The puppies whimpered and struggled in his arms. He kept looking at Ben, but his words were for me. "Those words, *Amofi himak nittak*, Choctaw for 'My dog today.' I brought these pups to town to find homes for them. The mama's ready for them to go."

Exhausted from my outburst, I slumped to the storefront walk. One of the puppies wiggled loose and fell to his owner's feet. With the overjoyed gusto of a puppy who had found a playmate, she scampered onto my lap. She licked my cheeks, the tears that ran down my chin, my mouth. It felt like Amazing Grace had come back into my arms. I knew it couldn't be so, but the old ache eased. I gathered up the pup, buried my face in her soft fur and sobbed.

—⟶⟶—

Mama looked up from the field. She straightened, stretched her back and groaned. Sweat ran down her face and she wiped her eyes. "About time, son! A trip for cottonseed and it takes all day. What took so— Oh my lord."

"Look, Mama. Look what Ben got me." I cradled the pup in my arms and whispered as though it were sleeping. "Her name is Pepper, and she's gonna grow up like Amazing Grace. She'll protect me from rattlesnakes and help me herd the chickens and—"

"Love you," she said.

PART TWO

We posed unsmiling—Mama and Annie Laurie in Gibson Girl pompadours, waists and bosoms corseted into pigeon-breasted forms. Ben and Joe, in black broadcloth suits with white shirts and starched collars. And I, at thirteen, forced into a sailor dress I abhorred. We stood outside our home for a photograph to send back to family in Missouri. To show them. Show them we'd made it. Sunburns concealed by sepia, our sacrifices layered under handkerchief soft linen and Dallas-bought lace. It was 1905.

Chapter Fifteen

Mama's sharp intake of breath made me look up as she stared out the kitchen window. Her hands fluttered as she rinsed a cup, fumbled and let it slip from her fingers before she could dry it. She started to bend to collect the pieces but stood again and gazed outside. I watched too but pretended not to recognize the familiar Missouri Fox Trotter as it paced from the main road down the turnoff to our place. Nathan. Mama turned away from the window, tore off her apron and turned back around to watch him. A private time to be sure, but I stared in fascination at the blush of heat rising in her face, her blue eyes obscured by darkened pupils, her lips parted, confirming how she felt about Nathan.

As he grew closer I saw he had grown thinner. His dark hair showed streaks of gray. Mama's hand went to her own black hair. Had she changed, too? If she had, the changes had been so gradual that I hadn't noticed them. I watched the transformation from her disbelief to nostalgia to a mask that closed off all emotion. Then she stood straighter, let her eyes go to steel and opened the kitchen door.

"Nathan Cage!" Her voice trembled, and she stopped to clear her throat. "My goodness. You've come a long way."

"Then can I come in and sit a spell?" He tried to make light, to hide his own reaction to seeing her after all this time. He had arrived with no letter in advance. In his hand, he held a bouquet of wildflowers.

Ben and Joe rushed in from the field. "I saw that Missouri Fox Trotter tied up outside," said Ben, "and knew it had to be you!"

"Sit down, Nathan. You must be tired." Mama scooted the chair out. "Boys, take care of his horse."

Nathan sank into the chair. "Sure feels better than a saddle." He leaned on his elbows. "Wanted to see the family here. See if y'all were doing all right. You heard Harriet passed away."

"I've had a chance to adjust to it, get through it a little bit." Mama sat across from him. "And you? Nan wrote several years ago, but I worried about you, too." She stood again and turned back to stare out the window she'd watched him through. "We're doing fine. It's been hard, but first chance you get, go out and take a handful of this land. You won't come up with stones. Blackland. That's what this is. Cotton land. You won't get me to go back to the rocks of Douglas County, Missouri." She opened the icebox, pulled out the jug of buttermilk and poured Nathan a glassful. She set it down hard in front of him. "Not ever." She gathered the wildflowers he brought, poured water into a canning jar and despite her habit of placing each stem in an orderly, fixed arrangement, even for flowers picked from the roadside, she bunched the black-eyed Susans into a rough bouquet and stuffed them into the jar. She sat down across from Nathan again and placed her hands palm down on the table. "Thanks for the flowers just the same."

I began to understand what all this meant. I remembered those Burpee puzzles he and Mama used to put together. How often he came to help when Papa felt too sick to work. And the way he looked at her. I liked him, had known him all my life, but there were times when I walked into the room, the topic changed, the words moving into shadows. When Nathan hung around, Mama's laughter altered, the tone of her voice. Now I watched as Nathan nodded his head and said. "I'd like to come visit every once in a while. You know, if it's all right with you."

"Come visit all you like. Who's taking care of your children while you're traipsing across the Red River?"

"They're staying with their grandmother. The oldest two girls have beaus. It won't be long until they're married and off on their own. The youngest, seems to be doing fine. She hasn't had much of a mother since Harriet got sick. Spent most of the time with her grandmother even then."

Curiosity killed me. "What about Jimmy? What's he up to?"

Nathan winked at me. "You mean, is he still giving away his clothes? Jimmy's being Jimmy, I guess."

Trying to take it like a lame joke, I smiled until I felt the heat rise to my face and decided to quick put the buttermilk jug in the icebox. "Tell him howdy."

Mama pinched her lips together. "I miss them. I miss them all. But you know how you feel when you have to do something. Just have to?"

"I do." Nathan reached out and took her hand. "Indeed, I do."

I glanced at Annie Laurie and then at the floor.

After supper that evening, Mama said, "Let me show you the cotton field, Nathan. The boys, all of us, have worked so hard, but come look at what we've got going." She stood holding the screen door open. The last sunrays created an aura about her, made her almost unreal. She had always tried to be so tough, so relentless, but here in this glow, she appeared fragile, part of the light.

I pretended not to notice how Nathan gazed at her. Ben cleared his throat, but Annie Laurie stared openly at Nathan and Mama, then exchanged glances with Ben and Joe that meant they would reexamine the scene later that night.

Nathan rose to his feet, careful not to make eye contact with anyone. "Be right there. Let me get my hat." He paused to settle the hat on his head and followed her out into the evening.

Looping an apron about her neck and cinching it tightly around her waist, Annie Laurie bustled about telling Ben that Mama wanted him to see to our milk cow first thing in the morning. "She recommends you pen her up before she calves out in the back pasture again. Always had a hard time that cow, she—"

"I've got a headache." I pressed my fingertips to my temples.

"Well, darlin', do you need to lie down?"

"No, I'll sit here in the parlor for a minute and see if it don't go away."

"*Doesn't.* You know, Cora. You are becoming a young lady and I think—"

With a smirk and a curtsy, I said, "May I please be excused to the parlor? I doesn't feel well." I laughed and bolted out of the kitchen to ensconce myself beneath the window where if I leaned forward, I could see Mama and Nathan, and if I held my breath, I could hear them talking.

Nathan paused on the porch. "Let's sit a spell." He took Mama's hand and led her to the swing. The perfume of the rose bush wafted about. "Reminds me of back in Missouri. Same kind of roses?"

"I brought a cutting with me. You know, something from the old home place." She didn't pull her hand away from his.

"Reminds me of us."

"Yes, some."

"You think about it then?"

She took her hand away. "Some, Nathan, but—"

"That's all I wanted to hear. There is no 'but.'" He laughed softly. "You said once they were called 'First Love.'"

She nodded.

"And you brought it with you, all the way here to Texas." He stopped the rocking of the swing.

"Oh Nathan, so much time has—"

"Time's got nothing to do with it, Crecie." He took her hand again.

I set my knuckles against my teeth. *Crecie?* No one ever called her Crecie. Not Papa. Not anybody.

She pulled him to his feet. "The cotton fields, Nathan. You must come see."

I waited to go back to the kitchen until they stepped off the porch leaving the swing still drifting back and forth as though they might still be in it.

"Feeling better?" Annie Laurie asked, "I could use some help with these dishes."

"No," I said, "I think it's gotten even worse. I'm going to bed."

Nathan left three days later, and I breathed deeper. Maybe this ended it. He didn't have any business coming down here and bothering Mama. Maybe he would stay in Missouri like he should. I thought for a long time about how I could help accomplish that. Maybe if I wrote Jimmy and promised him another agate, *maybe* he could help convince his father that the family needed him up there, not burning up the roads between here and Douglas County.

Chapter Sixteen

After months of going out in a waft of Clubman aftershave, Joe came in from town one night and sat at the table. "I've been thinking," he said, and stood up again and stuck his thumbs in his belt loops.

"That's a first," said Ben.

Annie Laurie shushed Ben and said, "Don't be so insensitive. What is it, Joe? You look positively stricken. Mama, doesn't he look stricken?"

Mama narrowed her eyes at Joe.

"Struck with Cupid's arrow, I'd say." Ben got up and gave him a little punch on the shoulder. "Might as well fess up."

"Why don't you tell it yourself if you know all about it?" Joe glared at Ben and turned to Mama. "He *thinks* he does anyway. It's stuck in his craw that I'll beat him to the altar."

"The altar?" Mama sat down faster than I had ever seen her. "The altar?"

"Yes, ma'am. Katy Marshall and I. Her father especially approved after he stepped in on us when we were sparkin'. Actually, he was emphatic about it." Joe hesitated. "It's not that I'm against it."

"This seems so sudden. You've only been seeing this girl a few months. I guess the most important question is—do you love her, son?"

"Actually, it's been nearly a year, Mama." Joe looked at the ceiling and then the floor but came clean. "And to answer your question—I guess. I guess I do."

"Oh, he does. He told me so. More than once. He's scared to say so out loud in front of y'all." Ben gave Joe a brotherly pat on the back. "It's a good thing, Joe. Don't let it slip you by like I did." A look crossed his face that I had never seen before. Somewhere between anger and angst.

I decided not to pursue any clever taunts. Besides this was Joe's day.

Mama sat there like she was thinking the whole thing over. "A banker's daughter."

Annie Laurie's eyes glowed with what I recognized as mail order fever, but I kissed Joe on the cheek and headed up the stairs leaving Mama and her to question and cajole and make plans.

—⧉—

As part of the wedding party, we needed new dresses. With a tape measure around her neck, the dressmaker made Annie Laurie stand like a mannequin as she basted the side seams with quick whips. I was next in line and dreaded it. Mama had picked out patterns for all of us with the new standing collar deeply pointed at the back and bolero bodices. At least my blue linen didn't go all the way to the floor, which would have only slowed me down.

"Mama," Annie Laurie said, "it's supposed to be a surprise, but I thought you might better appreciate the information if you'd had time to absorb it." She glanced at the seamstress as if deciding whether to speak in front of her.

"Oh, what, child? Such intrigue does not become you."

"Katy was too excited to contain herself and told me in confidentiality that her father plans to announce at the wedding that he's making Joe vice-president of Ladonia State Bank. If Joe does well, he'll transfer them to the Dallas branch. And make him president!" Annie Laurie twisted to take in Mama's expression.

"Stay straight, miss! You'll make me skip a stitch." The dressmaker's mouth was so full of pins it took a moment for us to understand her.

"What? All right, all right. But isn't that the be-all and end-all, Mama?"

"Sons have a way of doing that—marry some pretty young thing, go off and leave the rest of us waiting for a letter." Mama's voice caught and she turned to the window so no one could see her face. I stood behind her and put my hand on her shoulder.

Mama sniffed but faced us, a shine of tears in her eyes. "Guess that's the way of things—leaving."

Determined to improve the mood, I said, "Ben, Annie Laurie and I are here, Mama. He won't never get married if he don't admit how he feels. I'm pretty sure he didn't with that Smith girl." I tried to laugh enough to make light, but I hoped in my heart of hearts that Ben would forego romance and stay forever with us on the farm.

—⁂—

It hardly seemed possible that the wedding date could be set so quickly and organized. I began to wonder if there was a special reason for the rush. I'd heard of weddings that involved a shotgun, but Joe and Katy's celebration appeared not to be so influenced. It was certainly a nice enough affair—showers and hoopla the rest of us had never experienced. We smiled our way through it.

"One thing about marrying the banker's daughter," Annie Laurie said after the ceremony, "her daddy puts on a wedding for the society pages—small, but ever so elegant."

I thought Katy resembled a frosted layer cake, a froth of tulle and white lace. Joe looked like most bridegrooms, I supposed—a stiff collar choking him to death, striped pants and frock coat, trying to smile while men slapped him on the back and slipped him snorts of Jack Daniels.

Letting my eyes drift around the reception, I noted the mother of the bride and guests. They sipped their champagne delicately and nibbled their petit fours and patted their lips with linen napkins. Such stodgy folks probably never climbed a tree. I studied Joe. Before my very eyes, he was becoming one of them—smiling just so, his handshakes just so. Maybe the Jack Daniels factored in, but the brother I knew was fading like an old photograph right in front of me.

Chapter Seventeen

I caught glimpses of the boy from the dizzying height of the pecan tree that bordered our properties. So in the mornings before sunrise, I lay awake and reserved part of my day for spying.

I never saw that he had parents, just the old woman who must have been his grandmother. He looked about my own age, but I had never seen him at school.

I studied his habits. He milked the cows then set to gardening under his grandmother's supervision from the porch rocker. He didn't look up at her, but doggedly followed directions. Trees hid most of the unpainted house, but judging from the yard, which was flat out dirt and chickens, nothing could have been well kept. Maybe his grandmother felt sickly. Every afternoon before the evening milking, he grabbed a fishing pole and headed for Caney Creek.

This time I would be ahead of him.

At the creek with Pepper tucked in beside me, I waited in the hollow between bald cypress knees. I'd brought ham bits to keep the dog distracted and a large piece of cake to share if the situation looked promising. Annie Laurie called in the distance, but I sank deeper into the crevice and waited.

At last I heard the rustle of reeds and the boy's sigh as he settled down to fish. So much closer than I'd ever been. Shade dappled his tanned skin. His dark hair flopped over his brow, so I could not make out his eye color, but he had a fine, straight nose and a mouth full enough to be a girl's. He baited the hook, let it sink and leaned against the bank. Squinting at the flash of sunlight on the water, he closed his eyes.

And then, nothing. No fish, no frogs, no dragonflies. Just silence. What had I hoped for? For him to talk to himself? Break into song? Dearly wishing that he *had*—it would have been so entertaining—I tried to quell the disappointment. Mesmerized by the warmth and ripples spreading from leaves that occasionally fell into the water, I thought I might fall asleep too. Pepper slept beside me, an ear twitching every now and then. I pinched myself to stay awake.

When I thought I would have to scream from frustration, he pulled the hook from the water and stood. He turned to check in the direction he'd come and seeing no one, dropped his britches, lifted his shirt over his head and slid silently into the water. He shuddered with the chill before diving below and coming up downstream where he turned and floated on his back, letting the current take him away.

Smooth and bronzed from the sun, he reminded me of a boy from Greek lore. His shoulders had begun to broaden, but the rest was all angles. Like the Greek legends Papa had told me, I imagined him carried away by a dolphin.

The creek meandered through the cypresses, and before long he drifted out of sight. I slipped from the shade to pick up his shirt, warm from the sun and rough in my hands. I took in its smell—vinegary sweat and the yeasty odor of clabbered milk. I paused. Something I couldn't identify made me press my nose to the shirt again and breathe in before I folded it into a neat square along with the britches. On top of the clothes, I laid the piece of cake wrapped in a page torn from the Sears Catalog. "There," I said, before giving the bundle one last pat. "There."

What if I waited till he returned? "No, let's go." I slapped my leg. Pepper barked once before being shushed, and we sprinted back to the pecan tree.

Another hour passed before the boy returned to his grandmother's house. Waiting in the tree, I had almost dozed off when I heard Pepper stand and shake. The boy came trudging back up the hill, carrying two small trout and his fishing pole. I liked to believe I could make out the smudge of chocolate icing on his chin. I smiled when I thought about when I might reveal myself. Not too soon. I had much more to learn about him. He would be my friend, even if he didn't know it yet.

—⟨⟨⟨—

"Whatcha been up to, little sister?" Ben had come in from the fields. "How'd you get sunburned if you haven't been out pulling weeds like I have?

"I went fishing." I checked my face in the window's reflection. "I'm not burned."

"Will 'rosy' do then?" He opened the icebox and grabbed the buttermilk. He drank straight from the jug and wiped away his white mustache with his shirtsleeve. "Lord, it's hot out there."

"But Mama says we'll get a mighty nice field of cotton."

"That we will. Market prices right at fourteen cents a pound. Might be enough to get you a pony." Ben took another slug of buttermilk. "Even after seed for next year and paying the help, we'll be livin' in high cotton!"

"I hope Mama's satisfied. She's hard to keep happy."

Ben snorted. "I'd say that's true of women as a race of human beings."

"I'm sure I don't know what you mean. We are merely determined," I said and wondered if I'd contradicted myself. "And besides, what do you know about those neighbors down the road? Sure do keep to themselves, don't they?"

"Well, where did that come from? Weren't we talking about women and high cotton?"

"Doesn't look like those folks are in high cotton, does it? I mean they milk cows and grow tomatoes. How do they make a livin'?" I scanned my reflection in the hall mirror once more to see if I really was getting a sunburn. "Just an old woman and a boy. Looks sad to me."

Ben put his hat back on and headed out the door. "Met the woman once and I don't know much about the boy. There's rumors in town, but I don't hold with gossip. Gotta go. Find Mama. She's looking for you."

What could it be? He looked like a perfectly nice boy. "I can keep a secret. Tell me what—"

The door slammed behind him.

I stomped my foot. "Well, *murder!*"

"There you are! I've been looking all over for you." Mama deposited the bucket of men's shirts and long johns at my feet. "Mark Twain said, 'There ought to be a room in every house to swear in. It's dangerous to have to repress an emotion like that,' but unfortunately for you, you have neither the time nor the room, so silence yourself and put these clothes on the line. They'll have to hang there all night to get dry. And by the way, you are not to disappear for an entire afternoon. We were beginning to worry. Your sister combed the countryside."

"Worried, I bet. Worried who was gonna hang the clothes on the line, that's what." I stared the ropes of wrung-out clothing, sighed and slung the bucket on one hip. *Gossip, huh? I bet my sister will come clean. Annie Laurie never could keep a juicy story under her bonnet.* "C'mon, Pepper. Help me think while I hang these bloomin' bloomers."

"It's not for children's ears." Annie Laurie snapped the clothes off the line. "Why are you so interested in the neighbors?" She reached for the sheet. "Here, help me fold this." She pinched the corners together and handed one end to me. "Stop that! Stretch it out. You know what Mama'll say about the sheets being wadded up."

"I was smelling the sunshine in them," I said. "I love that smell."

"I'd say it was laundry soap. Whoever heard that sunshine smells." But to be sure, Annie Laurie put her face against the fabric and breathed. "Pearline." She breathed again. "Mama pays extra for it, and I'm going to pay extra for it when I get married."

"You think the schoolmaster is gonna ask you? He's been over here courtin' since last spring.

"Why, it's on the tip of his tongue every time he tells me goodnight. I can just feel it."

"His tongue?" I lobbed her end of the sheet at her and ducked behind the one still hanging on the line. I tried to control my laugh, but it surfaced like air bubbling up in a pond.

"You know very well what I mean. You little stink—"

"I was only teasing. You know I like Mr. Garrett fine." I hid my grin behind a pair of overalls. "Wanna see if I can find out for you? His sister's in my class at school, and I have been known to be clever in ways of intrigue."

"You have not." Annie Laurie paused. "Well, sometimes, perhaps. What did you have in mind?" She removed the clothespins and put them in the hanging bag. "That is, I mean if I were to consent."

"It's simple. I'll find something Belinda wants to know. Not even say that's what I'm doing. Make it like a gift of information. Then not too long after, ask her if she knows anything about her big brother's plans. She'll return the favor, but I'll make it all about how I don't want him to be joining the army or anything." I dropped my voice and ran my words together. "She'll never guess it's about you."

"Well, no. Absolutely not. It's not right to go behind his back. Unless you think—no! He'll ask me when he's good and ready." Annie Laurie reached for another sheet and paused. "Do you think she'll know if he's ready sometime soon?"

"I wouldn't want to do anything that makes you uncomfortable in matters of conspiracy, Annie. Who knows, though, maybe she'll be as anxious to see if you'll say yes. Maybe he's gonna get *her* to ask *me* what *I* know. And school's starting up." I grabbed three pillowcases off the line. "Here, let me fold those. You've already done more than your share."

"What do you want now?" Annie Laurie watched suspiciously as I tucked a pillowcase under my chin and folded it in half.

"Speaking of school, I think it's strange that some kids have to go to school but some kids don't." I glanced up quickly before rushing on. "I haven't seen that boy down the road at school. He wasn't in school last year either. Wondered why. Probably has a good reason. And since you and Mr. Garrett are lovey-dovey—"

"I beg your pardon. I would hardly—"

"Okay—*friends*. I hoped that in return for me doing a favor for you, you might—"

"All right. All right. I'll see about it." Annie Laurie stacked the clothes in the basket. "Let's get on in. It's nigh dark."

—⚌—

In September, the air—a thick and languid stew—stuck our clothes to us. Sweat soaked through the boys' shirts, and strands from the girls' braids stuck to their necks.

Mr. Garrett loosened his tie and spoke to the class. "I am going to break a rule, and y'all know how I feel about the importance of rules, but

I can't stand it anymore. Bring your lunch pails and let's go to the creek for an afternoon with Dickens."

"Not *Great Expectations.*" The boys moaned.

"Ah, perhaps if you imagined Miss Havisham with her bare toes in the creek water."

That set the girls to giggling, and I moved toward intrigue.

"I've got oatmeal cookies to share if anybody is interested," I said in almost a whisper, looking directly at Belinda Garrett.

"Well, sure." She followed me down to the stream where we found a shady spot and sat out of sight from the others.

"But let's soak our toes while we eat them. I think I'm gonna die if I don't cool off." I plopped down, took off my shoes and stockings and sighed as I sank my feet into the water.

"Ohhh, that is so much better. Aren't you going to take yours off?"

"My brother won't approve, I don't think."

"He can't see you so why worry? I mean, he sent us to the creek after all. I bet he's downstream wading with his britches rolled up, going, 'Ahh, that's the ticket!'"

Belinda laughed. "I can picture him, now that you mention it. He does funny things sometimes."

"Funny things? Like what? He always seems so serious to me." I knew exactly what she meant but considered naïveté the doorway to espionage.

"That's because he's a teacher. At home, he's very funny, but he wouldn't like me telling because he wants the respect of the students."

"Well, I certainly respect him. My goodness, yes. I don't think there would be *anything* you could tell me that would make me not respect him. Take my sister, Annie Laurie. She respects him, even if she's already finished school."

Belinda shifted her eyes back and forth before she spoke. "I think he respects her too."

"Does he talk about her?" I wiggled my toes in the sandy creek bed.

"No, not much. He looks funny when he does."

"Is that what you meant by 'He's very funny at home?'"

"No, it's a different kind of funny."

"Annie Laurie does exactly the same thing, but she'd kill me if I told you." I reached in my lunch pail. "Here, have another cookie."

"Well, if you don't mind."

"Mind? I made them special myself to share with a new best friend." This was going to be easier than I thought.

"I think they are sweet on each other. Do you?" Belinda put a prissy little smile on her lips and looked up expectantly at me.

"I wouldn't be surprised, but this needs further investigation. Let's be super sleuths!" I held up my little finger. "Pinky swear."

Belinda Garrett and I hooked little fingers and chanted—

> *Pinky, pinky bow-bell,*
> *whoever tells a lie*
> *will sink down to the bad place*
> *and never rise up again.*

Annie Laurie would owe me plenty when I came back with my undercover work results. I thought to consider it a career.

—⁂—

I sidled up to Annie Laurie while she washed dishes. "I don't have complete information yet, but I will soon. Belinda thinks he's sweet on you."

"I know that! I want to know if he has marriage in mind."

"I'm working on it. I'm working on it." I sighed in exasperation. "You have to be patient. These things need to be handled in a delicate manner."

"You've never had a delicate moment in your life." Annie Laurie set the last plate out for me to dry. "It's late and I still have to brush my hair."

"Patience, dear sister, patience." I swiped the towel over the dish and went to sit out on the porch. When I sat down on the swing, Mama was standing there in the dark. The climbing rose that she had nurtured as a cutting all the way from Missouri bloomed as though summer lingered about us. The fragrance filled the night.

"Could anything smell more heavenly?" Mama leaned into the trellis. "This 'First Love' rose?"

"That's why you brought it with us, isn't it? To remind you of Papa?"

"Oh, yes. Papa. Of course, your father."

"I think Annie Laurie has a first love."

"Mr. Garrett?" She loosened her high collar. "First love is a powerful thing."

"Like with Papa." This time I didn't make it a question. I didn't know why I said it again. Maybe it was her stammer when I first asked her that egged me on, but mostly the memory of her and Nathan Cage talking on the porch in that very swing niggled at Mama's credibility.

"Can you never stop prying?" Mama didn't try to keep the irritation out of her voice. "I remember my mother saying that to me once, 'Some things are not your affair, little Miss Lucretia.' And as they weren't mine, some things are not *your* affair either, little Miss Cora."

Little Miss Cora, indeed. That was a weak defense, if I had ever seen one. I wanted to chisel away at that veneer Mama sometimes put up. I was determined to do it despite the obstacles she threw in my path.

Chapter Eighteen

One afternoon without telling me where we were going, Ben suggested a ride on Blackjack. It had to be something special if my brother invited me to come along.

"It's a three-mile journey so stifle your impatience." Ben swung into the saddle, cleared the stirrup for me and slung me up behind him. Even in the fall of the year, the sun burned down relentlessly in East Texas. The sultry air made sweat form at my hairline and drip into my eyes. I gazed out over the fields of butterfly weed and marigolds. Coneflowers filled the shaded ditches. The steam of an Indian summer day misted them together like some blurry painting.

I rubbed my forehead against Ben's back and blinked the sweat away. "If it gets much hotter, you'd better check to see if I'm still on this horse. He's so black it's like sittin' on a stovetop. I might faint and fall off."

"I told you to bring your hat, but nooo, you couldn't slow down enough to go get it."

"It's not my head that's burnin' up back here." I grabbed Ben around the waist when Blackjack picked up a trot. "Slow him down! He's scaring me to death!"

"Let's try a lope. That's easier to ride. Hang on, little sister!"

The lope made sitting easier, but I felt the power of those haunches, the bunch and stretch of them that carries riders over ground at dizzying speeds. It did move the air around to cool us off, but my knuckles were pale from holding on and I had bitten my lip.

The low-slung ranch house and the barn that loomed beside it looked hand hewn. Three corrals housed several horses, but the main herd grazed on the pastures sloping to the river where sycamores grew. A man stood out by a corral, his hand outstretched to a small horse.

"Why, it's that Indian who gave me Pepper!" I shoved Ben's shoulder. "Just because he got rid of a puppy don't mean I like Indians."

"Well then, I guess you won't be interested in that pony I promised you last month." He put his foot back in the stirrup and started to turn Blackjack away.

"You never promised me anything! You said maybe, and I never believed a word of it anyway." Then I caught sight of a fine little buckskin peering at me over the corral fence. "But since we're here, we might as well take a look." I slid off Blackjack and walked to the split rail enclosure.

Ben and the old man smiled at each other and then followed me to the gate. I had already opened it and was whispering sugarcoated words to the little mare.

The man spoke to Ben in quiet words. "She don't spook. She don't buck. She won't run off with—"

"We'll take her," I said.

Ben talked like a real horse trader as we stood at the paddock. "The real truth, Mr. Birdsong—what's the story on that horse? Have you been dosing her with a little skullcap? It's been known to calm the most unruly critter. Even considered giving Blackjack there a dose ever' now and then."

"Mr. Allen, I am Caddo as you call us. Honesty is taught to us from birth. What I tell you is true. You may take the mare and if she does not please you, I will give you back the twenty dollars I ask of you." Mr. Birdsong dropped his voice. "You might be getting more than you bargain for. I have every reason to believe she is in foal. Are you still interested?"

I caught my breath. "In foal?"

Ben nodded. "I am indeed. My brother took his gelding with him when he moved to town. We could use another horse."

I hugged the mare's neck, and she curved her head to wrap me against her.

I noticed Ben watching me with a brotherly air, and his voice caught. "What do we call her, Mr. Birdsong?"

"Her name is Belle."

—⁂—

I sat the mare bareback and stroked her coat that glowed like shot silk, changing colors from dusky cream to tan to gold against her legs that were soot black from hock to pastern. She set out with eager optimism, her ears forward and head up. The wind whipped her mane and tail in a flash of coarse black that did not absorb the light but reflected it like ebony wood.

Blackjack certainly became interested in the new acquisition, but Belle squealed if he even looked back at her.

"That'll teach you to flirt with Miss Belle," Ben said. "She's taken."

"She certainly is! She's mine!" I called.

"She is that, for sure, Miss Cora." Ben lifted a rein to slow Blackjack. "It's going be a slow trot back home, boy. We don't want to rush the girls, do we?" He glanced back at me.

"I've got past being a little girl, Benjamin. Fifteen is practically a grown woman." I sent Belle up next to him. "I can ride and I can rush if I want to."

"All right. I can see you're not a little girl, but you are my little sister and will be to the day I die."

"Oh fiddledeedee. You'll be one hundred and I'll be ninety, and then neither one of us will remember who's the older." I loped ahead of him knowing it would take all he had to hold back Blackjack.

—⁂—

At the sight of me carrying a bedroll out to the barn, Mama shook her head. "This will have to stop come winter, you understand that?" I kept walking. Mama blocked my departure. "You *do* understand that, do you not?"

"Yes, yes, ma'am." I patted my leg for Pepper to follow. "Belle needs to know that she belongs to me now and that she's supposed to love me. Like I love her."

"Well, I can hardly imagine she has any doubt of that." Mama looked at Ben and Annie Laurie. "First Fanciful and Pepper, now Belle! This child thinks she can charm all the animals in Texas."

"Didn't you have anything you loved with all your heart, Mama?" I hoisted the bedroll on my shoulder and called, "I'm coming, Belle." From darkness of the barn interior came a shuffle of hooves and a nicker.

—⁂—

Like most afternoons after school, I took my books to the tree where Mama believed me to be studying. I waited for the boy. I set the books at the base of the pecan, tucked my skirt in my drawers and climbed to the best vantage point—forty feet above the ground.

"There he is," I whispered down to Pepper. He'd have to hurry to get back in time to milk, and I wondered if he'd still try to go to the creek. His grandmother appeared to be giving him continuous instruction, but he never looked up. Did he not like the woman? If he didn't like her, I wouldn't like her either.

At last, he snatched up the fishing pole and started for the creek. Even as far away as I was, I could see the scowl on his face. I scrambled down from the tree and skirted through the cornfield. Dried stalks slapped against my cheeks, but I cocked my arm across my face and burrowed through. Pepper tripped me twice, but I swatted at her and kept running. What would I do when I got there? What would I say?

I stood panting at the edge of the water. Maybe I should splash my face. Cool myself down. Look relaxed. Surprised by some boy I never saw before.

Only moments later, he appeared on the slope of the creek bank. And before I could smile, before I had a chance to explain, he turned to leave.

I started to call, "Wait. Please!" I had only wanted to be friends, to let him know I could be kind. That he could learn to trust me. He'd been so lonely looking. Surely, he needed a friend. Surely. But out came, "Hold on there, buster! What's the matter with you anyway?" I wadded my skirt in my hands and bound up the bank behind him. "You come back here this minute!" I tried to match his strides, catch up. "What are you so scared of?"

He turned around once. A hard stare. And kept walking.

What had I seen on his face? Not quite fear, but something like it. Not quite hate, but something like it. Scorn, perhaps. I had intruded. Despite my good intentions, he had no use for my offers of friendship. That much I could read. I stopped. "Sorry!" Although my words were probably lost in the rustling of the corn stalks, it proved just as well since I couldn't keep the irritation out of my voice. "I said I was sorry."

Chapter Nineteen

"I think my brother is coming to your house tomorrow night." Belinda nudged me and gave me a wink. "I heard him talking to my parents, and it's more than the usual visit, if you know what I mean." We stood at our halfway point before having to go separate directions.

"*Tomorrow* night?" I chewed my thumbnail. "Think he could give me two more nights?"

"Give *you*? Surely you do not think he's coming to see *you*?" Belinda let her mouth drop open in a guffaw. "That's the most—"

"Good heavens, of course not. It's that I want this to work out right, you see. Annie Laurie will want to look, well, perfect. And sometimes that takes her a day or two. The hair, the dress. You get the idea."

Before Belinda could confirm her understanding, I snatched my skirt to my knees and bounded across the cotton rows to meet Ben who waited to take me the rest of the way home.

Breathless when I burst into the hallway, I yelled, "Annie Laurie? Annie Laurie! Get yourself over here and listen to this."

Annie Laurie lifted her skirt enough to step across the doorsill without stumbling and said, "My heavens, Cora, how you do carry on. Calm yourself and you will be duly heard."

"Oh, yeah, Miss High and Mighty? Wait'll you hear this!" I skidded to a stop and produced a secretive arch to my eyebrow. "Well, never mind. I thought you'd be excited to hear. Remember our bargain—you'd tell me about the boy if I found out Mr. Garrett's intentions?" I smoothed my skirt and turned to leave. "I see I must have been mistaken, so I'll—"

She stepped on the hem of my dress. "Hold on there, missy. I'm willing to hear you out, provided—"

"Provided?" I leaned into the fabric that her foot held captive. "I think we'll make it provided *you* supply *me* with the information I required in exchange."

"I'm sure I don't remember what you are talking about. You simply volunteered to—"

"You, dear sister, were going to tell me why that neighbor boy don't have to go to school." I turned slowly so as not to rip the skirt hem. "Remember? I got news if you got news."

"Doesn't."

"Doesn't, doesn't, doesn't! Why doesn't he have to go to school?" I stomped my foot.

"All right, all right." Annie Laurie lifted her shoe from the dress hem. "Hearsay is, well, that he's not white. And if you're not white, you are not eligible for a white education. Now, cough up your news."

I sat. My skirt billowed about me. *Not white?*

—m—

I was right about one thing. It took Annie Laurie two days to prepare for Mr. Garrett's visit. He sent a note asking if he might come, and by way of encouragement, Mama issued an invitation to dinner. I sat on the bed the evening of his arrival and observed the flurry of activity. Annie Laurie had brushed her hair an extra 100 times, and I had to admit it gleamed. She cinched her waist to 18 inches and plumped her bosom up to the low neckline of her bodice.

"Mama is never gonna let you get away with that." I smoothed my own skirt over my ankles. "What are you thinking?"

"It's what *he's* thinking that concerns me, Miss Prissy Pants. When did you get so prim and proper?" She turned to study herself in the mirror. "We've barely got you to quit wearing britches. And I've seen you plenty of times tuck your skirt in your bloomers so you could climb a tree, so I hardly think you qualify as a fashion advisor." She glossed her lips, smacked them and added, "My goodness, no!"

"You know? Your accent's getting as bad as the rest of these East Texas folks! Or maybe you're puttin' on for Mr. Gar-rett."

"Hush, you! Get on out of here and take your opinions with you!"

I bolted from the bed and laughed all the way down the stairs, calling back. "Wait till I tell Mama!" A shoe sailed past, but that made me laugh even louder.

As I swung off the newel post, I blundered into a snappily dressed but strained-faced Mr. Garrett. Moisture erupted on his upper lip. Mama had yet to close the door behind him and stood aghast at my behavior.

"Howdy, Mr. Garrett. I'm sure Annie Laurie will be right down." I turned and bellowed up the stairwell. "He's he-re!"

With a rush of footsteps, Annie Laurie flung open the door and then descended with all the grace and decorum of an heiress.

"Miss Allen!" Mr. Garrett ran a finger under his collar and tried to breathe.

The sharpest intake of breath, however, was Mama's. "Oh my," she said.

I smiled, knowing full well the décolletage inspired the gasp and not Annie Laurie's beauty.

Mama had prepared roast chicken, sweet potatoes and thick sliced tomatoes with the skin blanched off. Because she'd had to dump the case of Wedgewood china to keep her piano, she brought out the Blue Willow dishware and the brilliant cut glass goblets. She had only been able to afford four, so she placed a jelly jar at the right corner of my plate. Other than that, she had gone whole hog on dinner. Ben eyed the layout Mama had prepared and seemed to recognize the significance of this particular event.

It was an opportunity I no longer had the discipline to resist. As Mama served the apple pie, I broke into Ben's tirade about Emperor Nicholas II of Russia. Mr. Garrett who had desperately been trying and failing to keep his eyes leveled above Annie Laurie's collarbone, seemed relieved at my interruption.

"Sir, I have a question that applies more closely to home." I ignored the warning purse of Annie Laurie's lips. "I have recently been made aware that our school only allows white children to attend. Everybody else is shut out, even if they look as white as you and me. Well, practically, so why—"

"That'll be enough, dear." Standing behind our guest, Mama glared at me. "Won't you have another piece of pie, Mr. Garrett?"

"Mama, he hasn't even finished the first. Ow!" I lifted the tablecloth to catch the pointed toe of Annie Laurie's shoe receding under her chair. I glowered at her but said, "Perhaps another time, sir."

After dinner while Mr. Garrett and Annie Laurie retired to the front porch swing, I took it upon myself to sit at the piano and tink out "Beautiful Dreamer," pausing long enough to catch phrases of conversation. Even if it proved to be a you-scratch-my-back-and-I'll-scratch-yours arrangement, I was instrumental in bringing Annie Laurie and her beau together. And as such, automatically made me privy to further proceedings. From outside a songbird called and the fragrance of the First Love roses lingered in the air. "They're my mother's favorite," said Annie Laurie. "They remind her of my father." She sighed. "It's sad to lose your first love, don't you think, Mr. Garrett?"

"Please call me William, so that I might call you Annie Laurie. And yes, it must be terrible." He stuttered a little but managed to continue. "I've wanted this moment to be perfect, but I'm afraid my emotions handicap me. Would you think me unimaginative if I borrow from a poet? A woman no less?"

"Why, I'm sure Mr. Garrett, rather William, I could hardly fault you for—"

He blurted out his next words in a great rush, empowered by ardor I supposed, but by the second stanza, he was able to address the beauty of their meaning.

> I love thee to the level of every day's
> Most quiet need, by sun and candle-light.
> I love thee freely, as men strive for Right;
> I love thee purely, as they turn from Praise
> I love thee with the passion put to use
> In my old griefs, and with my childhood's faith.
> I love thee with a love I seemed to lose
> With my lost saints,—I love thee with the breath,
> Smiles, tears, of all my life!—and, if God choose,
> I shall but love thee better after death.

"Annie Laurie Allen, will you marry me?"

Pretty syrupy, I'd say, all this love business, but if Annie Laurie was happy, so was I. And if Mr. Garrett kissed her, I couldn't tell without leaning from the doorway. She would probably never tell either. Not unless she had need of another favor.

Chapter Twenty

The next day when Ben rode in from town, he handed me a letter to give to Mama, which I noted came from Nathan Cage. It had been a long time since a letter from him had arrived. Mama had suffered increasing bouts of irritability, and I had held out hope that he had lost interest. The two-cent stamp was postmarked ten days before, so he had not written earlier, and the letter lost in the mail. "Here, Mama, it's for you." I stepped away around the corner of the parlor and busied myself with absolutely nothing so I could catch her reaction.

She took the letter to the front porch swing but didn't sit. Fumbling with the envelope, she paced about and scanned the page, then clutched the rose trellis to steady herself. A thorn caught the back of her hand, but she hardly seemed to notice. Wiping the blood from her hand onto her skirt, she sat to read again. That evening, she excused herself after preparing dinner and not eating, went upstairs to her room.

As my sister and brother and I sat staring at each other at the kitchen table, I reported on what I'd seen earlier and said, "Annie Laurie, go check on her and purloin the letter. It's our responsibility. Something has upset her to no end. How are we to help her if we are kept in the dark?"

Ben refused to have anything to do with it, but I could see I had made some progress with Annie Laurie. "If you fetch it pretty quick, we can read it and get it back up there before she even notices. She's probably lying up there with her head under a pillow. Annie Laurie, we have got to do something to help Mama."

Those were the golden words—"help Mama."

It always worked with Annie Laurie. She took the stairs two steps at a time and came down within minutes. "You were right," she whispered. "Had her head covered. Wouldn't tell me a thing, but the letter lay right there on the dresser. I told her I would bring her some tea, so we've got five minutes to peruse the contents. I'll start the water. Read it out loud."

I struggled with his nearly illegible script. *Plowing accident. Part of leg amputated. Okay. Will be okay. Feeling better. Can walk some with crutches. Not much for sitting a horse yet.*

"Amputated!" I stared at Annie Laurie. "Oh, wow."

"Poor Nathan," she said as she sat back down at the table. "Poor Mama."

"Well, yes." I refolded the letter and handed it back. "We'll have to be extra nice to her and maybe she will finally tell us. The tea's ready, you better get it up to her." I stuck the letter in her apron pocket. "It'll be our secret."

A shame about Nathan. Truly, it sounded awful. But maybe it would be the end of his plans to see Mama, and she could get over him.

The next morning, she strode to the parlor, pulled her writing paper from her desk drawer and wrote. She wadded the paper into a ball and started again. I watched from the doorway as she took rose petals from a book where she had pressed them, lifted a few and slid them into the envelope. Later that day though, before giving it to Ben to mail, she tore the envelope open, took out the petals and crushed them in her fist.

At last! I breathed a sigh of relief. Still, it does seem a little cruel to Nathan if she didn't love him anymore because he got his leg cut off. *Ah well, all's fair in love and war.* I couldn't quite make out which this would be.

Chapter Twenty-one

With Belle tied to the pecan tree, I climbed to watch the boy. "Does the same thing every single day. The same old thing." It had been months since I intercepted him at the creek, but the time had come to get a better look at him. He was certainly tan, although I had to admit he was brown over his entire body. I remembered that and recalled noticing Ben's chest once when he ripped off his shirt in front of the icebox after a day in the field. It glowed white as a striped bass's belly. Mama always nagged me to stay out of the midday sun and for heaven's sake, wear a hat. Ivory skin was the hallmark of the leisure class, and even though we were hardly that, Mama always aspired to it. If I could ever catch Mr. Garrett again without Annie Laurie attached to his arm, I'd see if I couldn't make him explain the exact definition of "white." And did it matter or not if the only white skin you had lay under your shirt?

I worked on a plan to walk down to the creek to see if I could entice the boy to help me with something. Annie Laurie used that ploy so many times with Mr. Garrett that I could mimic it in my sleep. What would I need help with? Boys always thought girls couldn't bait hooks. I'd go early and wait till he was half asleep fishing. I'd stick a hook in my finger, pinch it till the blood dripped and hold it up for him to see as I fought back tears and incidentally blocked his path of escape.

The creek swelled with the previous night's rain. The boy studied my footprints as he approached the bank, then searched the trees for a sign of their owner. But silent and still, I lay tucked away in the cypress roots.

Most of an hour went by before he dropped his chin and his hands went loose on the fishing pole. I eased from my hiding spot and sat within twenty feet of him. I arranged my fishing gear and the can of worms, then drew out the hook. I closed my eyes and touched the hook to my finger. Before I allowed myself to think another thought, I dug it into the flesh. I pinched my finger as hard as I could, and blood seeped from the spot. I squeezed again and pushed the hook a little deeper. "Ow!"

The boy's eyes flashed open, and ready to bolt, he pressed himself against the creek bank.

I had already begun to cry almost silently. I didn't have to work hard at it. It *did* hurt. I held up my finger and let the blood trickle down my hand. "I can't get the hook out. I can't! It's stuck. I was trying to bait the hook, and the dumb old worm slipped." Spontaneous tears flowed. I thought I'd discerned a glimmer of pity in his eyes and feeling assured that he'd let down his guard, I held out my hand and put my blue eyes to work. A little practice before the mirror at home had given me confidence. When my eyes filled with tears, someone, *anyon*e would want to quell them, surely. Maybe even kiss them away. "Oh," I cried softly. "Oh."

He had started to stand. Still not sure whether he intended to help or to run. I allowed a little panic to come into my voice. "Don't! Can you? Could you?" And then I diminished my voice to the point that he had to lean forward to hear. "Help me?"

He nodded finally after studying my eyes, looking for traces of lies. Convinced they projected pure helplessness, I had to drop my head to hide the smile.

He knelt beside me in a crouch that would allow him break away. I held out my hand and smiled with shy appreciation. "Will it hurt?" I asked.

He shook his head once, turned my face away, and when I looked back, the hook lay on the ground. He swished my hand in creek water and motioned for me to wait. When he returned he wrapped my finger in spider web. I gasped, but he pressed it to the wound. "Orb weavers," he said, "make good bandages." Then he stood, grabbed his bait and pole and left.

"But, wait!" I cried. "You're supposed to teach me how to bait a hook!"

He turned, raised an eyebrow and trudged up the bank toward his house.

"Murder, murder, murder." I skewered the earthworm onto the hook and flopped the line into the water. "He took the bait, but he got away."

Chapter Twenty-two

Annie Laurie set the wedding date for the first week of March. She insisted she could not wait another day. "If I am to have the perfect wedding, it will have to be with daffodils. And the redbud and dogwood will be pure heaven."

By mid-September she had bought up all the daffodil bulbs to be had in Fannin County and planned to have them in the ground before the end of the month. She designed her dress, and when Mama told her that an elaborate gown of Chantilly lace and silk were extravagances in which she was not prepared to invest, Annie Laurie announced she would make it herself and ordered the fabric from the Sears catalog. The day Ben brought the boxes in from the Ladonia Post Office, she sat down and touched the lace, its delicacy, its fine beauty. Tears came to her eyes. "It's beautiful, Mama. Look, it's beautiful."

"Yes, darling." Mama took Annie Laurie's face in her hands. "Yes, it is lovely."

Mama fought back tears herself. Annie Laurie probably still seemed like a child full of dreams to her, but I could see that she had become a young woman and was leaving me behind.

—ɯ—

Belinda and I continued to exchange secrets about our siblings' romance, but I spent more of my time thinking about the boy. Maybe he couldn't read or write. Maybe I could teach him, and in gratitude he would tell me why the townspeople didn't consider him white. I had begun to ride Belle to school, tying her to the tree each morning and every afternoon taking the long way home by way of the creek, hoping to see him. If I did, I planned to offer him a ride back to his grandmother's or ask him to teach me how to bait a hook. He couldn't resist forever.

I finally caught him trotting up from the creek in late October when leaves in colors of claret and mustard drifted down from the red oaks and sycamores. A cold front threatened above the tree line, and the air had gone still, silencing the papery rustle of cottonwoods. I cut off his retreat and offered a hand up on Belle.

The mare put her nose on him. She nickered. She searched his pockets and nudged against him.

"You better let her take you home," I said. "You're gonna freeze to death if that storm catches you."

"Ain't no storm gonna catch me. I can run about as fast as Belle can carry me."

I wondered how he knew the mare's name. Had he heard me call for her? Perhaps. "You cannot neither. Get on up here. I won't hurt you." I tried not to stare at him. I concentrated on the horizon, not wanting to scare him off. That look crossed his face again—fear or misgivings, defiance. But this time, he grabbed the pony's mane and swung up behind me. The closeness of him and his body heat surprised me. I glanced down to see his britches against my own legs bared to the knee below my skirt. Mama would have had a fit. Something about it made me understand why. Not specifically. But something in the way his body conformed to mine.

"That's Caney Creek back there," he said. "It rises thirty-five miles to northeast of here and runs southwest for five and a half miles to its mouth on the Cowleech Fork of the Sabine River." He rattled off the statistics as though I had asked the question of a mapmaker. "It goes from Grandma's, past your place on down to my uncle's."

I had no idea how to respond. Except to challenge him. "Well, how do you know all that? What did you do—walk it?" I straightened in the saddle. The only time I had walked that far was on the trek from Missouri. "I guess they put up markers for all the creeks and lakes for you."

He didn't answer.

"What's your name anyway?" I moved Belle into a trot.

He didn't answer. Good lord, it took the patience of Job to get him to say anything but creek names. "I'm Cora. Cora Allen. We came from Missouri." I waited as long as I could stand to. "How about you?"

"Around here." The wind picked up and carried his words away.

"What?" I turned to understand, but his mouth was too close—his eyes too reckless.

The clouds bunched and tumbled, and from them came the spit of freezing rain. Sycamore leaves clung to my hair, and around us, the sumac blurred red like thin flames.

"Stop here," he said, while we were still a hundred yards from his grandmother's house.

"But—"

He barely waited for Belle to slow to slip off her. I watched as the wind whipped his hair and stuck his shirt to his shoulder blades as he strode toward the house.

I swung Belle toward home at a gallop. How rude. He didn't even thank me or wave goodbye. Never mind answer polite questions. But then again came that rush of heartbeat and flush of heat.

—⟋⟍⟍—

That first cold front ushered in a long series of dismal days. In mid-November, Ben said, "Come on out to the barn with me, little sister. Something I want to show you."

We bundled up and trudged out in the cold air. In the dim stall I heard the shuffle of Blackjack's feet on straw and the rhythmic crush of hay as Belle munched her forage. In the hush and shadows of the barn, I found peace in the smell of alfalfa and horse, of faint turpentine and leather.

Ben ran his hands around Belle's belly and smiled. "That's not fat on her."

"I was afraid to really count on it," I said, "but it's a baby for sure, isn't it?"

"Yes, it's a baby." Ben laughed and hugged me close. "Goodnight, let's get in the barn. I'm freezing."

"When will it be, Ben? Isn't it too cold for a baby?"

"Naw, it'll be fine. A few more weeks is my guess. If Belle gets a good dose of cold weather every day, baby should come with a heavier coat. We'll still make a nice stall available and a good size run-out. Belle doesn't need to stand outside the schoolroom all day waiting for you. Blackjack and I will see you get to and from school."

More rides on Blackjack. I'd thought I'd become accustomed to horses after months of riding Belle, but Blackjack was another ride indeed. He still scared me, but it held more promise than walking six miles. He covered it in half the time it took me and the mare.

The thought crossed my mind that it would put an end to my waiting for the boy. Not that he wanted to see me anyway. I had not one glimpse of him since giving him a ride home. Maybe I could watch from the pecan tree, even though I'd be in plain sight with all the leaves gone. At least, I'd have the excuse of picking pecans if he spied me.

I stroked the mare. "I'll come out tomorrow after school and brush you good. Stay warm, little mama." I kissed Belle goodnight on her nose, and Ben and I huddled together to run back to the house.

—⁂—

Finally, in late December it looked like Ben had figured the timing of the foaling down pretty close. If I'd only had the stamina to have seen it. Determined to be a help to Belle, I spent the last two nights in the stall and then dozed off in the classroom the following days. After supper, I told Pepper to stay in the house and for the third evening in a row, I mucked and replaced the straw in Belle's stall. The night promised to be even colder than the nights before, but I had the towels ready to dry the foal immediately. The wind had come up and after a few moments of diligence, the soft breathing of the mare lulled me to sleep.

Only an hour passed, but the exciting event had gone on without me. As I blinked my eyes open, there stood the foal on shaky legs, but it had already found its mother's milk. I squealed and then shushed myself. I had every intention of rubbing the baby with the towels I'd brought out but couldn't work up the nerve. What if it hated that? What if I scared it? What if— I backed out through the stall gate and ran calling for Ben.

He sat at the kitchen table blowing over a cup of hot coffee. I grabbed him by the shirtsleeve, stuffed his coat in his hands and ran back out to the barn without ever uttering a word.

He met me in a few minutes. He looked under the foal's belly and announced, "Well now, that's a fine little colt."

"A colt? But I thought—"

"Well, you thought wrong. Let's see if Belle will let us rub the baby dry and we'll let her alone for the rest of the night." He spoke so softly I could hardly hear him.

Ben directed my hands over the foal, first without the towel and then with it. "He's gonna have a nice calm nature like his mama, I do believe. He's a handsome lad. We could call him Beau. Goes fine with Belle, doesn't it? What do you think?" Ben shivered. "Lordy, it's cold. Let's get on back to the house. You can check on them first thing in the morning before school. You need to get a good night's sleep even if Mama and Annie Laurie stay up all night working on that wedding gown."

The wind whipped through the open doorway and the lamplight wavered. "The baby's here, Mama! His name is Beau. Wait until you see him, Annie Laurie!"

Annie Laurie glared up from her sewing. "Y'all shut that door this minute." In recent months she had adopted the East Texas drawl and mannerisms that defined Fannin County. "I've got a toothache as it is, and y'all have made it worse."

Ben and I gave each other a look and shook our heads.

"Don't think I didn't see that! Mama, did you see—"

"You're tired, Annie Laurie. Go on to bed." Mama reached for the wedding gown. "I'll work on it a while for you. We could get a sewing machine you know. Sure would go faster. And it'd be of use for other things. Why don't—"

"I want it all hand sewn. You know that, Mama. I want it to be perfect." Annie Laurie started to cry and grabbed a hankie before tears fell on the Chantilly lace.

"Oh brother," I said.

"I'm sorry, I'm sorry. I know it's silly." Annie Laurie clutched her cheek. "My tooth is killing me."

"Go on upstairs. I'll bring you a couple of cloves crushed in warm oil." Mama patted her shoulder and sent her on. "It'll feel better in the morning."

—⁂—

But it was not better in the morning. So despite the cold, we took the buckboard into Ladonia. Mama drove while I sat next to Annie Laurie keeping a heavy blanket wrapped around her shoulders.

We waited two hours in the dentist's office. "That tooth is going have to come out." The doctor minced no words. "It's a wisdom tooth so far back, ain't nobody going to notice anyway," he said when he saw the look on Annie Laurie's face. He handed her a jigger of rye whiskey. "Take it down quick."

Even with the whiskey, Annie Laurie cried out as the doctor wrenched the tooth loose. I watched her knuckles pale as she gripped Mama's hand. Observing Mama's face, I couldn't tell who hurt the most.

Annie Laurie held her cheek and sobbed as we left the office. Blood stained the blanket Mama had wrapped around her and crystallized in the frigid air.

Mama murmured all the way home. "Try to think of something else, darling. How beautiful you'll look in that wedding gown. Imagine William's face when he sees you." She popped the whip over the horse's back. "Hurry on! Git up there." And to Annie Laurie she promised, "There's laudanum at home. Plenty of it. Just hold on."

When we pulled up at the front of the house, Mama called for Ben to take care of the horse we had put a lather on. She hustled Annie Laurie to our bedroom upstairs. She sent me for the laudanum.

I thought Mama kept it on a high kitchen shelf but couldn't remember where exactly. Shuffling through the bottles of cough syrup and bromide, my fingers closed around the angular shape of The Anchor Brand laudanum bottle. "Good." I clutched the bottle to my chest and rushed up the stairs.

After that Annie Laurie slept through the night.

She felt better the next day and came down but refused anything to eat or drink except for a little water. "I can feel a terrible hole back there," she said as she ran her tongue over the spot.

"Swish this salt water. It'll help." Mama handed her a glass. "Tomorrow you won't even know it happened."

Mr. Garrett came after school the next afternoon, but Annie Laurie refused to see him. She sent me down with a note as he waited in the parlor.

> *William,*
>> *How dear of you to call, but I am a fright and cannot bear*
>> *to face you quite so soon. I'll send word to school with Cora*
>> *as soon as I am presentable again.*
>>> *With affection,*
>>> *Annie Laurie*

—⁓—

At midnight Annie Laurie called Mama. "I'm so hot, Mama. Open the window." She flung the blanket from her.

"Sweetheart, it's 30 degrees out there, and look at you. You're shaking." She felt her Laurie's forehead. "And burning up. Cora, get the brandy and the willow bark. It'll take down that fever."

Clutching my nightgown in my hands, I hurried down the stairs and rushed back in minutes with the willow bark and a cup of brandy laced with laudanum. Mama supported Annie Laurie's head in the crook of her arm and touched the cup to her lips. "If it doesn't kill you, it should cure you." She tried to smile but couldn't make it believable.

As Annie Laurie pressed her mouth to the cup, she shuddered so violently that much of the draught splattered to her gown. She began to cry softly.

"It's all right. It's all right." Mama peeled the sweat-dampened hair from her forehead and cheek. "I'll get a cool cloth." The rest of the night, she sat on the edge of the bed dabbing the cloth in water and pressing it to Annie Laurie's face and neck.

I sat on my own bed trembling. I had never seen Annie Laurie like this. Sometimes she feigned headaches if she wanted out of a chore and she sometimes couldn't wash the dishes because the water wrinkled her hands and always, always she insisted on brushing her hair 100 strokes, but of late, I had witnessed her diligence of dress making, the tedious hours spent over Chantilly lace and satin.

Mama's eyes held a wild look.

By morning, she began to pray.

She called for Ben. "You ride. You ride hard and get the doctor. Something's gone wrong, Ben. Put that black horse of yours to the test."

Annie Laurie's moan interrupted her, and Mama turned back toward the bed. "You better stay out, Cora. Maybe it's the flu."

"But Mama, I want to help. Isn't there something—" I stopped. I could smell the fear like when Papa was dying and when Ben had been beaten to a bloody pulp by the Indians.

"Bring me a clean bowl of water and then. . . ." Mama smacked her fist on her forehead like she couldn't think. "Put on some coffee. The doctor will be here soon."

I stepped slowly down the stairs. *What if, what if?* "No, stop it," I said aloud. "It's going to be okay. The doctor will come and give her quinine or something. Get the water and stop thinking."

I brought a full bowl of water and set it by the bedstead. I stared at Annie Laurie as she lay flushed and restless, fighting Mama's attempt to bathe her forehead. At times, she called out for Papa, and tears boiled to Mama's eyes. At other times, Annie Laurie mumbled that she hurt. And all the while Mama pressed the cool cloth to her cheeks and almost silently continued to beg God for help.

Chapter Twenty-three

Cool and bright. The freezing temperatures of the preceding days were gone. And Annie Laurie was gone. We buried her in Chantilly lace and silk. Mama had stayed up long into the night finishing with tight, precise stitches the work Annie Laurie had begun. I could only think of one thing she would have wanted—that her hair would shine with the hundred strokes. And so I did that—brushed and brushed the dark locks until they glowed with the brushing and the tears that I could not wipe away quickly enough.

We all stood in the cluster of bare, white-trunked sycamores and said our goodbyes. I held on to Ben and stared up at him hoping to find some understanding of how all this could go so wrong. His nostrils flared as he took deep breaths, but he would not look at me. He stared up at the blue skies and clenched his fists as if to crush the angry words he wanted to say.

Joe and his wife stood beside Mama. The Garretts were there and Cousin Frank and Zora. Belinda could only stare at me as she stood holding on to her brother's arm. William crumpled his hat to his chest and never uttered a word. After the funeral, Mama had gone to her bed in grief, and Ben and Joe sat beside her. Words could bring no comfort, and so there were none.

It was a bad thing. I knew it. But in me surged some rage that had to be exorcised. The night fell as dark and as still as the death we had all witnessed.

Although it hadn't been long since Belle foaled, I thought she was probably up to it. Hadn't Ben told me to take her out on the trail and let the colt follow? A little sooner than planned, granted, but I had to go. I headed for the barn.

Belle nickered as I unlatched the stall door. The foal wobbled to his feet and hung behind his mama.

I led Belle out of her stall. "We'll go for a little ride—not far. I promise not too far." My hands shook as I haltered the mare and pushed the pad and saddle onto her back. "If baby here can't keep up with us, I promise I'll let you slow down. I promise."

Belle groaned as I cinched up the saddle. Milk flowed down the side of her leg. The foal danced around us, trying to get to her teats.

"I'm sorry. I have to—" I pulled the bit into her mouth and set the bridle into place. I grabbed the saddle horn and pushed my foot into the stirrup, but Belle swung away and blocked me from mounting. Never had she been so obstinate.

"Stand still!"

Belle swung away again. I hit her then. Twice. With the flat of my hand. I fell against her, still gripping the stirrup before falling until I lay sobbing in the dust beneath the mare.

How long I lay there I didn't know. At least until Belle nudged me hard. I spewed dirt from my mouth and smeared the straw and tears across my cheek. Shame, glittering and bitter, ran from my gut to my throat.

"I'm sorry." I rubbed Belle's shoulder as I pulled up alongside her. "I'm so sorry. You don't know. You just don't know." I released the cinch, slid the saddle to the ground and led her back to her stall. The foal followed, but when I reached to stroke him, he flinched and moved behind his mama.

In the dark, Blackjack shuffled in his stall, and I hit upon a plan—a death wish—but a plan. Blackjack had come all the way from Missouri and never seemed to tire. He could out-distance the pain—cool my fury. Halter in hand, I leaned over the stall door and studied his eyes. Kind enough. But did they lie?

"Want to get out? Go for a little excursion?" I reached out to touch his neck. He arched against my hand and blew—a good sign I hoped. Slowly, slowly I opened the gate and stepped inside.

Large and dim, the stall smelled of all things equine—the musky, indescribable power that was horse. The stallion snuffled. His feet danced in place, although he had never been trained to do it. He was a quarter horse, faster in the quarter mile than any two-year-old in the big races they held in Kentucky. I pushed away the fear I had always felt around this big animal. Surely, I rode better after all those months with Belle. I needed to run, and the stallion could do it for me. He could fly.

I led him out and tied him to the corral rail—up high like Ben had always told me to. Not too loose. Not too tight. He accepted the quick brush down. He accepted the saddle. Then I sent him around a few times on the longe line, like I'd seen Ben do. He pulled a few times but slowed to a trot when I asked and came in to me, his breath hot and impatient.

After tightening the girth, I sent him around two more times before cinching it up again. I pressed gently, and Blackjack lowered his head so I could guide the bit over his tongue back to the gap in his teeth. I chose a shank bit, the longest one. His ears were pricked in some confusion that it was me and not Ben at his head in this maneuver, but he submitted to the leather being drawn over his head and ears. I set the browband, buckled the throatlatch and ran my hands down his neck. I led him through the gate and turned him to face it in case he thought about bolting for the countryside. I gripped the horn and swung into the saddle. He stood. I locked my feet into the stirrups. He stood. Slowly I reined him around and headed toward town, planning to stay on the road, lit with moonlight.

Thoughts for emergency control ran through my mind. *Hold one rein. One rein if he takes off.* But he behaved well. I felt the strength—the haunches that bunched under me, the ligaments that stretched bone to bone. The tendons that strapped bone to muscle. He was everything Ben had bragged about him.

A canter. We would stick to a canter and try to forget that Annie Laurie lay in her grave. Her face, composed and stony, her skin blanched to pallor. I asked for a trot, then a canter and back down to a walk. Blackjack resisted but came down to a sidestepping gait. Surely, I could handle him with the four-inch shank bit. Before I thought clearly about what I asked, I touched my heels to his flanks. He nearly surged out from under me so powerful his response, but I managed to stay with him. Gone, the pain. Gone, Annie Laurie's last word—*Papa*. Flight. Lunging into space. Freedom. This moment was all that mattered.

Blackjack left the road. He charged forward, and I couldn't hold him. I had no control. No thought except to ride this creature. He became part of the wind and oblivion. And I, part of him.

I never saw the fallen tree until he leaped.

Breath gone, I lay stunned where I fell, my arm twisted beneath me. I didn't care. Pain felt good. This pain could be fixed, not like the pain of the last few days. That would never be fixed.

I lay there for a while staring at the moon. Hoping for forgetfulness. But along the road someone called. I felt annoyance, then relief, then self-pity. The boy.

"Here!" I called. "Here!"

In moments, he came leading Blackjack by the reins. "I heard you thundering past Grandma's house." He tethered the horse and knelt beside me. He touched my shoulder. "Can you roll over? Let me—"

"Owww! Don't touch me! Ow!" I grabbed my arm and gasped in pain.

"Uh oh. Broken? Think you can ride back with me? I'll put you in the saddle so you can hold the horn."

"I am not getting back on that horse. I can walk home." I rolled to a sit and let the boy lift me to a stand. "You've never ridden Blackjack. He'll kill us both."

"I can ride, white girl. Put your foot in the stirrup. I'll boost you the rest of the way."

"Nooo." I started to bawl. "I can't. It hurts too much."

"Do it! It's too far to walk, and I ain't about to carry you." He lifted my foot to the stirrup. "Grab on with your good arm."

I locked the fingers of my left hand around the horn, and the boy shoved me onto the saddle. He swung up behind me and took the reins.

"We'll go slow," he said. We rode for a long while in silence. "I heard," he said against my hair.

I leaned back against him. I had no words.

"It's gonna be all right after a while." He gave me a tentative pat on my good shoulder. "After a while it'll be all right."

"How do *you* know?"

"I said, after a while. Even if it's a long while."

The pain skittered up my forearm and into my shoulder. Exquisite. And I ceased to think about the boy except as means to an end.

Chapter Twenty-four

In the late afternoon of a March day, the sun glinted off the slope and set the daffodils to gold. I sat with Mama on the porch swing gazing at them. They covered the hillside where Annie Laurie had planted them last September and where she had planned to be married. Instead, her grave lay nearby, close enough to view the daffodils if her eyes could see. Would it be some cruel joke of God's? To give her eyes from the grave to see the flowers that would have adorned her wedding day?

"Mama? That poet who wrote 'A crowd, a host of daffodils?'"

Mama pushed the swing with her feet, moving back and forth as though hypnotized. "Wordsworth."

"Mr. Garrett loved that poem. Made us all memorize it. He said Wordsworth planted a field of them for his daughter when she died—in remembrance. Maybe we could think of it that way, Mama. In remembrance?" I wondered if Mr. Garrett had seen the daffodils since they had begun to bloom. Of course, he had if he'd been to visit the gravesite.

I studied my arm that was still pale and wrinkled after having the cast removed. "Mama?"

No answer.

"Mama? Let's go on in."

"I'm coming. Go ahead. . . ." She mouthed the words *without me*. I started to close the door quietly behind me as I'd closed it so many times before in the last weeks, but she sighed and pushed herself up.

Ben came down the road in the phaeton buggy he had bought with his share of the cotton money. "Never know when I might need to go a courtin'," he had said at the time. He had a passenger, but no young woman. They were coming directly out of the sunset. I shaded my eyes with my hand. His dust-covered pants leg pinned at the knee, a man sat with him.

"Who's that with Ben? Is that Nathan? Look, Mama, it's Nathan!"

Ben hopped down to assist him off the carriage, but Nathan waved him off. He stood waiting for Mama, maintaining his balance on a cane. He didn't seem sure of her or himself.

She clenched one fist as she offered the other hand to him. I didn't understand her reaction. I thought she would fall into his arms and take consolation in his being there. But when I thought more about it, I doubted she would want anyone to see how shaken, how almost destroyed she was. Even Nathan.

"Why, Nathan," she said, "what a surprise." She turned to direct a stabbing little frown at Ben, but with some effort smiled at Nathan. "You needn't have made such a long trip. I guess Nan must have told you about— Well, it's kind of you to come, but I hope you didn't think it necessary."

"Crecie."

Mama looked away into the sun. Nathan took one step closer to her, never letting go of her hand. She tried to pull away, but he held her. She looked over his shoulder and finally into his eyes.

Obviously shaken, she still managed to remain aloof until after supper when she directed him to the front porch swing and joined him with a bottle of Hennessy and two snifters. I assumed my position at the couch by the window. "May be a bad habit," I heard Mama say, "but it gets me through the night."

"Lots worse habits in this world than a glass of brandy at the end of the day. Got me through a few rough times myself."

I moved nearer the curtains where I could watch.

"If you don't want to talk about it, I understand. You know how women are. We think we've got to talk everything out. Purge." Mama smiled and took a sip of the brandy, but her lip fluttered on the brim of the glass and she tried to conceal the spill in a quick dab with the back of her hand. "Men seem determined to play the strong silent type." She glanced up quickly at him. "But sometimes it does help to talk."

"Talk brings it all up again. And it can't change what happened. But to satisfy your need to know—"

"I lied. I do need to understand. How can something so terrible happen to you and I not sense it somehow? Not know until I got your letter."

"Well, it was stupid to start with." He laughed softly. "I wish I could stand and pace about the porch, my drink in my hand. Like a man telling a war story. Better to sit. That way I can maintain some degree of dignity. The story is undignified enough as it is. Had myself in a hurry. And I knew better. Had me a two-horse sulky that could plow two rows at a time and I intended to get done by dark. The incline wasn't that steep, and I had one turn to make. Can't remember too much after that. Maybe one of the horses stumbled. Felt the reins go tight and then slack, and I felt the sulky shift. I jumped but couldn't quite get clear."

Mama listened and then spoke quietly so that I had to strain to hear her. "I wish I could have been there to take care of you. But we'll get through this. Like we've got through everything."

"I wanted to be here with you," he said, "after Annie Laurie died. I wanted to take care of you instead of you taking care of me." He stared off into the fallow fields of the past winter.

"Oh Nathan, you shouldn't have come though. It's such a long trip, and the pain must still be hard to bear."

He gripped her fingers with his own and pressed them to his lips. "It's ugly—the leg."

"But it's not *you*. You are still beautiful." She ran the back of her hand across his cheek. Her voice broke. "We'll be fine."

All this talk nauseated me. Beautiful? Really. Mama seemed to have completely reversed her initial reaction, which I preferred.

He turned her hand to kiss the palm of it. "Just keep puttin' one foot in front of the other." His laugh sounded tinged with bitterness. "I might be a little slow on that score, but I'll be damned if I let it make me less a man. I'll find a way to get around this somehow."

His vehemence startled me.

Mama seemed to search for words to say. "Why, I don't doubt—"

"Of course, you do! I did and still do sometimes, but you wait and see. I can't be a farmer anymore but I'll find another way." Nathan held on to the porch swing and stood. "It's getting late, and I must prevail upon Ben to take me back to town."

"Stay here, Nathan. You don't need to go all the way back to Ladonia."

"Naw, but thanks for the invite. I hate to admit I can't get up them stairs."

I rushed back to the kitchen and grabbed the plates off the table. When Mama and Nathan came in, I had my back to them washing the dishes.

Ben looked up from the newspaper and leaned back on two legs of his chair. "I got afraid I might have to do those dishes. You must have been real busy with something else."

Wouldn't it be fun to kick the back legs of that chair right out from under him, I thought. Instead I said, "I hear the pretty girl you've been courtin' went on a picnic with that new boy in town."

Chapter Twenty-five

The redbuds had bloomed, the dogwood flowered and green began taking the place of the delicate daffodil blossoms, overrunning the memories of Annie Laurie's wedding. No longer the brilliant yellows and fuchsias and spiritual whites of early spring. Green, green everywhere.

I sat in the warm, stuffy classroom and watched Mr. Garrett forget where he was in his lecture and stand at the blackboard with his back to us, the chalk poised but never making a mark on the board. He gave us homework but never remembered to collect it the next day, so nobody was too surprised when he stopped what he was doing and announced that he would not be returning for the fall semester. Uncertain about his plans, he said he hoped to take a business position in an accounting company or become an assistant to a professor at The University of Texas in Austin. Or somewhere. He didn't seem to know where to go or what to do. "Maybe a soldier," he said, "but there's no war going on. I really wish I had a war to go to."

"He probably would make a good soldier," said Belinda as she and I were leaving the classroom. "He's very brave. You know he didn't cry once when—" Belinda's hand slipped over her mouth. "I mean. . . . I did find this under his desk. I bet it's about your sister." She unfolded a small piece of paper. On it was written

Whippoorwill, your song with melancholic tone
Doth fuel the sorrow in my heart
And make me dread the fall of night.
And now I feel I must petition thee
To leave for winter so I might

Recoup my life and faith in God
Then when the spring arrives again
Your song will only bring to me
Remembrance of a love that was.

"That's really sad, isn't it, for someone who never once cried—that I ever saw anyway."

I flung my book strap over my shoulder. Why did she have to show me that? I knew Mr. Garrett loved Annie Laurie. It only made me feel worse to read his pain. Leaving seemed the right thing for him. He needed to get past the grief and move on with his life. The whippoorwills' call is lovely, not so melancholic, and maybe someday instead, he will hear their refrain as the sweet promise of spring. "Ben will meet me halfway," I said walking ahead so she wouldn't see the flash of tears in my eyes.

"Oh, Cora, I didn't mean. . . . What I meant to say—"

"Whatever you meant to say couldn't possibly make any difference, Belinda." I turned back to her and clasped her hands. "I know you mean well, it just won't make any difference." Ben and Blackjack were visible on the road ahead, and I walked resolutely to meet them.

—⚏—

Nathan stayed two weeks this time. He borrowed Ben's buggy and spent much of his time in Ladonia wheeling and dealing with local businesses. Mama began to wear a rose in her hair. Every day. I pretended not to notice.

One night while Mama cooked supper, she said to Nathan, "What exactly do you have in *mind*, if you don't *mind* my asking?" She looked over her shoulder at him as she fried chicken.

He sat at the kitchen table with his good leg stretched out before him and massaged his thigh. "This leg gets more than its share of the workload."

"That is not what I asked you and you know it."

"Excuse me," I interrupted. "I seem to be in the way here." I stopped peeling the potatoes and wiped my hands on my apron. "I'll go check on Belle and Beau."

"You're not in the way, Cora. We were—"

"No, no. It's all right. I need to check on them anyway." I stepped outside to the porch and called Pepper, but then stepped back to the window. A kitchen mirror angled so I could see them quite clearly.

Nathan spoke above the popping lard. "I'll tell you more tonight."

"No, you won't. You never do too much talking when you—"

He reached up and pulled her to his lap. "When I what?" He murmured against her throat.

"Hush, the children might come in, and you know very well what I mean." She swatted his hand with the spatula and tried to get away.

"I don't think we're foolin' anybody."

No, you're not, I thought.

"Maybe not, but there is a certain value in keeping up appearances. At least until I've agreed to marry you." She couldn't stifle a laugh.

"You'll marry me. I have to make you an honest woman." He sat up and let her get to her feet. "I've got a few details to work out back home, but I'll be back before the end of summer."

"The end of summer? That long, Nathan?"

I rolled my eyes. It wasn't all *that* long. All this eavesdropping was getting to be too much. I was finding out way more than I wanted to know.

"Before then," he said, "if I get lucky."

Mama speared the chicken out of the skillet and spoke over her shoulder. "Betting on horses or do you have a plan?"

"Yes, I have a plan. You bet I've got a plan—a deal on a Lummus gin and compress." He grabbed his cane and stood. "I could start up the fastest cotton gin in Fannin County. This machine can produce one and a half bales of cotton every hour. As many as fifteen bales in a twelve-hour workday. You and your farm can double your production, and I wouldn't charge *you* a penny to gin it." He stopped, and the tone of his voice changed in a way I found particularly annoying. "Providing," he said, "you and I are on *real* good terms."

"Fifteen bales a day?"

"Yes, ma'am. Fifteen bales."

"And when do you and I get married?"

"The minute you see me coming back down the road." Nathan sat on the edge of the table and pulled her back to him.

"So, are you going to rob a bank?" She smoothed out the cowlick his hat had created in his hair. "Better get a haircut first." She used her coquettish voice.

Nathan took her face in his hands. "Whatever it takes."

Chapter Twenty-six

To expose the colt to various experiences, I took Belle on trail rides with Beau gamboling after us. Pepper darted a black and white dash in and out of our path. We rode over every obstacle I could think to try––bridges, stumps, fields of flowers and fields of rocks. I encouraged the colt with soft words, and even when he showed hesitation at the bridge, he followed Belle. The creek would be the last challenge. The rain had turned the bank into a muddy slide. I thought this might be the most likely place Beau would balk. I started off at a brisk trot hoping the momentum would override his anxiety.

Even the mare paused when she saw the muddy drop and danced on her feet for a moment before taking the slope almost on her haunches. Pepper nipped at the colt's feet until he floundered after her in a great spew of creek water and exuberance. The excitement thrilled Pepper and she set up a tirade of barking but refused to follow. The spray rainbowed and glistened from the cypress's needle-like leaves so they hung like fine icicles.

"Yippee!" I squealed. "Beau, ain't you a corker!"

"Corker's one word for it." The boy stood up, drenched and angry. "I got another word."

"But you can't say it because I'm a lady." I put an impudent smile on my face.

"A lady? That *is* a corker!"

"Why you—" I started for him on my horse, but Belle stopped abruptly to put her nose in his outstretched hand. I caught myself to keep from tumbling, but he grabbed my hand and pulled me into the water beside him. "How's your arm?"

That night came back to me in a rush of emotion—the pain and grief, the relief that he'd found me. I had never told anyone exactly how I broke my arm the night after Annie Laurie died. I had waited for the boy to finish rubbing Blackjack down and feed and water him, then I limped into the kitchen holding my arm against my side. My brother Joe rode for the doctor who came to set and splint my forearm. No one had pinned me down on the hows and whys. They were too heartbroken themselves. Laudanum eased grief as well as the pain from my broken arm. The doctor asked, but I had my lie ready. "Fell off the fence trying to feed Blackjack."

Now that the boy and I stood face to face, both dripping, I couldn't decipher exactly what I felt. But it didn't feel like I should trust it. I responded to his question. "Fine. My arm's fine."

"You scared all the fish away," he said. "You realize that?" He waved his hand at the churning water where Beau pawed with great pleasure.

"Is that all you care about? Fishing?" I tried to regain some dignity. "Certainly not gardening or milking. I know you don't like taking orders from your grandma."

"Fishing is one way I get some peace." He looked at the horses wallowing in the water. "I used to think so, anyway." The horses stood and shook and sprayed us again. The boy turned to leave.

I wasn't going to let him get away so quickly. I reached for his shirtsleeve. "Wait!"

When he stopped to stare at me, his black eyes bored into me and frightened me for a moment. I gasped a little at the sensation but softened my voice. "I don't think I ever thanked you for saving—helping me back last winter. Especially the part about not telling anyone." I had to look away from those eyes. "There are so many things I don't know about you. I mean, would you tell me your name? You know mine."

"Jesse. It's Jesse. That ought to hold you for a while."

I pressed my luck. "Just one thing." I ducked my head and looked up at him. "It's personal."

Jesse wrenched his sleeve from my fingers and began collecting his fishing gear.

"Why don't you go to school? People say you're not—"

"None of their damn business why." His fury made me step back.

"I don't need school. I can read and I can write."

"I'm sorry! I'm sorry. Don't be mad. I was only trying—"

He grabbed a branch and pulled himself up the slippery bank. Within moments, all that remained were his muddy footprints.

—⁓—

Like the apple in the Garden of Eden, the open letter lay in plain view on Mama's desk. I dropped it into my apron pocket and ran up the stairs to my room. "Waiting for an appointment with the president of First National Bank in Springfield," Nathan wrote. I wondered if a bank would be willing to lend money to a man with a dream and only half of one leg? Even if they knew him well, even if the idea had merit. And how much would this Lummus gin and compress cost? If it promised as good as Nathan said, it would be a small fortune. What did he have to mortgage? His farm in Missouri? His fine Missouri Fox Trotters? Would he ask Mama to put up her farm?

Mama would never talk about what she spent, but she had bought more acres with the cotton profits. They were plowed and planted. She'd hired tenant farmers, moved them into quick-built houses and paid them with shares of the cotton crop. Full summer and with cultivation underway, Ben worked from before daylight until dark supervising the men.

While I sat out on the porch swing, I listened to Mama at the piano playing the slow sad repetitions of Für Elise. It seemed that playing that piece would make her feel even worse, but she played it over and over. At last, she left the piano to come into the twilight and sit next to me. We watched the workers come in from the fields backlit against the setting sun, their shadows flowing like ink ahead of the old oaks. The daffodils had long since withered and roses bloomed. Neither of us would say what we were thinking—how we longed to hear Annie Laurie's prattle. Neither could bear to say her name. It had been ten months. Maybe one day we would reminisce about what life had been with Annie Laurie here, but for now it festered a wound that had not scabbed over, still too fresh to be touched, too raw to be bandaged.

Late that night, I heard Mama's sobs. I stood at the door and knocked softly. She answered in a voice girded with stoicism. "It's all right. Go on back to bed." I wished Nathan would hurry back. At least, he would be there for her, and maybe she wouldn't have to put up a front with him. Or maybe she would. No tellin' with Mama.

"C'mon, Pepper." I patted my leg and the border collie followed me up the stairs to where we both slept and where I wished I could sit and watch Annie Laurie brush her hair.

Chapter Twenty-seven

Summer turned to fall and still no Nathan. Mama had made me dress for Sunday dinner, even if just the three of us sat down. Afterward, I changed into some old britches and pulled Papa's hat low over my eyes and wandered out to the barn. Out of sorts was the only way I could describe Mama of late. I understood why she felt unhappy with so few letters from Nathan, but nothing made her happy. "Stay out of her way, Pepper, and hope 'out of sight, out of mind' works for us." In addition, I decided that I couldn't make that Jesse boy mad at me again. I stroked Belle's thickening coat, wrapped my jacket tighter and talked to her. "I'll fix up a pecan pie and take it to his house. Well, even that might make him mad, but if he's got any kind of sweet tooth, he'll get over it. He ate the cake I left for him after all." The mare's ears twitched back and front as if considering the feasibility of such a plan.

The pie felt warm against me as I rode through a small grove of denuded peach trees toward the boy's grandmother's house. The ground was spongy with rotten fruit and the fog redolent with the fermented perfume. Belle bent her head and snorted at the fetid layers but moved on almost silently through the mist. Pepper whined and sneezed and trotted behind us.

Among the trees, the house with its unpainted planks and broken windows wavered a mirage in the mist. With a quilt across her lap, the old woman sat in a rocking chair on the porch. She puffed a pipe, and cat-like, the smoke writhed around her like a familiar. She reminded me of the Cheshire Cat. "What you want, girl?" she asked from the side of her mouth—her smile more a grimace with the pipe clenched between her teeth.

"Mama sent me. Thought you all might like a pie. We've been here a while and neglected to make your acquaintance." I looked all about me. The boy was not to be seen. I dismounted Belle and walked up the worn path leading to the front of the house. The screen door hung on one hinge and cardboard covered some of the windows. The cows lowed, and the echoes sounded eerie in the gray morning. I stood respectfully at the foot of the steps waiting to be invited up, but no invitation came. "Well, uh, here." I extended my arms, the pie balanced on my outstretched hands.

The pipe clacked in the woman's teeth. "Set it there." She nodded at the edge of the porch. "Tell your ma I'm beholden."

"Does Jesse like pecan pie? It's pecan. Is he—"

"Loadin' horses with his uncle 'bout three mile from here out toward the river. Too far fer a gal like you to be traipsing."

"Well, maybe if you would tell him I came by and brought the—"

"The pie," the old woman finished for me.

"And I'm Cora, Cora Allen. If you'd mention—"

"Best be runnin' along, girl. He ain't got time to be foolin'."

I wanted to argue. The old biddy. I wanted to explain that he seemed like a nice boy and everyone needed friends and I thought I'd like to be kind. "I didn't mean—"

"I know what you meant. Git along. I got chores to do."

"Yes, ma'am."

"Ma'am, indeed." The old woman closed her lips around the pipe stem. She sighed with a great breath. "I know you mean well, Miss Allen, but he ain't your kind. His ma paid the price for foolin' with a redskin. Church ladies paid a visit. Encouraged her and her injun to stay to theirselves. No need to come to their church meetings. No need to shop at their husband's stores. Best to leave town. 'Heathens not fit for polite company,' said. Five years later the boy shows up on my doorstep. Don't know if my gal died or run off with her man. Nah, it'll only lead to heartbreak. My advice? Nip it in the bud."

I stumbled back to Belle and mounted quickly as I could but turned when I'd gone a few yards. A low growl came from Pepper's throat, and the specter of the woman wavered in the fog. She didn't pick up the pie. She didn't make a move to do chores. She sat on the porch and rocked back and forth. I thought again of the Cheshire Cat and his words to Alice—"I'm not crazy. My reality is just different than yours."

Maybe so, maybe so, but all I could think about were those bloody stripes left on Ben's back, Mama's wedding ring spinning in the dust and Amazing Grace's little yelp as the renegade pulled her by one leg onto his pony.

And here I had gone and made him a pecan pie. It took me three tries to get it right. I had so wanted him to like it, to like me. I endured his grandmother's grumblings. I had almost *begged* him to be my friend. I knew gossipers held that he wasn't white, but why did he have to be *a damn Indian?*

—⁓—

The next day, I waited in the drifting leaves of the old pecan tree on the outside chance that I would see Jesse returning home. He held a different fascination for me now. Last night, I spent the hour before sleep stewing about him. Maybe I would get even. Maybe next time it would be a poison pie. But then I thought about the night he brought me home on Blackjack and how he hadn't said a word to anyone. After all, he was only half injun. Maybe the white half would be the stronger of the bloodline. No, not likely considering the way he insisted on being so standoffish. I thought he probably liked being part redskin. It suited him fine, and the disconcerting thing was that it began to suit *me* better the longer I thought about it.

The autumn fog had not lifted entirely, and the countryside lay in a smoky haze. Someone burned a brush fire close enough to smell the woodsy, comforting aroma that promised colder weather. He came trudging in a slow deliberate stride, and looking down, did not see me scramble from my perch and walk out to meet him.

"I brought you that pie," I called as an introduction, as though I were asking permission to join him. "Gave it to your grandma."

He walked on like I wasn't there, neither slowing for me nor making me trot to stay up with him.

"You know, to thank you for bringing me home that night." I grew breathless with the pace.

"It's been a year."

"I'm slow to learn to bake pecan pie. I got it there as fast as I could, Jesse."

He looked up briefly from over his jacket collar, and although I couldn't see his mouth, I swore I saw a flicker of amusement in those dark eyes.

"I hope you like it. Do you?"

"Do I what?"

"Like pecan pie?"

"Look, Miss Allen." He stopped and turned to face me. He shook his head and looked at the overcast sky above us.

"Please don't call me 'Miss'. I don't even know your last name to call you and keep you a stranger to me. All I know is Jesse, Jesse." I whispered the last word to him and wanted to touch his jacket sleeve but feared he would leave me standing alone in the chill air.

"My last name is Birdsong." He stared hard at me waiting for me to remember the name. "You met my uncle. I heard how that first little skirmish went."

Choosing to ignore the sarcasm in his voice, I said, "Well, I was very young then." My eyes widened. "That's why Belle knew you! You're an Indian." I corrected myself. "Half-Indian. And that's not nearly as bad."

He smirked. "But not nearly as good as full Caddo."

Chapter Twenty-eight

When Ben brought in the mail, Mama barely scanned Nathan's letters. If they were left long enough for me to peruse, I deemed the platitudes obvious.

One morning before Mama knew I had come down, I heard her whisper to herself in tight, clipped words, "Takes more than stickum on a stamp to hold two people together." With each syllable, she tore off a new piece of the last letter and fed it to the cast iron stove. The flares were trivial.

But the piano served as a medium for her moods. Although still obsessed with Mozart, Mama leaned on the keys playing "Moonlight Sonata" in C sharp minor. Dark and brooding. Over and over.

One night at dinner, she said, "I have a cotton farm to run. I've got a remaining son and daughter. Ben needs to be thinking about finding a wife." But she hesitated there like she didn't know what she'd do without him. "Cora, you need to stay out of trouble. And that boy you know nothing about? Stop pestering him and start paying better attention to your studies. The College of Industrial Arts is a possibility if you keep your grades up."

Most afternoons she tended to farm business, the workers, the expenditures and profits, saying, "What do I need a man for?" Then she sat at the piano again.

In his letters, Nathan had said he'd be back by the end of the summer at the latest. But August had gone by along with the months of September and October. Mama put down the tally sheets and took up her writing stationery. When she left to give instructions to one of the workers, I stepped within reading distance of the desk. "Faith is one thing," she wrote, "but foolish is sometimes a close companion."

Ben had gone to town, but I thought I heard him ride up as I watched Mama hurry to complete the letter. The light was dimming, but she bent close to the paper and scribbled her signature. The door opened and closed quietly. The footsteps off cadence, Nathan stepped behind her and stilled her hands as she completed the address.

He kissed the back of her neck. I shouldn't have been watching. I should have give them their privacy, but it was too compelling a scene.

Without turning around, Mama stood, pressed her hands on the desk, her arms rigid. She shoved against the weight of him.

Nathan had been smiling, holding out his arms, but he stepped back, stunned.

Anger seemed to flood her. She turned away and steadied herself with one hand against the doorframe. But then she drew up, empowered by cold, white fury. She marched past him, throwing him off balance and brushed past Ben as she stormed out the door. The screen slammed behind her as she strode out into the yard, the chickens scattering.

Nathan caught himself as he staggered, a look of confusion on his face. He looked for an answer from Ben.

"I'm sorry, Nathan. I guess I should've warned you. Well, the thing is." Ben shrugged. "You know, Mother is, well, has been known to be challenging. She sent me to town twice a week to see if a telegram had arrived, a letter, anything from you. There were so few, you know. At first, she seemed hurt, but then she got mad. I'm afraid you've got your tail in a crack." Ben lifted his hands as if to say he would never be able to understand women. "Man to man here."

From the porch, I could see Mama standing at the gate as if debating whether to leave the yard altogether. She gripped the gatepost and stared out at the stripped cotton fields.

"Dear God." Nathan leaned heavily on his cane and then limped forward to meet his fate. He paused in the doorway before taking slow steps toward her.

With new resolve on her face, Mama turned to face him, the fury gone. No tears, but instead some eclipse of emotion, some cool haze spawned the gap between that first unvarnished fury and the gaze she leveled on him as he approached her. "It's not that I don't love you anymore." She held up her hand to stop him from coming any closer. "You've just worn me out."

He lifted his hand like he wanted to remove the red oak leaf that adhered to her hair like a decorative feather. "But Lucretia, I intended it to be a surprise."

"You go on." She stepped away from the gate and jerked her chin toward the dirt road. "You've taken your time, and now I will take mine." A smile full of irony slipped across her mouth.

"I had to have it all planned out and secured. I—"

"You left me out of it though, didn't you. You forgot that we should have shared the planning and whatever trouble came along with it. You forgot. You forgot me in favor of your wheeling and dealing." Mama skirted around him and headed back to the house. "I'll have to forget you while I make my own plans." She turned to face him full on. "I'll get my life perfect. And you get your life perfect. And maybe if our luck holds out, we can find something perfect together. If we're not too old to give a damn."

I looked at Ben and then down at the porch steps. Embarrassing, this love business. Sometimes it sounded like hate when I knew it wasn't. Whatever it was, it was very complicated. I thought of Jesse.

Chapter Twenty-nine

I had always thought Jesse exotic—his golden skin like some ancient people of mountainous regions of the west or forests of the east. And his black eyes that revealed almost nothing except vexation. No doubt I provoked that stormy reaction. I asked too many questions. But I had wanted to understand him, have him like me. How could I know it would be so offensive to him? After all, he didn't have a brother who had been beaten, his back stripped raw. For no reason. He didn't have his dog snatched and done God knows what to. I felt perfectly justified in my anger.

I spent afternoons in the pecan tree, chucking down the nuts as though the boy stood beneath me. The November sun ran tepid over me and fell like lantern light through bare branches. As the days cooled, so did my indignation. My conscience pricked at my self-serving logic. Probably being a half-breed had its drawbacks. He couldn't go to school even if he wanted to. And why did he have to live with his grandmother? Where had his parents gone? Because of the name, Birdsong, I figured Jesse's father had to be Indian and brother to Jesse's uncle. Sounded like the old woman was the girl's mother. The questions etched into my sense of right and wrong. But about one thing I was absolutely right. That boy needed a friend. And I would be the one. Self-righteousness crowded out my suspicion and hatred. How could people treat Jesse that way? They wouldn't if I had anything to say about it. I did not intend to consider the irony of this new way of thinking.

The way to his uncle's place was not completely cemented in my memory. I would have to ask Ben and that would entail one or more lies. He would never let me approach Mr. Birdsong about personal matters.

"I've been thinking, Ben." I arranged to brush my mare at the same time he groomed Blackjack. "I might go see if that old Indian man has any more puppies. Pepper here could use a friend. Mr. Birdsong would probably consider it a favor if I took one off his hands."

"Mama will kill us both if we bring home another animal. You know she's been out of sorts lately." Ben glanced back at the house.

"You mean since Nathan came back." I raised an eyebrow and nodded. "You won't even need to go. I just want to know which road to take after we passed the Turnbow's place."

Ben made no response and bent to check Blackjack's hooves.

"We could say it wandered up."

"Cora Allen! No! Wipe that thought out of your mind. Let's allow things to calm down around here before we stir up trouble. And in Mama's way of thinking, a new dog is trouble."

"If you really think so, Ben." I gave the mare's coat a lick and a promise. My mind was made up, and anyway, Belle probably knew the way herself.

—ᴡ—

The day I started out for Birdsong's reminded me of coming into Texas. It had been autumn then too, and the trees had taken on even more loveliness with their dying leaves. They would come again every spring, making it not so sad to marvel at their final beauty. The tree would live on after the ritual of letting go, but for now it seemed as though they had written their own epitaph.

I thought again of Annie Laurie. All that would come again of her was an old photograph or two and the memories, but even those would fade. If I kept thinking along those lines, I would be in a state by the time I reached Mr. Birdsong's, so I swept those thoughts aside and concentrated on the horizon.

The possibility that Jesse and his uncle would consider my intentions do-gooder smugness never entered my mind. Pride I understood. Independence I understood. But only when it revolved around my own immediate pride and independence. I moved Belle into a snappy little trot and glowed with the milk of human kindness.

Belle did indeed know the way. Her ears pricked forward, and she moved into gait with enthusiasm, as though she remembered the old man, his leathered hands, his kind voice and slight smell of wood smoke that always seemed attached to him.

We gained the top of the ridge, and I could see the small farm down in the valley below. It lay in the fog of early morning and assumed a mystical effect. Even though Belle danced in her eagerness to go on, I held her back. This would be very special. I would make a difference in Jesse's life. I could see it all from my perspective there on the hill. The oaks and elms in shades of butter yellow and crimson, the fog blurring them to watercolor vagaries painted the morning to perfection. The future played out before me, unwinding in my imagination, smooth and seamless. I took a deep breath and smiled. I gave Belle the rein and trotted down to the farm.

As I rode up, Mr. Birdsong moved among the yearlings, stroking them along their haunches and flanks, his hands knowing their muscle and sinew. I waited for him to look up. His guinea hens had already given notice of my arrival, and his border collies that knew the mare well, stood quietly by waiting and wagging their tails.

Instead of calling out, I dismounted and stood at the fence, my chin resting on my forearms against the pine logs. "Don't let me disturb you, Mr. Birdsong. I just came to watch."

He laughed but obliged me. He continued working with the colts, sending them around until he turned and walked away. They followed him, pressing their muzzles into his hands. He called over his shoulder, "Miss Allen, kindly bring me that bucket of sweet feed over there by the barn, and we'll give them a handful. Belle won't want to miss out either."

I handed him the bucket over the fence after giving Belle a handful and watched as Birdsong offered the treat with cupped hands to the yearlings. The only noise was the soft muffled sounds of horses snuffling against his palms.

Wiping his fingers against his britches, he walked over to where I stood. He nodded toward Belle. "How's our little mare?"

"Why, she's fit as a fiddle, sir." I reached up to scratch Belle's neck. "She takes good care of me, and I take good care of her. Thank you for asking." I tried as hard as I could to not rush into my list of questions.

He grinned. A couple of his teeth were missing, but it didn't diminish the guilelessness of his nature. "I heard your Belle delivered a foal for you. A bonus, no?"

"Yes, sir. And he is becoming a fine gelding. Thank you very much for including him in the deal." I tried for a little curtsey. It was more like a bob, but I thought it might charm him anyway.

Mr. Birdsong directed his attention toward the filly that kept nudging his pockets for more sweet feed. "That's all for now, my little shoat." And to me, "Tie Belle up at the post. Let's sit." He nodded toward the two cane rockers on the porch. "We'll talk about the real reason you came to see me."

I sat on the edge of the rocker, not daring to lean back and get too comfortable. "First, I want to say I'm sorry about calling you an old codger the first time I saw you and I know you wouldn't eat little girls' dogs and you wouldn't beat people with a bullwhip or anything like that. I was so upset, I didn't stop to think and I was just a kid." Out of breath and worried that the memory of my tirade years ago would forever poison Mr. Birdsong against me, I waited for him to reassure me that he understood. I studied the woodbine's orange and burgundy colored leaves that were beautiful even as the vine strangled the chinaberry's trunk and put feelers out for the lower branches. "Pretty vine," I said at last when he hadn't responded.

"Woodbine can be real nice especially in the fall, but it grabs hold and don't let go. I tried many times to cut it back, but it never gives up."

Would he think me like that? Grabbing hold and never letting go? I recognized the trait in myself. But couldn't it be a good thing? It just meant persistence, concern, caring.

"You came to ask about my nephew. Isn't that right?"

His intuition took me by surprise. I wished I had brought a hanky to wipe away the moisture I felt collecting on my upper lip and my palms. If I wiped my hands on my skirt, it would give away my fluster. "I want to be his friend. He helped me out one time, and I hope to return the favor." I made a quick swipe at my lips and pressed my fingers into the fabric of my blouse sleeves. "Do you think you could put in a good word for me?" I smiled up hopefully at him. This was not going how I had planned. What exactly had I wanted? For the old man to divulge the whereabouts of the parents and who they were and why they weren't around? And why did the boy appear so unhappy? Yes. That and more. But even I could not bring myself to come right out and ask. I couldn't help Jesse if I didn't know the truth. And I had to help him even if he didn't know he needed it.

I studied the old man. How could I have ever hated that face? Even in his wrinkled cheeks I saw humor and kindness. Would Jesse have this when he grew older? Maybe not. This man who sat before me seemed born with the kind of generosity of spirit that was hard to come by. What crosses had he to bear? I only knew how I had misjudged him. In spite of it all, he didn't seem embittered by it. You could tell that in the way he cared for the horses. I would have much to learn from him. I hoped to know him for a long time. Perhaps someday he would reveal his secrets to a satisfied life and then he could explain Jesse to me.

The squawks of the guinea hens broke the silence. I jumped at the sound and rose to my feet. "I better go. I don't know what I wanted, anyway. Sometimes I get carried away." I rushed through the last words. "Would you not, please don't mention—"

But too late. Jesse had opened the gate and stood glaring at me.

He did not come any closer but studied the colts in the corral. "Grandma kept me late worrying with the new calf. I got here soon as I could. Too soon, I see." He turned and headed away. "Which one of these yearlings you want me to help start?"

"That sorrel with one white sock." Birdsong used the arms of the rocker to push to a stand. "He needs more patience than I got."

I stood, turned away and clutched my hands together. Mr. Birdsong spoke to me in a low voice, "Just be steady. Maybe someday he will talk to you himself. Until then, I do not feel it would be truehearted to speak for him."

I nodded furiously. I wanted to disappear, be already on the back of Belle flying toward home. I forced myself to step slowly and raise a hand in goodbye. Only at the last minute did I walk to the boy, his back rigid, his shoulders resolutely squared, and touch his arm. He flinched, but I felt glad I had done it. I hoped the touch of my hand on his arm still burned. Maybe touch would unlock whatever he guarded so fiercely. Surely trust would follow if I kept trying. I turned and stepped on the upping-block to mount with decorum. I rode, smoothing Belle's mane to calm myself, and waited until I made the crest of the hill to urge her into a dead run. It was a relief to become oblivious to everything but the clearing air and the bright blue of an autumn day.

Chapter Thirty

B en brought home the Ladonia Herald and left it open on the table to the local news page. There each week, was a quarter-page write up about Nathan's Lummus gin and compress. This one read:

> Nathan Cage, recently of Douglas County, Missouri, has announced a new facility for cotton ginning that will become available as early as June 1908. Reportedly able to gin 15 bales in a 12-hour period, the machine promises to make Fannin County first on the market with cotton. Within the second year of business, Cage hopes to offer shares in the business to prominent businessmen and looks forward to the creation of additional production facilities.

Mama rolled the newspaper into kindling-size tubes and fed it to the cast iron stove. Its flame a brief blaze that threw no warmth. "'A flash in the pan' I believe is the term." She smiled, but she couldn't keep the bitterness out of her voice.

Ben sat with one leg cocked over the other and leaned back in his chair. "What's the matter, Mama? Nathan's likely success getting on your nerves?"

"You hush, Benjamin Franklin Allen! You're flaunting that newspaper just to get a rise out of me and you know it." She slammed a skillet onto the stovetop and slung a scoop of lard into it. "What do I care about his cotton gin?"

"Well, looks like I did." Ben slid back from the table and stood to go.

"Did what?" She turned to face him.

"Get a rise out of you." He dodged the saltshaker that flew past his ear as he exited the kitchen laughing. He turned and looked back through the open window. She knelt on her hands and knees picking the broken glass off the floor and muttering.

"Now, if you were to marry Nathan," he called, "you'd have sterling silver ones to chunk at me and not be there cleaning up that mess."

"Wipe that grin off your face, mister," but she had to look down quickly to hide the amusement even I could see from the doorway.

Later that evening before dinner, I offered to set the table and lied about how I had spent some of the day. I'd been up in the pecan tree again but had no excuse to be there, so that wouldn't do. All the pecans had been picked the month before. I decided to put some truth into my lie. I admitted I'd gone to visit Mr. Birdsong to tell him how much Belle pleased me and how well the colt had developed and how much I loved my dog, Pepper.

Mama raised an eyebrow. "I see you've overcome your grudge against the Indian race."

"Yes, Mama. I've come to understand they are not all treacherous. Mr. Birdsong is a kind man, and I aim to make it up to him for my poor behavior way back when."

Mama studied me for a moment. "I sense there is more to the story but I'll let it go."

I arranged the bowls and spoons. Such sparseness. I hated setting the table with only three places. It had been a year since Annie Laurie's death, and although I could smile again, it didn't feel much better. Maybe it never would. Even when I grew to be an old woman I'd lament the friendship and memories I'd have shared with my sister. Mama felt worse, but I said it anyway. "If you'd let Nathan visit, we could set four places, then it wouldn't seem so—" I silenced myself and set off in another direction. "What will we use for a saltshaker since you threw our only one at Ben?" I tried to suppress a laugh but couldn't do it.

"I'll get Ben to pick up another one in town." Mama never looked up from stirring the stew. "I've been hankering for one of those pewter saltcellars anyway. They've got the little spoons to dish the salt out and—

"Mama?"

"What?"

"Really? You always hated that stodgy old stuff."

"Never mind then. We can just spoon salt out of an old teacup." Mama stopped talking when she heard Ben come through the front door. But when we did sit down at the table, just the three of us, she hardly touched the stew. She sat turning her fork from back to front and back again.

Ben kept his eyes down and his fork moving, careful not to look up or make any clever comments to Mama. But she reached across him and served him an extra portion of apple pie and smiled an apology for the saltshaker incident as she did so. "Go on. Invite him out for Christmas dinner. Since Katy's parents are visiting Joe and her in up Dallas, they can't be here. It'll be good to have company to fill that chair." She nodded at the ladder-back across from her. "It's been empty too long."

Making every effort to avoid a triumphant smile, Ben said, "That'd be nice, Mama, but I'd just as soon you send a written invitation. Nathan will think I'm playing matchmaker. I'd be happy to deliver it by hand." He glanced at me, my fork poised in mid-air.

"So you think he'd be so coy as to not accept word of mouth?" Mama buttered her cornbread with savage little flicks that reminded me of a fencing maneuver.

Ben parried with his own tactics. "No, no. It's just that even if it's a little formal, the invite should come directly from you. You know?"

"No, I do not know. Ask him. If he doesn't come, he doesn't." A fragment of desperation crossed her brow. She set down the butter knife and stared at Ben. "I don't intend to beg, and a written note has the flavor of entreaty."

Nonetheless, the following morning, an envelope in Mama's flourished script lay on the parlor table addressed to Mr. Cage. Ben chuckled as I saw him slip it into his breast pocket and said to no one, "About time."

—◦◦◦—

Once again, I stared out the window and watched Nathan Cage ride up. He rode that same Missouri Fox Trotter, and the horse still paced, two legs on the same side moving together. Although a flaw in most horses, I imagined that it provided a smoother ride for a man with an amputated limb. He waited there in the saddle as if considering what challenge might lie before him, and I wondered how the missing leg would affect his getting down from the horse.

He descended slowly but efficiently, and for a moment I forgot which leg had been affected. It was his left leg, but he dismounted on that side. Did he have a peg leg? I thought Mama might be repulsed by the idea of a false leg replacing the flesh and blood one he once had. Almost better to see it gone than substituted with something so foreign and artificial. But she might not have to see it, not for a while anyway and perhaps never. I called out that Nathan had arrived and watched her as she pasted a smile on her face and opened the door.

Dinner was careful. Mama and Nathan smiled, but still managed to avoid eye contact. But just as we finished dessert, she rose and covered her shoulders with a shawl. She paused behind Nathan and laid her hand on his shoulder. "It's surprising balmy for a December evening. I do believe I'll sit out on the swing."

No fool, Nathan. Just that touch of her hand, so casual, so unassuming, but a summons without a doubt, invited him to join her. He studied her face as he pushed away from the table to heed the call. Ben glanced briefly at me, a sly smile of satisfaction on his face.

"Tell me about your new ability to walk," she said, before he could stand. "Your limp is hardly noticeable." For the first time all evening she looked directly at him.

Without answering, he reached down and lifted his pants leg.

It wasn't so awful, after all. No metal contraption or a peg stump like I'd imagined. The wood grain looked smooth and formed a perfectly shaped artificial leg strapped on above the knee.

"Does it hurt any?" She touched his knee that could still flex.

"At first, but since the callus has formed, it's not nearly so bad." He smoothed the pants leg back down. "I practiced so I could show you, in case you ever forgave me."

"There seems so little to forgive you for now. I suppose your male pride was more to blame than a desire to exclude me."

Nathan didn't venture into discussing why she had not tried harder to understand his point of view. He seemed content to have her at his side, looking like she would accept his arm around her to keep her warm as they stepped to the front porch.

Chapter Thirty-one

The days were so dreary that it felt as though dark, heavy opera drapes had been drawn around me. My future seemed obscured. This would be my last year at school. Ladonia High School did not go beyond the eleventh grade, and I would have decisions to make or Mama would make them for me. Girls my age would be getting married. A few going on to normal school. Well, I wouldn't think about it. I'd go riding in britches and boots if I wanted to. No one would tell me what to wear or that I had to go to college or get married. With marriage, I'd be caught up in never-ending housework, with scrubbing pots and washing diapers and cooking for grumpy children and a demanding husband. College would be hours and hours of unrelenting reading and writing at a desk, my fingers ink-stained, my eyes word-strained.

For a while longer, I would be free. I flung on Ben's shearling jacket and wrapped the scarf around my head that my wagon train friend Mildred had given me years ago to keep me "warm in the winter and cool in the summer," she had said. I held the scarf to my face and wondered how Mildred fared now and if they'd made it safely to California. Pressing the flat brim of Papa's hat onto my head, I stood before the mirror and found myself a caricature of an old cowpoke. It pleased me.

I rode out late in the afternoon, the border collie trailing. The air closed around me, cold and damp and utterly comforting. I became like the fog and knew no separation between the chilled haze and myself.

My little mare picked her way along the path toward the creek, and I let her lead the way. The mist settling on my eyelashes blurred the images of trees to unreal specters. I pulled the hat down farther on my forehead and blinked away what felt like tears except for their coolness. "We'll get a fire going just as soon as we get down there." Even as I said it, I feared the wood would be too damp. "With a little luck, anyway." I patted Belle's neck, which had become slick with moisture, but still warm to the touch.

I gathered small pieces of wood for kindling and found that if I stripped the bark off larger branches, the underneath was dry and burned well. Congratulating myself on my competence, I pulled Ben's jacket over my knees and stared into the flames. Except for the fire crackling, the evening fell silent, blanketed in the fog's secrecy. Belle nickered. Pepper stood, ears perked.

"Fire is a pretty interesting thing," he said.

I gasped and turned to look up at Jesse. "Is this your old Indian trick? Sneaking up on white women while they try to stay warm?"

"White women who build fires advertise their whereabouts."

"I did not advertise anything." I straightened and sniffed indignantly. "I came out here to be alone. And it's foggy, anyhow, and who needs—"

"An Indian to keep them warm?"

I searched my mind for a reason for his sudden bravado. Had I been too forward myself? I remembered how he had flinched when I touched him before leaving Birdsong's place. I had thought it aversion, but maybe something else came into play. Had I invited this male to light down from his horse and presume such audacious—whatever it was? "Jesse Birdsong, if you think you can intimidate me, you have another think coming." I wrapped my jacket even tighter around me and turned back to gaze into the fire.

"You think I don't know what 'intimidate' means? Scoot over, girl. Even Indians get cold on evenings like this."

"I've got a knife, you know." Appalled by his laugh that followed, I turned to face him but was arrested by his profile illuminated by the firelight. He could have been any other boy instead of a red Indian. His features softened one moment and sharpened in another with a change in the flames. In that moment I fell a little bit in love with him.

Without looking at me, he shook his head and spoke so quietly that I almost couldn't hear him, "You have no reason to need it, Cora, but even if you did, it would do you no good."

"Why, I could—"

"Shh. Just listen to the fire."

"Well, I—"

"Shh."

I turned my attention back to the flames, letting the heat disguise the burn of frustration in my cheeks. Refusing to look at him again, I felt as though the fire consumed me, turning me into some red flower I had seen in floral still life books. Ben's jacket felt heavy and hot, the hat crushed my face. I dragged it from my head. My hair caught in the scarf and tumbled about my shoulders.

"Your hair's as black as mine," Jesse said. He stared briefly at me and went back to poking at the burning wood. "But your eyes are blue . . . ." He didn't finish the sentence.

I didn't know what to say or what to make of the sudden flush of heat, but I could hardly remove the jacket. Perhaps if I just unbuttoned the top buttons and let the shearling slip away from my throat, I would feel better. As I did, I felt the need to explain, at least justify the action. "That fire's hotter than I thought it would be."

"It can keep you warm or burn the hell out of you. Hard to get it just right." Jesse gazed into the burning logs. "My uncle says we get to flame for a while, burn up what we can to stay alive until there's nothing left to keep us going."

"Your uncle's got plenty left to keep going."

"If you asked him, he would say he is mere kindling compared to what he used to be. What's left is a little wisdom, many regrets."

"That's sad, isn't it?" I turned toward Jesse. "Do you think we'll be like that? Not much wisdom and a lot of regrets? I don't want to look back on my life and feel that way." My voice dropped to a whisper. "Do you think the regrets will be caused more by what we did or what we didn't do?"

He stoked the fire with a stick. "See this here wood? It's bois d'arc, hardest wood around, but even it will burn. Slow-like, but it'll burn."

"That's not what I asked you, Jesse." I took the stick from him and waved it in the air. The jacket slipped from my shoulder. "She who holds the stick asks the questions here. And you have to answer."

With a laugh more like a grunt, he answered. "I'd rather make mistakes. No use passing up chances." He glanced at me to check my reaction.

"Me too, Jesse, me too." I reached for his hand, just to touch it—not hold it, but he wrapped his fingers around mine and held them there. What was this shyness I felt? I had used all of my charm and piquancy just to get him to notice me. Now that he responded, I didn't know what to do with him. "It's deciding what risks are worth taking, I guess." I hoped my voice didn't shake.

"I guess that's where wisdom comes in," he said. He leaned over and kissed me. Without being impure or passionate, it was intimate—secret, private and forever cached in my memory.

"But we'd be in too much of a rush to listen." He kissed me again.

Chapter Thirty-two

Rumored to be a solitary man, the new schoolmaster, Charles Ingram, came to teach at the beginning of the second term in January. But when I met his gray eyes as I walked through the door of the Ladonia High School, I knew he'd likely change his mind before school was out.

He could only be a few years older than I. He tried too hard to appear mature, sporting a vest, high-buttoned collar and a pocket watch he pompously referred to. The bowtie that wobbled on his prominent Adam's apple got on my nerves the most. Before the start of regular classes, he made appointments for an interview with each student planning to graduate that spring. As the highest achiever in the class, I intended to make it a memorable one.

Attempting to avoid my eyes, he spent most of the introduction staring at my widow's peak. When a lock of my hair escaped my pompadour coiffure, I left it there, choosing to project an air of the ungovernable. His eyes traveled from my hair to my mouth, which I pursed slightly. When he looked even more dismayed, his eyes strayed to my hands that I folded primly before me. Ingram leaned forward to recover a pen he had fumbled to the floor when first I seated myself before him. Unsnapping the pen cap, he mustered an air of authority by clearing his throat and saying, "When planning the curriculum, I like to be apprised of the goals of my students."

Although not bad looking at all, he appeared slightly anemic despite his short blond slicked-back hair and an attempt at a fashionable mustache. In an effort not to give away my amusement at his stuffiness and transparency, I let him wait for me to say something. When he glanced for the second time at his pocket watch, I said, "Where are you from, Mr. Ingram? You don't seem remotely like a Texas man." I lifted the strand that had fallen on my forehead and very slowly tucked it back into place. I never took my eyes off the schoolmaster's face.

"As a matter of fact, I am from. . . ." But his eyes widened with the obvious realization that he had already lost the purpose of the interview, which amused me to no end.

He stood, scooting his chair back with a grating sound on the floor. "It is I who will ask the questions, Miss Allen. It will help me assist you in the achievement of your goals if you will please give me some indication of what you might do after graduation."

"Why, anything I *want* to, Mr. Ingram." Keeping a straight face began to be challenging, but I leveled my eyes at him and said nothing more.

"What would be most helpful to me would be to hear you read. If you would kindly do so, it would be a true source of enlightenment." He strolled to the bookshelf and perused the few books there and handed one to me. "If you would, then?" He thrust the book at me and stood waiting.

I noted the title and opened the book. In a voice heavy with Southern expression I read:

> "He had been able to repress every disrespectful
> word; but the flashing eye, the gloomy and troubled
> brow, were part of a natural language that could not
> be repressed   indubitable signs, which showed too
> plainly that the man could not become a thing."

Since I hadn't stumbled over "indubitable," I paused for a moment before lifting my eyes. I cocked my head and blinked twice before asking, "Are you a Yankee, Mr. Ingram?"

He had seated himself again. He leaned back, his hands behind his head and one leg across the other to assume, I felt sure, an air of casual intellectualism. But he was so taken aback that he nearly lost his balance. "Miss Allen! Surely you cannot imagine the remnants of the War of Southern Rebellion are still a matter of contention."

I laughed loud enough to distract the other graduating students who had come for interviews. "Why, Mr. Ingram, whatever do you mean? The War of Northern Aggression has been over for nearly fifty years. I was born in Missouri, southern Missouri to be sure, but I have no great sympathies for the Confederate States, even if Texas is my home now. I had just thought another reading choice might suit you better." I turned and pulled Walden from the shelf. With purpose, I flipped to a particular page, traced down it with my finger and read aloud.

> The virtues of a superior man are like the wind. The virtues of a common man are like the grass—the grass, when the wind passes over it, bends.

"And you are the superior man. Are you not, sir?"

Since he sat there with his mouth open, I placed both books back on the shelf, saying I hoped my reading ability satisfied him and that I looked forward to beginning my final months of school. "I do plan to further my education, Mr. Ingram. I intend to be valedictorian of this class."

Bending my knee in the mildest of curtsies, I excused myself. As I headed back to the surrey I had trained Belle to pull, I thought perhaps it *was* braggadocious to predict my being valedictorian when it was most often reserved for boys. Still, I could not conceal the smile that kept coming to my lips. He would not find me remotely "like the grass," even if he thought himself to be "like the wind." Poor Charles Ingram. He was mine for the taking.

Chapter Thirty-three

I planned to meet Jesse that evening, although I knew I'd have to concoct a plausible excuse for leaving after dinner without doing the dishes. I had frequently neglected Belle's grooming, and that would do, I supposed. Ben raised an eyebrow at Mama, and I saw it.

"What is that supposed to mean?" I drew on my coat and headed for the door. "I am fully aware Belle hasn't had a good brush down in several days, but tonight she will. I've had a lot of reading to do for this new schoolmaster, so it's infringed upon my horse grooming duties."

Ben leaned back on the chair legs and laughed. "Ooo, 'infringed' she says. The new man must be challenging her vocabulary as well."

"I'm sure I didn't hear that, Benjamin Franklin Allen." I left the door ajar, so he would have to get up and close it after I left.

Jesse had said he would come around to the barn and wait for me there. It was so quiet, I could hear the mice scurrying in the grain barrels. With no wind, the night would be even colder than last, and Belle would appreciate a good rubdown. I kept her in her stall and worked closely against her. I leaned into her for the smell and heat. She turned and enfolded me in the curve of her neck and nuzzled my shoulder. I spoke against the warm throat. "You are a good girl, Belle. Mr. Birdsong trained you well."

"I trained the mare." Jesse emerged from the shadows. "And she taught me in return."

"Do you always have to do that? I swear, you must think it very authentic—Indian and all." I smiled and turned to face him while propping myself against Belle. "Do you want to help out here? Her mane's got a rat's nest in it."

Jesse ran his hands over the mare. He stroked her neck and ears until his fingers finally settled over the knots. He began unthreading the fine hair that tended to tangle into stubborn clumps defying even the nimblest of fingers. "Give me some axle-grease."

"Please?" I said. I found the bucket on the shelf but held it behind me.

He stopped and turned, a wicked smile on his face. "Yes, ma'am, please." He walked very slowly toward me until he pressed me to the wall, his mouth against my ear. "Pretty, pretty, please." He took my face in his hands and kissed me. This time the passion was there, the demand for more. The polite entreaty I had bargained for became something altogether different. It frightened me, but only a little, just enough to make me daring. I felt myself flush against his touch and I myself wanted to beg "please."

"Cora!" The barn door jimmied. "You still in there? Mama said to get on back in the house before you freeze."

Jesse became part of the shadows and left me there—anything but frozen. The heat of his kiss filled me, and I knew it had to be wrong.

Chapter Thirty-four

As much as I wanted to best Ingram, his attempts at gaining my attention through the explanation of remote facts and melodious readings of Shakespeare disarmed me and gave me a glimpse of who he really was if he removed the pretense of sophistication. Despite his obvious desire to maintain intellectual superiority, he could not hide his passion for the coming of Halley's Comet. I could hardly keep from smiling as it shone in his eyes, put a bit of color to his face and stationed him on the level of any enthusiastic schoolboy.

Although the redbud and dogwood had yet to bloom and Halley's Comet was not at its most visible, Charles Ingram spent part of every day in the classroom extolling the amazing features of the phenomenon. I watched his cheeks grow ruddier as he paced about the classroom drumming up every fact he could about the comet. "Do you know?" He stopped and gazed out the window. "Do you know that Mark Twain has predicted his own demise based on its coming?" His voice rose in preparation for the quote I waited for him to deliver. "Mark Twain said, 'I came in with Halley's Comet in 1835. It is coming again next year, and I expect to go out with it. It will be the greatest disappointment of my life if I don't go out with Halley's Comet.' What do you think, students? Does Twain have but a few months to live?" I looked about me. If Mr. Ingram waited to see a reaction among his students, he was disappointed. I alone nodded in response, lifting my eyebrows in interest.

"And past these mystical bodies of light," he said as he pointed toward the orrery, a moving model of the solar system he had brought to class, "it will arrive again this coming spring!" His voice cracked with the thrill. "Halley's Comet!" He paused, waiting for some cry of excitement from the students.

I did not intend to disappoint him. I gasped and covered my mouth with my hand.

His fingers drifted over the orrery. "This is what our world would look like if you were God or an angel." He appeared to try not to, but at the use of the word "angel," his eyes strayed to me.

—⚶—

April was breaking my heart—its beauty, the sweet, sweet promise of spring. Charles Ingram's lack of guile made it perfectly clear to me that once I was no longer his student, he would declare himself. He did have a way about him. His thrill of discovery of *terra incognita*, as he was so fond of saying, proved a passion at least. He always made such an effort to impress me that I found it endearing. He assumed literary stances, his hand in his vest pocket as he spouted words that I had to secretly look up in the dictionary, so on the next day I could appear to have known them all along. His announcement that Mark Twain had, in fact, died as Halley's Comet became more and more visible, had carried with it that thrill of the unknown.

The stars held some mystery for me, too. The vastness of the heavens seemed never-ending. That, Charles Ingram and I had in common. I found myself drawn to his excitement when he promised students that he would lay hands on a telescope, and we would all have the opportunity to see the comet on the southern horizon.

I sat in the classroom and watched his mouth, trying to imagine what it might be like to kiss him. Annie Laurie had fallen in love with a schoolmaster and she had been such a romantic. Maybe there was something to it, after all. But when I thought of kisses, all that filled my mind was Jesse's mouth, Jesse's arms. Forbidden and irresistible.

—⚶—

"Have you heard about the comet?" I sat with my back to the cypress knee and waited for Jesse's response. "I said, have you heard about Halley's Comet?" I punched his arm for an answer.

"Who hasn't heard about it?"

"I swear, Jesse. Sometimes it's like you don't hear my question or you don't care to answer." Again, he said nothing. "Well, Mr. Ingram—you know who Mr. Ingram is, right? Next week he's bringing a telescope for us to look through so we can get a close-up view of the comet." I tried to touch Jesse, impart the excitement, but he jerked his arm away. "It will be a special night class. Isn't that something? I mean, can you imagine?" Without stopping to wait for a response, I went on. "A close-up view! Mr. Ingram is so well versed in matters of scientific phenomenon that he just knows about every—"

"Then he probably mentioned that it showed up in 1066—around the Battle of Hastings. Made William the Conqueror think God blessed his invasion of England. God don't bless such stuff. Just like God don't bless white man's takeover. Ain't no God thing at all."

"Mr. Ingram didn't mention anything like that. And he certainly didn't discuss blessings of any kind. I think you just—"

"It's getting dark and I better get back. Grandma ain't been feeling too good lately, and if she finds out I'm—"

"Hasn't."

"What?"

"Grandma *hasn't* been feeling well lately."

But Jesse rose to his feet and was gone.

He didn't kiss me. Not once. Didn't even try. What could be the matter with him? I thought for a minute more. Well, it wouldn't hurt him to try to better himself. I stood and walked up the creek bank. "Come on, Pepper." I walked out from under the canopy of cypress and stared up into the night. The stars were brilliant, and somewhere out there beyond the tree-blanketed horizon, Halley's Comet moved toward Earth. "Pepper, look! There are millions of them, and we are just a tiny dot on a tiny dot. Can you imagine what it would be like to ride that comet, circle Earth and go out again past Mars, even Jupiter?" I wondered what Mr. Ingram would have to say about that, but the night had some perfume about it, the breeze felt gentle on my skin. A longing came over me and made me weep, for it was Jesse I wanted after all. The moon hung on the horizon, a dark amber crescent. Fog began to form above the creek bed, threatening to obscure the night, the spring, and who Jesse and I had been to each other.

Mr. Ingram announced in class the next day that he had secured the telescope for the upcoming Wednesday evening, and if weather held up, all the students would be invited to view Halley's Comet. "This is an opportunity you cannot miss! A chance you won't have for another seventy-five years." He looked at me and very softly said, "In 1985, we will all have passed our century mark."

It seemed as though he promised that he and I would see the comet again together, whether from Earth or from Heaven. How romantic Mr. Ingram could be. I doubted very much that Jesse would ever promise me anything so extravagantly poetic as that. Given more to action than pretty speech, and although the action was quite thrilling, it did not evoke the dreamy imagination Mr. Ingram's words could. Perhaps he could be as passionate as Jesse. I would have to wait for graduation to find out.

—ɯ—

The night of the viewing was perfect, and Mr. Ingram had arranged for the telescope to be set up at the hill on Honey Grove Road. Imagining myself a vision in white, I preened before the mirror wearing my new Edwardian windowpane lawn dress. I ran my fingers around the boxes formed by the embroidered vertical and horizontal lines. The fabric was a luxury I had begged Mama for. I had known it would be worthy of some heart-stopping occasion, and if ever one occurred, this was it. I stole into Mama's room and patted Vivaudou's Talcum Powder on my shoulders.

When I stepped into the parlor, Mama's eyes narrowed. "The air bespeaks a thievery of sorts."

"All right, Mama. Surely you don't mind missing a few flakes of talcum. I promise to return with them."

"Let's hope you do." She wrapped a light shawl around my shoulders and kissed me on the cheek. "Later in the week, Nathan will come get me when the rest of us get our chance to look through the telescope. But you young people will get to see it first." She saw Ben and me to the door and stood on the porch to watch us leave. "Ben," she called, "you are appointed chaperone."

I thought her too old-school for words.

As we climbed into the surrey, I whispered, "You don't have to stay with me, Ben. It's just going to be some old blurry streak of light. You'd probably be bored."

"I've been assigned your guardian for the evening, dear sister, and I take my charge seriously. I've had occasion to see how Ingram looks at you." Ben gave Blackjack a flick of the reins and the sudden motion pushed me back against the seat.

"Oh, you have not!" I wound the shawl tighter. "Besides, I am practically a grown woman and hardly need anything except a chauffeur. In fact, I may not need one of those for very much longer. I intend to learn to drive a car."

Ben turned to stare openmouthed at me. "Let me know when. I'll set out an alarm for the townspeople."

"Hush. You're just putting on. You have every intention of doing the same. I saw you and Nathan looking at Model T pictures just the other day. Surely you don't think he's going to buy you one."

"My dear, once Mama marries the man, and you get out from underfoot, I'll have plenty money. Mama will turn the farm over to me and cotton's bringing high dollar these days."

"Until some pretty little thing comes along." I pursed my lips and resettled myself on the seat. "I've had a few occasions myself to observe whose eyes are on whom."

"All that grammar coming from a girl who used to say 'ain't' all the time." A smile lurked about his mouth. "You are such a character, even when you try to assume some worldly attitude. A chameleon."

His profile changed from the tease to a sudden melancholy expression, and I wanted to bring back to our gentle cajoling. "I believe a chameleon is a slick green lizard that changes colors at will. How can you say that about me?" I laid the feigned outrage on thick. "Maybe I'll just go off to college, work in a millinery shop and break the heart of some handsome well-to-do businessman."

"Why do I not doubt you'll do that very thing?" A lighthearted lilt returned to his voice. "Well, unless Mr. Ingram can intercede." Ben lifted the reins and Blackjack slowed to a halt.

"You never mind. Look! There they are—everybody waiting to look into that telescope. Can you just imagine?" I breathed in deeply.

We pulled up to the small crowd. The hill sat so far above the trees that there would be no trouble viewing the horizon where Mr. Ingram had promised the comet would be. He had chosen the night of a new moon and the stars hung low over the crowd. A few had already been to the telescope and were buzzing in amazement and fear. "It's caused wars, you know, fire and pestilence, and I've heard—"

Quick to interrupt, Mr. Ingram said, "The scientific world has repudiated such unfounded rumors. The comet is simply a celestial occurrence that is utterly predictable every seventy-five years—a fascinating phenomenon. My students have studied this event for the past few weeks. I'm sure if you ask any one of them, your fears will be allayed." He turned to watch us light down from the carriage. "Ah," he said, "here is someone who can set your worries at rest. Miss Allen?"

"Why indeed," I said with great authority to the group. "Mr. Mark Twain was an expert on Halley's Comet and he said, 'If you don't read the newspaper, you're uninformed. If you read the newspaper, you're misinformed.' So some of you may be misinformed. We all know Mr. Twain had a personal connection to this comet. Isn't that right, Mr. Ingram?"

"Why yes, it is, Miss Allen." Before he turned his eyes back to the telescope, he called to Ben and asked him if he wouldn't like to take a look.

Surprised, Ben looked quickly at me to gauge the degree of outrage I might express that he'd been chosen before me. With some effort, I subdued the epithet that formed in my throat and almost ventured to my tongue.

When at last it appeared that Ingram would call me to view the comet, I turned to a younger student and insisted she go ahead of me. And when most of the remaining viewers had put their eye to the telescope, I stood aloof, waiting to be persuaded into viewing the same. He didn't fool anybody. He intended to prove he was not in any hurry to get me up close to him. Silly boy.

Appearing somewhat confused, Charles Ingram held out an encouraging arm. I looked around briefly as if to confirm he actually summoned *me* and finally stepped forward.

"Why, I'd be delighted, Mr. Ingram." I leaned forward and looked. It seemed as though the heavens opened. I was so taken aback with the myriad of stars, I couldn't speak for a moment. The stars swam before my eyes, some red, others green or blue in swirls I'd never dreamed of. "My gracious, there is a heaven, after all."

"Yes, there is." Mr. Ingram leaned very close to my ear and breathed the words. "Yes, there is."

I looked away from the telescope and up into his face. Even in the starlight I could see the intensity in his eyes.

"Why, Mr. Ingram, I think we both agree." Let him take that as he will. I produced the seductive smile I had practiced in the mirror more than once. And who knew? Maybe some passion other than his enthusiasm for books and science lay hidden behind those spectacles. I had a sudden urge to lift them from his face, move very close and ask him to tell me what he saw. My heart beat a little faster just thinking about his answer.

Someone in the crowd muttered about how long my turn was taking, and I closed my mind to all the possibilities Mr. Ingram might have to offer. "But the comet? Where exactly is the comet? All I can see," I said, "is so many millions of stars. How important can a comet be among the stars that are the most extraordinary display of God?"

"Oh, my dear," And he cleared his throat before he could go on. "Look to the bottom left. See that exclamation-like brilliance along the horizon?"

I felt his slight tobacco breath against my cheek. "This is a once in a lifetime experience." He whispered the last words, and I knew they were meant for no one but me.

"We'll see about that, won't we, Mr. Ingram. We have to look forward to 1985." I looked again and did locate the comet before turning away and calling, "Ben! Ben! We have so much to tell—" I wanted to say Joe and Nan and Annie Laurie, but I couldn't bring myself to utter the words. I looked back up at the sky and wondered if Annie Laurie could be one of those stars.

Ben and I stepped up to the surrey and I put my hand on his arm. "Let's wait a minute. Even without the telescope, the sky is just filled, isn't it, with so much brilliance that we don't understand. I don't think we ever will. But just to think we are a part of it somehow."

I sat there so quietly that Ben waited a good while before clicking the horse into gait. The whippoorwills called into the night. "They're back, aren't they? The whippoorwills. Just in time to welcome the comet. Do you think they know? Birds and stars seem to go together."

"You're quite the romantic, aren't you, Cora. I doubt very much there is any connection, but if you want to reckon so, then there's no harm." Ben sent the horse on at a pace that befitted the evening—a slow walk under the starry sky. "It's a sad song, isn't it? Mournful." He gazed up at the sky and said, "Some old legend says a whippoorwill knows when a soul is leaving this life and can catch it before it escapes."

I turned to him. "If it had only been April when Annie Laurie died. The whippoorwills would have been here. Oh, Ben, what if?"

"Little sister." He paused like he wanted to say something more, but only said, "Yes, if only."

I sat back and turned my eyes to the sky again. The night held no wind, and the new leaves of the sycamores stood in relief against Cassiopeia. How peaceful and quiet it was with just the turning of the carriage wheels, the occasional horse's huffs as Blackjack bent to the traces and pulled us through the night.

As we made the turn toward home, I finally took my eyes off the heavens and gazed out into woods. Ben didn't seem to notice, but I had. There in the shadows waited a rider so much a part of the opaque night that he stood but a smudge against the pale form of the horse he rode.

Chapter Thirty-five

Being seventeen did not keep me from scaling the pecan tree that overlooked the property between ours and Jesse's grandmother's, nor did the fact that Mama had vehemently objected to my wearing overalls and a chambray shirt. I sat ensconced in the afternoon shade of leaves and waited for Jesse to start the trek to the creek or his uncle's. Belle stood untethered, and Pepper circled three times at the base of the tree and sighed heavily as she settled into the concave earth where she had carved out a spot over the years of waiting for me. A comfortable place, my tree, one of habit and peace since childhood even if surveillance was the goal.

When at last Jesse mounted the gray gelding, I could see the beauty of the way he moved with the horse. They were as one with communication unlike anything I had ever witnessed. I remembered Jesse's body against mine and knew how it must feel to the animal with no need to ask or wonder what Jesse wanted.

I followed him to his uncle's all the while knowing he knew it. He might have watched when Mr. Ingram and I stood at the telescope. He might have seen how much closer to me the teacher preferred to be than to the others. Although Jesse had no claim on me, and neither did Charles Ingram, Jesse's disapproval excited me most.

Jesse had already begun with a grullo colt when I rode into the compound. Mr. Birdsong nodded a welcome as I dismounted and leaned on the split-rail fence. I watched as the young horse stood on the far side of the corral. He only moved toward Jesse when Jesse had turned his back and strolled away. When the animal came close enough to breathe on his neck, Jesse turned to the side and offered his palm before stroking the colt's neck and back. It gave me chills as he ran his hands beneath the belly that quivered at his touch. I recognized the faint glimmers of trust as the colt blew and blinked his great soft eyes. So this was what it felt like to be under Jesse's hands.

With a blanket, he rubbed the silver dun coat, the black tiger-striped legs and along the dark streak that traveled from mane to tail. The horse blew again and dropped his head. Jesse leaned into the horse's shoulder and shifted his weight onto the withers until he lay sideways across the colt's back. He soothed the sides and back again. And then he walked away.

It seemed the breeze stopped blowing and all sound silenced around us. After long moments, I whispered, "Is that all? Aren't you going to ride?"

"In time, Cora. You will find that trust takes a very long time to grow and is too easily broken. I must accustom the animal to associate safety with the human, who is by nature a predator. The colt must never feel the spur or bit that comes too soon. When I do, it will be with consent."

Chapter Thirty-six

If sleeping with her hands creamed and gloved could be the direct result of the frequent presence of a man, Mama could have been said to be under the influence. She made excuses to remain out of the sun, so her complexion gradually returned to the almost porcelain white I remembered from my childhood. I smiled as I observed the small pots of rouge and blotting papers she concealed in the drawers of her dressing table.

"Don't you look lovely, Mama." I squinted to peer at her face as we prepared yet another dinner for Nathan and the family.

"Oh, thought I'd try some of the newer things. I'm not getting any younger, you know." She looked away quickly to avoid exposing the blush that bloomed more obviously on her whiter skin.

"I think I might like to try some of that rouge, myself." I offered an apron to her and spun her to tie the strings.

"I used to tie your apron strings when you were little." She turned to take my face in her hands. "Do you remember?"

I nodded but didn't remember. I found it hard to recall anything before Papa got sick.

"But as for you experimenting with rouge, I think young girls give the wrong impression if they dabble in their mother's make-up. Perhaps when you're older."

I'll dabble if I want to, I thought and wondered if I would always be a child to her.

Pepper set up barking and then pranced alongside Nathan's mount up to the gate. I watched as Mama whipped off the apron, checked her hair in the parlor mirror and stepped out onto the porch, not waiting for him to come to the door. The change in her tone of voice annoyed me. The minute Nathan set foot on the steps, she sounded years younger, girlish and soft. Why should it bother me? It had been nearly a decade since Papa died. Did I expect her to remain alone? A widow to waste away? I ought to have been glad for her happiness, but somehow it rankled me. I made up my mind to be a bigger person than that. I would begin at dinner.

When Nathan and Mama stepped through the door, I put a smile on my face and gave Nathan a brief pat on the shoulder. "Come on in and sit down. Supper's almost ready. I'll call Ben."

At the table, Ben narrowed his eyes and tried to determine my motives for being so nice to Nathan. I could almost read his mind—was I dangling a lure that would lead to an ambush later or did I truly have a change of heart?

—⚬⚬—

Nathan had come to dinner every Saturday since Christmas. But this time spring filled the air, and he had regained his confidence. He had a different look about him. Ben and I exchanged glances over dessert while Mama chatted as if she suspected nothing out of the ordinary. But something was afoot. Her eyes were glassy in their sparkle. Nathan intended to propose. I knew it.

"You two go on and sit outside. It's a beautiful evening," I said. "I'll take care of all this in here." I smiled broadly at Mama and began to clear the table. As soon as they stepped out the door, I put the plates on the floor for Pepper and then stacked them in the sink. I gathered up a pair of socks and the wooden egg for darning and situated myself by the window nearest the swing where I knew they would sit. Eavesdropping and watching were so simple in a house with thin walls and unsuspecting subjects.

Evening shadows climbed against the blackjack oak and cast silhouettes on the Eve's necklace that bloomed pink clusters. "That's one of my favorites," said Mama. "It's got more character than the redbud."

I could agree with that. Redbuds were everywhere, but Eve's necklace was a delight when you could find it.

"It's poisonous," said Nathan. "Kin to the mountain laurel. Hearsay is you eat one of those pods and you can see the face of God. That'd be right before you see St. Peter."

"That's why it's got more character. Makes you choose between good and evil."

"I guess we know how that worked out for Eve and her boyfriend."

"Nathan Cage! Don't you be irreverent." She picked up the pace of the swing. "It's a perfectly beautiful little tree."

Nathan dragged his shoes on the porch to slow the swing. "You've got to be wise around beauty. Can't say I've been able to do that."

Inside the house, I put down the sock and rolled my eyes.

"Don't make me go down on one knee." Nathan took Mama's hand and turned to her. "Wood don't bend that easy."

I scooted up to get a clearer view through the window. He slid a ring onto Mama's hand.

"Since we were children," he said, "we've known we belonged together. We let too many other things—people, circumstances get in the way." He kissed her fingers and turned her hand to kiss her palm. "Marry me, Crecie."

They sat there without saying another word while the sun set and the air went sweet with the fragrance of Eve's necklace and mountain laurel. Nathan could be romantic. I had to give him that.

Mama began to swing again. "There's something I never told you. I left Missouri so long ago because it seemed like the only thing to do."

I put down the sock I had darned to the point of leaving a tangle of thread in the toe and leaned closer to the window. All I remembered was her being hell-bent on farming on good blackland instead of the rocks of Douglas County.

"The one thing I never told you. I never told anyone."

"You don't need to tell me anything. Nothing could make any difference to me."

"But I must. At least, you have to know. For me, if for no other reason." She put her fingers to his lips to silence his objections. "I couldn't take any chances. I didn't know for sure. There had been no quickening. Maybe I chose not to know. There were so many things that could have caused the nausea, but by the time we reached the Red River, I had no doubt. Then that awful Indian thing. I think the cramps started then. We were all so upset about Ben that I don't think anyone noticed the blood or that I was in pain."

"Crecie, what are you trying to tell me? Were you—?"

"Let me finish. Let me get through this so there won't be any secrets between us."

"I hate that you went through that alone," he said. "All the more reason for us not to let any more time go by."

The whippoorwills began to fill the night with sad tremolos that plummeted through the pines. I couldn't listen anymore. I sat there in the darkened parlor. The night I had followed Mama into the woods. It was all coming back to me—the clean smell of the pine needles and something else—blood, but more than that, something complex and intimate. I remembered the stifled breaths and the sounds that escaped her lips. My own fear. It had been so dark. Even small animals had ceased to twitter and rustle. I had tripped and fallen against the rough bark of a tree, but then sat silently, not daring to move while I watched Mama burying something. I remembered thinking it a secret we shared. Even if I didn't understand it then. So that was the secret. For the first time I could ever remember, I had witnessed my mother's vulnerability, and the first time I ever remembered worrying for the woman who packed us all up and herded us to Texas.

I laid the sock beside me and stood. There was nothing more to hear. Of course, Nathan, the cause of it all, would understand. Why wouldn't he? And Mama. All these years with her First Love roses.

Chapter Thirty-seven

Nathan insisted on a blue Victorian house on Paris Road with its wraparound porches and shuttered windows that sat among tall oaks and pecans. Mama should have it, he said. She deserved it. She'd lived long enough in that country house.

Taking my hand as we walked the halls, Mama said, "You'll have your own room, your own choice of wallpaper. It even has indoor plumbing." She went on and on, unable to stop herself. "There's so much more opportunity here in town for you. And what comfort! In the evenings, there're electric lights!"

It looked like the houses I remembered in Springfield. The house, beautiful with its varnished floors and bright wallpaper, was veneered for outward show—modern, polished and unmindful of the past.

I hated it.

Like someone flipping through a calendar penciled in with dates and times that dictated my life, Mama's plans reeled past me. I begged her, "Let's wait until June. School will be out, and I'll be able to help you more. Until the summer, Mama, please!"

"Waiting until June or July will not present any problem at all, my dear. I can't imagine getting ready even that soon. When you've waited as long as Nathan and I have, a month or two will make no difference." She paused. "Well, what I mean is, it certainly seems like a long time." She looked into my eyes. "It's more than that, isn't it? What's the real reason you don't want to move to town?"

"Sentimentality, I guess. Memories in that old place won't be here in this house. Annie Laurie never lived here. Neither have Joe or Ben. You know Ben will stay at the farm."

"Yes, but we'll make new memories here. It's the people, not the house, after all." She ran her hands along the walnut banisters and remarked about the sheen of warm wood as we came back down the stairs. "Smooth as satin," she said. "I wonder if I'll ever get used to it."

I wanted to argue with her. Didn't she realize she'd contradicted herself? It was the people and not the house that mattered. And most of our people were gone. Instead, I tried to placate her, so I said, "Well, I guess *you'll* be able to sit and look at the rooms. Didn't Nathan promise you a maid?" I stared at the detailed carving that would need perpetual dusting. "You'll be quite the lady, won't you?"

But she had gone on ahead and didn't seem to hear. "And, oh, Cora! The kitchen!" She turned the faucet on and off and watched the water ebb and flow with the turns. "Won't Annie Laurie love this place?" And then before the tears could start, she covered her mouth. "Sometimes for a moment, I forget. I just forget. She loved pretty things. She would have been married, by now and in her own home." She turned toward me and offered her hands. "I'm sorry."

"You don't need to apologize to me, Mama. I do understand what you mean. But this will be your house. Yours and Nathan's. I'll be in college, or married or oh, I have no idea, but I'm supposed to move on, aren't I?" I tried to laugh, but it didn't quite work. "Unless you want an old maid hanging around all the time."

"That would be fine with me. But not with you, I know." She squeezed my hands. "What do *you* want?" She waited, but I let my fingers slip from hers and walked to the window. She continued. "There's always East Texas Normal College."

"Mama—"

"I know. I know. I don't mean to prattle on, but I'm trying so hard to understand you. You might ask Mr. Ingram about it. I believe that's where he matriculated. Or are there any marriage prospects on the horizon?" She tried to make light of it. "You were always such a devious child."

"Devious?" I laughed. "Hardly, Mama." But I didn't turn to face her. My mind had already gone to being pressed against the barn planking, the kisses that made me want to yield to the heat of that moment. Had she felt the same with Nathan? But she had been married. Well, barely widowed, and it had all started when Papa was still alive. I knew it had. I pressed my cheek to the window glass and hoped its surface would cool the fury I felt. "Not compared to some."

Chapter Thirty-eight

Graduation proved to be a simple affair. And Mr. Ingram did name me valedictorian. I wore the white lawn dress I had worn to the comet viewing and carried my handkerchief soaked in Florida water. Its sweet orange fragrance with spicy lavender and clove helped cool me. This time I carried a parasol to keep the East Texas sun off my face and to hide the dichotomy I feared lurked there. My life was coming to a crossroad. I tilted the parasol to place my face in its shadow and mask the indecision that might show in my eyes.

Furiously waving the hand-painted fan with mother of pearl sticks Mama had given me as a graduation gift, I dabbed at the perspiration beading my temple. The 90-degree heat of full sun made it hard to be elegant, but when Mr. Ingram stood calling my name and announcing me as valedictorian, I rose to accept, knowing I would at least have to try to make the customary gestures, act like a lady and meet the demands of custom. Well, except my speech I had practiced for hours in front of the mirror. It should be a bombshell. I had rehearsed the eye contact, the challenge and projection of my voice, and ready, I folded the parasol despite the heat and delivered.

"As we near the end of the first decade of this twentieth century, I speak to this generation of young women and men. Let us step forward with noble goals. Let us have enthusiasm for this new world and make a difference so that our power will be felt not just in education but in the worlds of business and politics, medicine and science as well. We must rid ourselves of prejudice toward other races, the Indian and the Negro. It is long past the Civil War and however entrenched these attitudes have become and the limited expectations we have of our fellow man, it is time to step out of our cocoons of habit and hatred to search our souls and behaviors in order to remedy our long record of the inequitable treatment of others. Don't let us sleep through this time when change might awaken us. Let us go down in the annals of history as having contributed to the welfare of our country in general and to the betterment of humanity in particular."

"Well, aren't you the little bee in a bonnet?" Ben hugged me. "Oh, when I think of your first visit with old Mr. Birdsong!" He chuckled as he went to stand in the shade with a new interest who stared back at me but looked away when I met her gaze.

Gossip buzzed at the tea for graduates. "You don't suppose Cora Allen will become a suffragette, do you? Or worse? I always thought she was such a sweet girl. Her mother must be mortified!"

Mama stood at the end of the receiving line, but when she finally got to me, she leaned in and whispered, "I always thought you to be unrestrained, but my dear, you have outdone yourself."

I was eight years old the last time I heard that. Nan had remarked on my cutting all my hair off. I smiled but wondered exactly what Mama meant. Did it mean I had really ripped my britches this time? Was she proud of me? Or did her eventual move to town skew her thinking toward appeasing the ladies?

Having waited until the crowd thinned, Mr. Ingram stepped toward me and murmured, "I am quite pleased with you, you know."

"Why, Mr. Ingram, I do believe you are a Yankee, after all." I offered my hand and looked up at him through my eyelashes. The last issue of *Ladies Home Journal* had reported the expression to be devastatingly alluring.

"I think we might make quite the future team," he said.

A mental picture flashed in my mind. Charles Ingram and I would be applauded by the church and school as the perfect couple. I, the prim lady, would support in word and deed everything my husband favored. The town would forget my valedictory address, assigning to it the fervor of an impressionable young woman. Mama would be so pleased. Ben would be amused. Jesse? The only word that came to mind was disdain.

—⁂—

A few days later Mr. Ingram came for an unannounced visit, with a peony in hand and a posy in his lapel. What lay in his heart mattered most, I guessed, and I tried to find it in his eyes. I stood in the doorway and despite myself put a hand to my hair as if to adjust it. "Why, Mr. Ingram. What a surprise!"

"Is it, Miss Allen? I rather thought you'd expect it." He tried to appear debonair, but it came off as arrogance.

Despite my annoyance, I stepped aside and held the door for him. "Mama! Mr. Ingram has come to call." And to him— "Please forgive us. Mama has us preserving blackberries before we move to town. I'm afraid we are a bit disheveled." I held up my purpled fingertips as I led him to the parlor.

Ignoring the berry stains, he said, "My dear, there is a certain charm in your disarray. Allow me." He lifted his hand to my forehead and tucked back an errant strand of hair.

It irritated me to no end. I shook my hair loose again and stared at him. "Sit down, please." I turned away to the kitchen and called back over my shoulder. "Tea?"

"That would be lovely." He sat and placed his hat in his lap.

I set the water to heat and hissed to Mama, "He didn't even send a message!"

"You be gracious," she hissed right back. "He's come all the way here to pay his respects, so get in there and behave like a lady." She bumped me with her hip. "I'll take care of the tea."

I set my mouth into a tight little smile and returned to where Ingram sat, his knees pressed together, his fingers drumming his kneecaps. Despite his obvious discomfiture, his posture somehow achieved a prim aspect that peeved me even more.

"Mama's bringing the tea." I jerked my chin toward the kitchen. I plopped down in the rocking chair and began a pace that more resembled a spasm than a sway.

Mr. Ingram moved to the edge of his chair and fiddled with something in his pocket.

Mama smiled as she carried the tray of tea and cookies into the parlor. "Why, Mr. Ingram, what a pleasure. Do have some tea." She placed the silver service that her mother had given her as a wedding present on the table beside us. "You'll excuse me? I am hard pressed to get this work done, but I can let Cora go for a bit, so do take your time and enjoy." She squinted her blue eyes at me in a deadly glare and returned to the kitchen.

The import of the silver tray was not lost on me. Nor on Charles Ingram. We had no need to impress him, but I lectured myself as I poured. I told myself to be good, that I had nothing to lose. I lifted the sugar prongs. He was trying to be nice. *Kindness is a virtue. Rise to the occasion.* To my suitor, I said, "One lump or two?"

Signaling one, he let out a deep breath. "What are your plans since you have graduated valedictorian of your class?"

I handed him the teacup but left mine untouched on the table. "I guess there's always the teacher's college in Commerce." The rocker lurched back and forth.

"Would you be a teacher, Miss Allen? It does have its moments." His expression became transparently sentimental.

I thought of the night of Halley's Comet and wondered if those may have been the "moments" he referred to. I had led him on, of course. Let him stare into my eyes a little too long. But I, too, had been seduced by the night sky full of stars. It didn't seem like toying with him at the time. Why was I so irritated with him? I resolved to mend my attitude. I could suggest a walk perhaps. Give the man a chance. "Would you like to see the garden? Mama has worked so hard in getting an early summer crop, although I can't imagine why since we'll be moving any day. Well, Ben will stay here so I guess he'll have some squash." I rambled and didn't understand why.

Ingram jumped to his feet. "A walk would be stellar, Miss Allen." He dabbed at the tea he had spilled on his tie. "Simply stellar."

I patted my skirt for Pepper to follow and led the way out the front door. "Mama's begonias should bloom any day, and the gardenias have already faded. I guess there's not too much color this week." I avoided mentioning the riotous First Love roses. And I wasn't about to sit in the swing. Too much of Mama and Nathan and their love to associate with Charles Ingram. For what seemed like hours, we strolled about the rows of green beans and squash, tomatoes and okra with their seed packets staked at the end of each row. "It's warm out here. Perhaps we should go in." Beads of moisture began to form on my temples.

"There is one thing, if you don't mind." He shuffled in his pocket and retrieved a piece of paper. "I had you in mind when I penned this and wondered if I might get your opinion."

Oh my, a poet. Although I admired the Romantics, I found it hard to appreciate the local version that inspired catcalls and aspersions, which usually challenged the poet's masculinity. The humidity and the heat blurred my vision. I could only hope that the impatience he might see in my eyes would be interpreted as eagerness to hear what he had written. I clasped my hands and steeled myself. "Why, my goodness, Mr. Ingram. Of course."

Snapping the note from its corners to straighten it, he cleared his throat and assumed an oratory stance with a hand tucked inside his vest. He cleared his throat again. "If you will, think of the night we shared the telescope."

> "Under light of a million stars
> Your glow outshone them all.
> And I, a victim of your charms
> At your hem in ardor fall.
>
> So prithee list my gentle verse
> And give your heart to me
> For I can hopefully disperse
> All your doubts that be."

When he had finished and looked up, I was wiping a drop from my eye. I let him think I shed a tear. Perspiration stung enough to make me dab at my eyes again and perpetuate any delusions he might have.

When I said nothing, he clarified. "You know, the night of the comet."

"I understand, Mr. Ingram." I searched for the word. "Lovely. How kind of you. Is that Mama calling?" I turned toward the house. "My, it is so warm, I do believe it has given me a headache. Will you forgive me, Mr. Ingram, if I retire?"

"Charles, please call me Charles. And if I may—"

"Look, here comes Ben. I'm sure he has a thousand questions about the comet. He seemed astounded at the sight." I hurried to meet Ben who came up from the barn. "Ben! Look who's here! I thought you two men might like to catch up on, oh, whatever you'd like to catch up on." I headed back to the house but turned before I forgot my manners. "Lovely of you to come out, Mr. Ing. . .Charles. Ben might like to hear your piece. He dabbles in rhyme himself."

With his mouth open, Ben stood wiping his hands on a red mechanic's rag and stared at me.

"Come along, Pepper. I must bathe my face. Goodbye now." I flapped my hanky behind me as I traipsed up the steps and into the cool of the parlor.

Chapter Thirty-nine

"It's that Indian boy, isn't it?" Mama and I sat out that evening on the swing.

"I'm sure I don't know what you mean." I peeled the petals from a rose and slapped them into my lap.

"That's why it didn't go so well with Mr. Ingram today. He seems like such a nice young man, well-educated and sincere and he certainly seems fond of you." Mama rocked for a while without saying anything more.

"But he's too easy."

"And your Indian boy?"

"He's not my Indian boy, and I don't know where you get all these ideas. He's interesting to watch when he trains horses, that's all."

"I may understand more than you think, my dear." Mama snapped off a rose and brought it close to take in its fragrance. "I was young once, too."

"Really?" I turned to face her. "You married the first boy who came along and didn't think twice." I wanted to say she should have thought twice if she were going to dishonor those vows. But I only said, "At least, Papa was a wonderful choice. I never thought there could ever be anyone else for you except Papa. And if he hadn't died—but he did, so now you and Nathan can have everything you've always wanted."

"Cora, why do you resent. . . ?" But she didn't finish. She stood to go in.

I let it go. I was not prepared to confront her. Not yet.

—⟋⟍—

I lay in bed that night, studying the wallpaper that was so out of fashion and traced the trellis design that had gone brown with age. Ten years ago, Annie Laurie and I had thought the flowers and ivy that intertwined on it beautiful. I remembered how we bumped our heads on the rafters if we didn't remember to crouch a little when we walked toward the edges of the room. As if a bruise might still be there, I touched my forehead. I reached across the bed where we sisters had lain together, telling secrets and hopes and dreams.

Annie Laurie had been in love with a schoolteacher and never thought twice about marrying the man when he proposed. Perhaps Charles Ingram deserved a second chance. I had been unkind. I knew I had. He had professed devotion, and his poem deserved consideration. Why couldn't I appreciate that? Maybe if I let him kiss me, some spark of romance would ignite. The project of Mr. Ingram began to take on an entertaining scope.

In fact, I made up my mind to take advantage of Mama's pot of lip rouge. If I had in mind to bring out the best passion Mr. Ingram could offer, then no stone should be left unturned. I imagined the scene. I'd arrive at the schoolhouse where I knew he'd still be doing paperwork or reading or writing or some other abysmally boring task and I would offer my apologies for succumbing to that silly headache. In my white dress, I'd stand above him, very closely so when he stood, he'd be shockingly near. I'd tilt my head up ever so provocatively, look into his pale eyes, my lips reddened by passion, I hoped he'd believe, and right then and there offer those lips for a kiss. That ought to set him on his heels.

—⟋⟍—

With Mama's little pot of lip stain in my purse and my hair done up in the vogue of a Gibson Girl, I helped myself into the surrey, drove myself into town and dropped the reins in front of Ladonia High School. It had once been a small white church and still touted a steeple, which seemed ironic for the scene I aimed to enact. The thought amused me as I applied a stain of lip color with my pinky finger.

Mr. Ingram sat hunched over a book. Just as I knew he would be. Not attempting to stifle my footsteps on the oak floor, I entered with such unflinching boldness that he was taken aback to the point of failing to rise. Just like I knew he would. I reached his chair while he gained composure and staggered to his feet inches from my bosom. Just like I knew he would.

"I have come to offer my heartfelt apologies for suffering the headache that prevented me from attending your lovely poem well enough and now I hope to have the opportunity to give it the proper attention it deserves." I flashed my eyes, pursed my lips ever so slightly and laid a gloved hand on his shoulder. "Right now."

He stood stupefied.

He rifled through his pockets, then his desk, but couldn't produce the page of poetry. He looked at me with a frantic expression that almost made me laugh.

"Never mind," I said, struggling to keep the impatience out of my voice. "You may kiss me instead."

His hands that had been so frenetically shuffling through papers, clenched and snapped a pencil lying among them. He turned to stare at me.

"Yes, I've decided that if you cared enough to write a poem for me, you might like to kiss me and so you may."

"Thank you," he said.

I wanted to roll my eyes but once more pursed my lips in an effort to direct his attention to the task at hand.

He jumped a little as if reminded and put his hands on my shoulders and leaned to kiss my upturned mouth.

Tasting vaguely of cornbread and trembling slightly, his lips pressed against mine with a tentativeness I could hardly call passion. Somewhere outside the window a cardinal advertised its incessant whistle and added to the headache once again forming at my temples. The pungent odor of lantana around the schoolhouse drifted through the window.

Why couldn't I concentrate? This was important, but the stupid bird and nettlesome wildflower were all I could take in. I had caught him by surprise, but today I intended to come to my decision about an important aspect of my future.

Shrugging his hands from my shoulders, I reached around his neck, drew him down to me and kissed him the way I remembered being kissed. I couldn't tell if Ingram's lips quivered this time since the pressure I applied with my own did not allow for any motion on his.

When he came out of his daze, wearing a carmine stain on his lips, I was waving goodbye, promising to visit another time. I had my answer. Jesse remained the one I wanted, and that would never do. What if the church ladies paid a visit to object to our relationship? What if we were run out of town like Jesse's parents? I couldn't imagine where in the state of Texas it would be possible for us to be respected as married folk. Perhaps if he stayed out of the sun and applied lemon juice to his skin, he could pass for white and if he cut his hair and pomaded it back and if he dressed in a high collared shirt, a wide tie and a waistcoat. If he became someone he wasn't.

Maybe I should be the one to change. Give up who I am. Mama would never forgive me. She had worked too hard for a better life here in Texas. I played the whole scene in my mind. The ladies would be nibbling their tea cakes and sipping lemonade on Mama's veranda. With Jesse by my side, I would ride up astride Belle, dismount and present Jesse to the ladies' afternoon club. Like in Victorian novels, the ladies would crush hankies to their lips and gasp little tight breaths that would suggest they might faint if he took another step. Mama would rush to her upstairs room with the vapors. The ladies would snap their parasols open and bustle down the steps not bothering to murmur their apologies. I would shout after them, "Don't y'all remember my valedictorian address? I was not joshin'!"

Well, maybe that bordered on high drama, but the bottom line lay the same. If I had really been sincere standing up before all the townsfolk condemning the injustices of the world, would I be doubting myself now? It took a lot more mettle to back up those pretty words with action. Mama would think I was throwing my life away, but it remained my life and I could throw it anywhere I wanted.

More than anything, I wanted to see Jesse. At least, experience the way he made me feel again—the way Charles Ingram was incapable of making me feel with his own insecurities, his trembling lips, his dainty poetry.

If Annie Laurie were here, she'd disapprove. Of course she would, but she'd have something to offer. Even if it meant my leaving everything here and going away to school to gain perspective. "Gain perspective" would never be her words. She would say, "Now, darlin', you owe it to your future to find yourself first." She'd hug me tight, then hold me at arm's length to say, "Worry about those old boys later. Later comes sooner than you think."

—⁂—

Summer day activities left no time for Jesse. The wagon arrived to send on ahead what little Mama wanted to take with her, the sentimental things that new money could not buy. Including, of course, her piano. It began to feel like leaving Missouri—saying goodbye again. Although the distance was only six miles, hardly from Missouri to Texas, the gap would divide our lives much as it had before. Ben would stay and no doubt bring a bride to the place someday. The pecan tree remained beyond the cotton fields. And Jesse. Jesse remained.

Whether he knew exactly when we planned to leave, I didn't know. We had not seen each other since April, and summer was halfway over. Did he want to avoid me so he wouldn't have to say goodbye? Or had he watched the comet viewing and seen Ingram with his cheek next to mine as we gazed into the heavens? Jesse had taken rude interest in the comet party, trying to compete with Ingram's expertise. He did have some interesting facts about the comet. I checked. I wanted to understand him, but he hoarded his words like they were precious pearls belonging only to himself. He garnered his emotions, stockpiling them in a private cache. Be careful what you want to know, I thought. Remember Pandora. Could be a whole lot of troubles let loose if Jesse ever opened up.

Chapter Forty

In the tailored walking gown she had insisted on, Mama sat before the mirror and watched as I stood behind her and coiled her hair beneath the feathered hat. "I'm a little embarrassed by the extravagance, but Nathan gave it to me, so I guess I must wear it." She studied me carefully in the mirror, no doubt looking for a smirk, but I arranged my face in concentration on the task of tucking and pinning.

"What do you think, Cora? I feel so overdone." Mama stood and straightened the pale green silk of her hobble skirt. "It's nothing like my first wedding dress to be sure. Back then I borrowed my mother's lace gown that she spent hours refashioning. I wore a bonnet, not this ostrich-on-the-loose affair. My, how dress styles change. Times change, lives change."

"I know." I did want Mama to be happy. I kept telling myself I did. If she and Nathan had loved each other for so long, then they should be married. Nothing to stop them now. Not a dying husband, not a wife with consumption. I reminded myself that her life belonged to her, not to me. "It's what you want, isn't it, Mama?"

"Yes. Yes, it's what I want. But change always brings surprises. I guess life does that." She turned to face me. "With college coming up, you have big changes, too, don't you?" She leaned in to kiss me, but the brim of the hat caught me in the forehead. We laughed and for a moment forgot about how our lives would be altered.

"How's Nathan to kiss the bride?" I said. "He may have to duck and come in from your bosom."

"Why, Cora, you are a shocking child!" She flapped at me with her lace hanky.

—⁓—

Ben brought the surrey around to the front and jumped down to help Mama as she tried to inch down the steps in her new skirt. "I can see why they call those things hobble skirts," he said. "You can hardly maneuver walking. How are we ever gonna get you in the buggy?"

Mama hiked the garment above her ankles and managed to climb up into the carriage. "These had to be designed by men. We women won't put up with this much longer."

"Why, Mother dear, are you becoming a suffragette? How will Nathan like that?" Ben clucked to Blackjack, and we began a smart pace into town.

"Slow down, Ben, before these feathers actually do take flight." Mama gripped the brim with both hands. "And as for Nathan—"

I could hardly stand the banter. "I believe I'll look into a suffragette group when I get to college. I do not intend to mince around in tight shoes and a hobble skirt, even if it is the very height of fashion. Do you all know that in Japan, women's feet are—"

"Let's talk about roses, shall we? We are, after all, on our way to my wedding!"

"Yes, Mama, of course, you're right."

It was a beautiful July day, with the scent of roses Mama had picked for her bouquet from the First Love that climbed the porch trellis. I intended to think about roses, despite the niggling resentment that those blooms should have been reserved for the memory of Papa.

—⁓—

Only the four of us attended the wedding, so it took place in the preacher's study of the United Methodist, a structure that smelled slightly of mildew and layers of Old English Floor Wax. The room had one stained-glass window. Hues of blue and purple rained down on the pale green dress Mama wore, as well as on my own white linen. It made for sad colorings. Nathan looked so proper—his high collar and pinstriped pants—proper, proper, proper—when Mama and Nathan weren't proper at all. I thought about that long ago night shortly after Papa died when Nathan came to the door, and Mama followed him out to who knows where and did who knows what. Well, I knew what now, didn't I. But with their marriage, everything would be legal, and nobody could fault them anymore.

I couldn't help but think of Papa, lying in his grave while Mama looked forward to a new life with a new man. Well, not so new man. The longer I thought about it, the more distraught I became. Maybe she would think they were tears of happiness. God knows I tried to smile. I held my hanky to my mouth and nodded when she came to tell me goodbye and I stood as long as I could tolerate waiting for them to climb into Nathan's new 1909 Buick Model F that was painted some stupid color they called Purple Lake. Maroon. Just maroon, for God's sake. With red wheels and shiny brass.

The ride back to the farm house seemed terribly long despite the beauty of the day and the songbirds—some crazy mockingbird on a fence post feeling the need to belt out a tune. Ben remained silent. Platitudes were my contributions—lovely service, handsome Nathan, beautiful Mama, so in love. Until I opened my mouth and said, "I don't think I'll ever wear this damn dress again."

"Well, good lord, girl. Why don't you say what you really think?" Then after a moment he said, "What's the matter with *you* anyway?" He reined in Blackjack and stared at me. "Are you sad because you'll miss Mama? Or do you still hate having to dress up?"

"I've worn it to the comet viewing, I've worn it to graduation, and I've worn it to Mama's wedding. I am sick and tired of it, that's all." I crushed my hat to my head and looked away. "Never mind."

"I'd say that's a pretty pampered way of thinking." He clicked for the horse to move on again. "Pretty pampered indeed."

"Oh, what do you know?" I should have never started. I had worked myself into a dither and couldn't seem to stop thinking about Mama and Nathan and how long they had been carrying on. Even while Papa lay dying. I wanted to be happy for her, but it seemed I didn't even know her anymore. All those years so strict and proper acting when all along, *all along*. "Shut up, Ben."

"It's not too far to walk, missy. Blackjack might like to lighten the load by ousting your pretty little lawn-dressed self and letting you mince the mile and a half back to the house in your pretty little pointy-toed shoes." He paused to turn and stare at me. "Not like you to be so bald-faced fractious."

I didn't say another word the rest of the way back to the house.

Ben stopped at the front steps and seemed eager to make amends. He came around to offer his arm as I stepped down from the surrey, but I swatted his hand away and jumped. If he had not caught me, I might have broken my ankle. As it was, I twisted it. I couldn't help the grimace of pain that must have crossed my face, but I didn't utter a sound.

Using my parasol as support, I limped up the steps and stood for a moment glaring at the climbing rose my mother had toted all the way from Missouri. It bloomed lush in the full throes of summer growth. She had probably already taken a cutting to start at the new house. Would the thing never die?

"Well, this is going to be a pleasant evening," Ben said to Blackjack. "Let's go get you unharnessed and brushed." Shaking his head, he put his hand to the bridle and led his horse to the barn. "It's a good thing she's got Pepper. That dog will put up with anything."

I ignored him.

—ᴍ—

I didn't know why I did it. What difference would it make? But I had, and there would be explaining to do.

I didn't bother changing from my lawn dress. I was sick and tired of it anyway. If it were torn, then more the reason to turn it into dishtowels. First Love. Well, Mama was happy, and I didn't have to look at the bush anymore. I limped down the stairs and out to the barn where the scythe hung on the wall.

"What are you up to?" Ben stopped his attention to Blackjack and watched me as I lifted the tool down from its hook and turned to leave.

"Just trimming a few weeds," I said.

"In your dress?" he asked but got no answer. He shrugged and went back to brushing. "No use inviting an argument with you so well armed," he called over his shoulder. "That thing's sharp."

Starting with the top branches of the bush where they had crept up beyond the trellis, I swung hard at a horizontal angle—completely wrong for the use of the tool. And somewhere after the first blows, I began to weep. The scythe only nicked the heavier branches that intertwined through the plaits of wood, taking wedges from the thorny bark but not severing them. I kept on hacking at the leafy stems and the blossoms. They fell in pink beheaded clusters to the porch, the steps and the ground. The butchered profusion lay there in shades of delicate coral to deeper cerise like some sunsets. Fragrance filled the air as though I were closed in a dark room with thousands of the flowers and nothing to distract me from the cloying excess of roses on my hands, my skirt, my face and hair.

Tears blinding my vision, I threw the scythe as far as I could, gripped my skirt with blistered hands and took the stairs to my room one slow step at a time, Pepper at my heels, whining quietly as though the blade had been directed at her.

Chapter Forty-one

I smelled the smoke before I saw it—that dense, acrid fume that was flesh and pine. When I turned to the east, black plumes climbed above Mr. Birdsong's place. The sun rose a dusky orange against the dawn. It would have been beautiful but for the fear that bloomed in my belly.

I screamed for Ben, but I saw Blackjack missing from his stall. I ran for Belle, slapped a saddle on and rode toward the pillars of dense smoke that lifted straight into the windless air of early morning. I had no thoughts of what I would find there or what I could do to help. My mind held no premonition at all, its awareness focused only on three sensations—the mare's hooves pounding the road, the long shadows of dawn and the awful odor of burning. I would not let my mind go beyond those perceptions. Despite the ground I covered, it all seemed far away and unreal.

As I approached the hill above Mr. Birdsong's, Belle veered to the side. When I corrected her, she spun in place nearly unseating me. In an effort to control her, Pepper circled, nipping at the mare's hocks. When one foot slipped from the stirrup, I gave up. I slid from Belle and with a slap, sent her back home. Still centered on the panicked horse, Pepper scampered after her, but stopped and returned to me, panting and whining.

I ran on until I felt the heat of the flames, saw the conflagration that consumed Mr. Birdsong's home. Smoke rose from the barn in thick, heavy coils. Even the split-rail fencing smoldered. Ben, his nose and mouth covered by a bandanna, was trying to move the blindfolded lead mare out of the pen. She reared and circled and emitted a human-like scream. Then she bolted, knocking him to the ground, but he held on, clambered to his feet and staggered through the gate ahead of her. The mare lurched right and left until she hit the smoking logs where she changed directions and charged through the gate after him. The rest of the herd followed as Ben let go and dived to the side. Pepper skirted and barked escorting the horses away from him. They ran as far as the hill where they turned to stare back at the fire, their heads high, eyes wide with panic before they wheeled to disappear over the rise in the land.

Whining, Pepper returned to Ben who sprawled in the dust. She licked his face until he grasped the fur at the base of her neck and pushed her away. He stood, hands on his knees until he could push himself upright. He walked away from the smoke and flames toward me and took me in his arms and held me without saying a word.

I stood there in his embrace, my cheek against his shirt and felt the rough fabric, its dirt and sweat. Why hadn't Mr. Birdsong come out? I couldn't think about what might have happened to him. And his dogs? Where were they? None of it made sense.

Staring back at the collapsing structure that had been Birdsong's home, I never closed my eyes although they stung with smoke and tears. A border collie's charred body lay in the doorway. "Where is Mr. Birdsong? Is Jesse. . . ?"

"I don't know. I don't think so."

I broke away and ran calling, "Mr. Birdsong! Jesse!" Ben blocked me from going any closer. When I did look up at my brother, I saw the flames reflecting on his face, his cheek already beginning to bruise, and I began the question I already knew the answer to.

"Did. . . ?"

"He must have been sleeping when the fire started, but the smoke probably overcame him." Ben let go of me and dropped his head. "I could only free the horses."

Something leaden lodged in my chest. I banged my head against Ben's shoulder and looked away to the hill where the horses had run. Framed against the blue sky, a dark figure on horseback stood motionless for a moment. The only movement came from the horse braced on its haunches, his forelegs beating a hard staccato on a blanket of purple thistle.

For that one moment, my heart leaped in relief. Jesse was alive. He had not died trying to save his uncle. He rode past us, headed for the smoldering barn. Throwing his reins to the ground, he stood for a moment before locking his elbow across his face and ducking in through the opening. The smoke swirled and engulfed him.

"Ben! You've got to stop him!" I started forward.

"I never thought about the colts!" Ben started back down the slope at a run. He threw a horse blanket into the water trough, lugged it over his head and went in after Jesse.

I covered my nose and mouth with my skirt hem and followed Ben to the barn door. The hay, the fire licking from within it, released threads of smoke, precursors of its potential. It singed my lungs and skin. The stalls where the colts were kept had collapsed like kindling, the walls blackened and charred, but still emitting tongues of flame. The stench of burnt hair and flesh overrode everything. Knowing its source sickened me.

I heard Jesse call out, "Old man! I'm here." His uncle *was* old, and I knew Jesse would feel like he should have protected him. Then Jesse fell. He had been careful to stay low where the smoke lay less dense, but he sprawled forward across a dark form. A waft of air briefly cleared the lower levels of smoke even as it fanned the fire. He scrambled away briefly before returning to run his hands along his uncle's thin shoulders, the braided gray hair, its twists and folds that must have been so familiar to his touch.

Then as Jesse groped for a hold to lift with, his hands stroked across the body of that old border collie that never left his uncle's side. She lay across the old man's knees, her head resting against him. Birdsong had probably died before her, but she refused to leave him. She had chosen to be by his side for years, and that day she would choose no differently.

A timber groaned above Jesse and his uncle. Layers and layers of gray smoke obscured daylight. Somewhere toward the back of the barn, a plank collapsed. The heat renewed as if it were a river itself, its eddies spiraling toward the opening above them.

Jesse slipped his arms beneath the body of his uncle and lifted him to his chest. I was not sure he could rise, but he tucked his chin against his uncle's neck and tried to cough. Ben threw the horse blanket across the two of them and led Jesse out.

—m—

It was not really a funeral. Only a few gathered at the gravesite. I wanted to place my hand on Jesse's shoulder, but he stood so rigidly at the mound of his uncle's grave, I was afraid to touch him. He spoke to the old woman, his grandmother. "I'm starting over at his place. You'll get along without me."

The woman shrugged and spit tobacco.

Chapter Forty-two

Mama invited Ben and me to the new house for Sunday dinner. It was no surprise that she had ulterior motives. "Come stay with me. You'll love the house, darling. Really you will. Nathan is gone all day and it's lonesome. Bring Pepper. Bring Belle. Just for this little while. We've got that empty little stable out back. Soon we'll hear from the colleges, and then you'll be gone. Ben will be fine out there."

I looked at Ben for confirmation but got as non-committal a response as I had ever seen from him. So I agreed. What did it matter anymore?

I couldn't deny the serenity and shade of the home, and neighbors did come to call despite my valedictorian address, but when I could get away with it, I lay in my bedroom and stared at the designer wallpaper—little aqua palms on a beige background. Gone were the bold florals of the past. I wondered if I could count all the small designs—if I concentrated, if I focused hard on something, *anything to* keep from remembering Jesse's face, the soot-stained tears that seeped down his face as he knelt over his uncle's body.

—⁂—

The heat would be unbearable by noon, so I chose dawn that morning to take Belle from the stable behind the house and ride out toward our old farm. Eager to be out of the stall Belle picked up a trot, and I let the beauty of the day, the morning glories that hung on fence lines and the sweet fragrance of honeysuckle override my anxiety that Jesse would refuse the kindness I so wanted to show. We were almost to the old Birdsong place when Belle slowed to a walk, almost as if she remembered the last time we were there and had refused to approach the flames. Once again, we came over the ridge. This time I prepared to resist a spin and push her on, but the mare only hesitated before nickering and heading down the slope.

Jesse had done what he said he would. He had moved to his uncle's place and begun the clean-up and rebuilding. His back to me, he bent over a sawhorse, hand-planing pine logs into smooth planks, the strokes in time with the cadence of cicadas that throbbed from the canopy of trees above him. Long curls of shavings fell at his feet and the scent of pine filled the air.

I stood as quietly as I could to watch him—watch the muscles in his back stretch and contract in the sunlight, the suspenders dispatched from his shoulders, his shirt thrown across the newly built corral fence.

He was beautiful. And stubborn to a fault. I wanted to touch him, run my hands across his shoulders, my fingers over his lips. The desire surprised me. As if he were privy to my thoughts, he turned. He studied me a moment and then went back to his work.

Refusing to dismount, I said, "You will not ignore me again this time."

"Go away," he said without turning to face me. "Stop scheming my rescue."

"Listen, Indian boy." And this time I did swing off the mare. "I will say I admire your tenacity—your intention to rebuild your uncle's home." I took a step closer. "I do." I dropped the reins to ground tie Belle and took one more step. "But sorrow should not be borne alone. There's no point in it except self-punishment."

Looking over his shoulder, he didn't say to go away again, but his eyes, dark and brooding, said it.

"So that's it. You intend to punish yourself because you weren't here in time to save him, because you should have been all-knowing, all-powerful, precognizant." For a moment, I felt superior to have used the word I had found when studying for college entrance exams but felt immediately ashamed of myself. My hand extended, I stepped forward. "I mean—"

"I know what you mean."

I touched his arm. He flinched, but I pivoted around him. He opened his mouth to tell me to leave him alone, but I put my fingers to his lips and slowly shook my head, no. I looked into his eyes, and despite the brightness of the morning, I could see that they were dilated—black almost. It could be that he had murder on his mind, but I chose to believe something else provoked him. He was a young man, after all.

The wanting to kiss him, have him hold me almost overpowered me. Almost. I intended to make good my intention of accompanying him in his sorrow, by working beside him and not asking anything of him. I stepped around him and took up the planing tool.

—⚏—

I lay in bed that night, and despite the hat I had worn, a fierce sunburn bloomed on my cheeks and nose. Mama stormed in and slapped the bottle of calamine lotion on the new dresser in my room and walked out.

The lights were off, and the full moon shone bright outside my window. Through the leaves, it slid in and out like puzzle pieces that didn't resemble a moon at all but like snatches of the truth I knew about Jesse—just pieces of who he really was.

I brought sandwiches and lemonade the next morning. Even Jesse might step out of the noon sun long enough to eat. Maybe he'd sit with me. I didn't expect him to talk. He'd barely acknowledged me except to say, "Plane with the grain."

Why not put up a log cabin? Why all this hand-planing? It seemed like a long project, but then was not the time to ask. Would he speak to me before I left for school or merely wonder some early fall day why I never came back? Or would he even concern himself with my absence?

I'd left Belle down by the creek and at high noon said I thought I'd go there to cool down. "Lunch." I held up the bag. "Come on," I said to Jesse and walked away, hoping to hear footsteps behind me.

When I'd given up on his coming, I slid the overall straps off my shoulders and stepped out of the britches leaving on the chemise I had stuffed down into them that morning. I bathed my feet in creek water and then my face. Red dragonflies skimmed the shoals and flitted above the water catching mosquito larvae before darting away from the disturbance I caused. I sighed and closed my eyes and slid to my shoulders in the stream. The hum of bees and a peace I didn't feel I deserved filled the summer air. I resolved to quit thinking. Thinking had never done me any good. I would listen to the bees.

I felt the water eddy about me and only opened my eyes enough to see bare legs stretched out into the deeper water. I slammed my eyelids shut, trying not to let my brow crease or my mouth give away the dismay. Or was it anticipation that pounded in my chest? I commanded myself to be still. I waited long moments before I said, "If you are trying to shock me, Jesse Birdsong, you have misled yourself. Now that you have cooled off, you get on back up the bank and get dressed. I am not the least impressed with this violation of courtesy." I tried to think what possessed him. He had ignored me for days and then plopped himself down next to me stitch-stark naked.

The water stirred. I could hear it sloughing off his body and opened one eye to see if he had gone. I opened both eyes and turned to see him walking up the embankment, his clothes in the crook of his arm. There was something about him that I couldn't deny—the smooth musculature of him, his brown skin, his grace that was powerful and vulnerable at the same time.

After a while, I stood, water running off my chemise, and there he waited, dressed and sitting on a smooth stone eating the sandwiches I had brought. He looked up but never changed his expression as his eyes traveled from my face to my breasts to my hips and thighs that the drenched fabric no doubt revealed.

I gasped and turned away and then thought, well, if he can flaunt his body. . . . I turned back to him and said, "What's good for the gander is good for the goose."

"Don't you have that mixed up?"

"Turn it any way you want, at least I showed some restraint."

He smiled and let his eyes explore the cotton shift I wore. "Not as much as you think."

It was the longest conversation we had had in weeks.

Chapter Forty-three

The letters came in quick succession—the first from nearby East Texas Normal School in Commerce and the second from Southwestern University in Georgetown over 250 miles away, a long train ride. The second one made me hold my breath as I stood in the post office and peeled open the envelopes. Both schools had accepted me. My life would change forever, one way or the other.

That evening I lay in bed. I had turned off the lamp and listened to screech owls usher in the night. Whoever named them screech owls was misled—their call was nothing akin to a screech, but a shuddering solo descending an octave in its wavering fall. Would I hear them when I left for college? I would if I stayed. *What if I did stay?*

I'd take the letters with me the next day when I rode out to Jesse's place. Funny referring to Mr. Birdsong's place as Jesse's. I let the scenario run through my head. I wouldn't say anything to him but hand him the letters still in their envelopes so that he'd have to think about it for a longer time. He would look up at me questioningly with a sad smile on his face as he understood the significance—the crossroads our lives had come to.

"I don't need to read them. I know they accepted you," I imagined him saying. He would step around the workbench and take me in his arms. "I have so little to offer you, but I need you. If you have to go, then come back to me. There's more to life than stone buildings and trolley cars and people crammed up next to you like chickens clucking and scratching." I would look into those dark eyes and see the passion—

What was I thinking? It would never go that way—not in a million years—but I would take those letters out to show him anyway. And I would give him his chance.

Mama had been so pleased with the colleges' acceptances. "You do realize what an opportunity this is, don't you, Cora? Why, if I'd had this opportunity—"

"What *would* you have done, Mama?" I cut my toast in triangles and then remembered she had always done the same. Irritatingly so. "I bet you'd have married Papa anyway and done exactly the same things."

"I did go to school, you know." She paused. "Well, perhaps you didn't know. I was awfully young—barely sixteen. Against Papa's persistent objections, my mother insisted that girls had need of formal education. Women in our family put a high value on their daughters' schooling, going back several generations." She turned and walked to the window, reminiscing more than informing me. "My sister became a school teacher. I spent two years at Columbia Female Baptist Academy. And then I met your father." She sighed. "And that was the end of that."

She'd left Nathan out of the story. "Well, Mama, good for you."

She turned, anger coloring her face. "Something about you has changed in recent weeks, Cora, and I don't understand it. You're so quick to find fault. You rarely sit down to eat dinner with us and when you do, you excuse yourself without a word to Nathan and without dessert." She sat, as though she feared continuing. "Never mind. I know this is a difficult time of change for you. For all of us. We'll talk about it another time. Maybe it's the result of so much in flux." She patted my hand. "Perhaps if I'd finished college, the wisdom of a few years would have made me less impulsive." She laughed softly. "We'll never know, will we?"

I wanted to say I thought her impulsiveness lasted far into her thirties but all I said was, "Or maybe we will." I tried to keep the irony out of my voice, but it leaked through the words, "You never know." I glanced at her to see if the impact of my words had registered.

She turned away, but not before her face had blanched.

"Going out to Ben's," I said. "I may stay the night. Keep Pepper here."

With her back still to me, Mama lifted her voice to portray light conversation. "What shall I say if Mr. Ingram comes to call? I saw him at the post office yesterday, and he mentioned he'd like to see you before you left for college." She turned to face me. "You know, to see if you needed any advice. I think he secretly wants to visit with you whatever the reason. He certainly keeps trying, doesn't he? Well, faint heart never won fair lady."

"First of all, I ain't no fair lady. And he wouldn't have the least idea what to do with me if he won me." I had walked halfway to the stable and called back, "Tell him he can go soak his head."

—⁓—

I thought myself as pretty as a picture as I rode Belle toward the old homestead. I watched my shadow play in and out of the sunlight with my hair flowing behind me. The sight suddenly reminded me of years before when I looked down at my shadow from the back of Ben's horse on the way to the front of the wagon train. Then my hair had stuck up in butchered tufts where I had scissored it off. I had never been quite able to forget that image—like a gnome I had thought and how I had wished for hair like Rapunzel's. Who knows, maybe I would never wear my hair up again. I had often been a defiant child. The attempt to conquer that characteristic wasn't even a cloud on my horizon.

I rode up to our old farmhouse, and although it had only been a few weeks since I'd packed my things and moved to Paris Road to satisfy Mama, the home place seemed a thing of the past. The front porch still sagged, the swing motionless in the heat. Still, we had all been together there—Annie Laurie, Joe, Ben and Mama. Where we had tried so hard to make a better life, where Annie Laurie died, and Joe had gone his own way.

Leaving Belle under the shade of a tree, I sat for a minute on the swing. Serious about assuming his role as the new owner, Ben worked out in the field somewhere. The house and yard, however, missed a woman's touch. Weeds cluttered the garden. A spittoon sat outside the screen door. Mama would have pitched a real fit about that, but she had a new life now and had cut herself loose from the old one. I stood, gave the swing a shove and opened the screen door to let myself in.

The musty odor of sweat and burned oatmeal permeated the kitchen. I stopped and tried to remember what the kitchen used to smell like. There were Mama's apple pies and biscuits. And fried chicken. Suddenly homesickness for those days and for her overcame me. But those memories were before I had overheard the confession. Before, when I believed Mama to be challenging, but always, *always* virtuous.

The screen door slammed behind me. Ben strode into the room. Robust and sunburned, he filled the space. "Saw Belle out front. Surprised to see you here. Thought you'd be fanning yourself on the veranda of the new house."

"You did not. You know very well I can barely abide that place." I turned with my hands on my hips. "But I declare, I believe you eat out of the pots." I scraped the crusted lima beans from the bottom of the saucepan and tossed it into the sink. I opened the icebox and scanned the contents. "At least you put the chicken back in here." I sliced off the remainder of the chicken breast and smeared butter on bread for the sandwiches I planned to take to Jesse.

Ben sat and leaned the chair back on two legs. "Going out to visit the new Mr. Birdsong? Taking him lunch?"

"As if it's any worry of yours. But yes. He's trying hard to rebuild that place. The least I can do is offer a little support."

"Why, the very least." Ben couldn't wipe the smile off his face. "What would Mama say if she knew you only came out here to 'support' Jesse Birdsong?"

"I hardly think I care what she says. I'll be soon gone, and neither Jesse Birdsong nor I will be her concern." I slapped the sandwiches in a handkerchief and tied it into a bundle.

Ben stood and reached for me. "I only meant that—"

"I'm sorry, Ben. I don't mean to be so grumpy. I think maybe the thought of leaving scares me more than I'd like to believe. Forgive me?" I kissed his cheek and stepped away.

If it weren't for the honeysuckle, I don't think I could have tolerated the heat of late morning. Its fragrance, seductive in its intensity, steamed from the fencerows in the humid summer air. I breathed it in and followed the old trail toward Birdsong's place. It was as though I moved through a memory—a haze of dandelion pinwheels and grasshoppers scattered before me in the dust.

The sound of his industry reached me as I came over the rise. I imagined him pounding away at the planks oblivious to my arrival, but the horses called out, and I had no moment of secrecy to watch him even from a distance. He looked up from his work and turned to face me as I rode down from the hill into the yard, but when I dismounted and walked to meet him, he turned back to the labor at hand. Blistered and bronzed, his shoulders flexed with the work, and perhaps tension I knew I elicited.

"Why do you always do that?" I asked.

"Do what?"

"You know very well what I mean." I stood talking to his back, knowing it would be a while before he turned to face me. "Do I so intimidate you that you can't face me?" I pulled the letters from East Texas Normal School and Southwestern University from my bag and placed them on the planks. "Read them."

"I'm busy."

"You're always busy. Read them."

I studied his face as his eyes raced over the words. I could detect nothing in particular of a reaction.

"Does the next one say the same thing?"

"Essentially, yes."

"Well, congratulations then." He turned back to his work.

"Aren't you going to kiss me goodbye?" I accentuated the challenge in my voice.

"That sounds like a dare."

I turned away, but he grabbed my arm and spun me around. His mouth was on mine before I had a chance to object. Satisfied, I yielded. I had got his reaction—the kiss felt almost like punishment. When he released me, I stepped back and caught my breath. His eyes were fevered—black and intense. I had angered him and aroused him and I was glad.

Keeping my voice light and mildly provocative I said, "I bet you're not too busy to meet me down at the creek. It's high noon and hot as blazes. I've brought lunch."

Without waiting, I walked back to Belle and led her down to the black willow trees that lined the creek bed. I stripped off my shoes and stockings and stood in the shallows to wait until I heard the rustle of sedge and elderberry.

"You're dressed up," he said with no note of appreciation in his tone.

"Why, yes I am." I held my skirt out to the sides. "It's a new bifurcated skirt—for riding astride. What do you think of it?" I turned front to back and looked over my shoulder at him in the prettiest pose I could manage with my toes sinking into the sand of the creek bed. "Well?"

"Seems practical."

"Is that all you've got to say?"

"I liked that shift you wore under your overalls better." He stripped and waded into the stream and standing behind me, lifted my hair and let his lips travel from my ear down my neck.

"Oh, Jesse." I turned to face him. "You have no sense of fash—"

But then it didn't matter. His lips shut off any words I had planned to say.

He lifted me and brought us both down into the stream. "Cooler?"

With my lips against his skin, I protested. "How will I ever explain this to mother? She'll—"

His hands went around my waist and released my skirt that floated about us, buoyed up by the water. I felt entwined as if by seaweed and resisted a moment longer before stretching for darker depths and slipping from the entanglement of the yards of fabric and my chemise. The water glittered clear, and through the wavering light I saw blue-hued shadows and a thousand filaments of refracted radiance from the sun amid the shade. I had it in my mind to get away, to tease, nonetheless to escape, but the resolve failed me.

I turned to face him. A sudden light beam caught him and made him incandescent. I let my hands run over his shoulders, along his torso to his hips and I pulled him to me. Although I had seen him naked before, I was not prepared for the masculinity of him—no softness, except for his mouth, no give to his body. It was designed to take. And it took my breath from me.

Chapter Forty-four

A half-moon sat above the tree line when I returned to the old home place. The call of the whippoorwills reverberated through the night like echoes of each other, calling and calling. I knew they would be gone soon to wherever they went for the winter.

Ben was still finishing up his work. I could hear the clank of metal. A lantern light emitted a beam from the open barn doors, and I paused and thought to go closer to watch him unannounced. How often would I have that chance again? To watch my brother in deep concentration in his work and have that to remember him by when I left for school?

Turning back to the house, I opened the screen door and stood for a minute longer. My life had changed. And would change again in the next few weeks. I looked back at the climbing rose. In an effort to save it, Ben had conscientiously trimmed it back. Despite my attack, a few hesitant tendrils had begun to cling to the trellis. "That damnable bush will never die," I said and let the door slam behind me.

On the kitchen table, I left a note for Ben saying I planned to retire early. With a glass of buttermilk and half a pan of cornbread, I climbed the steps and opened all the upstairs windows. As the room cooled to the evening air, I undressed, stood at the mirror and studied myself. Remorse briefly overwhelmed me. My skin still appeared flushed, my lips swollen and bruised to the touch. I had thought all evidence would have been washed away in the cool spring waters, but something existed that had not been there before–the blue of my eyes almost eclipsed by the pupils, my hair curled and clinging to my neck. I was reminded of that rosebush—its tendrils, its cleaving, unrelenting persistence.

I heard Ben come in, the icebox door opening and closing, the scoot of the chair on the floor. A sudden wave of nostalgia swept over me. So few nights would I stay here, so few times with my brother. I wanted to go down, sit with him at the table and listen to him complain about whatever tool had broken and the possibility of boll weevils. I wanted to study his blue eyes that were made impossibly vivid by his tanned face. But I couldn't. Not this night. He would see. Guilt wouldn't give me away or shame, but something elusive yet defining. Ben would see it and I couldn't quite bear to face that.

This was about Jesse and me. I would leave this part of my life that I might never find again. What if I met some sophisticated, learned man who might introduce me to a newer world? Or what if I never met anyone who could challenge me like Jesse could? I would see where these last few days would take us before I had to leave and perhaps never come back.

After the house got quiet and Ben had gone on to sleep, I slipped downstairs and chipped some splinters from the ice block to carry back to bed with me. I lay there and ran the ice over my forehead and temples, across my chest and let it melt between my breasts. I watched the moon grow whiter and higher and before I slept I thought it looked like a sliver of ice itself, so cool and isolated on a summer night where down on earth everything else seemed steeped in a hot, heady brew of pine scent, honeysuckle and something more I could not name.

Chapter Forty-five

The next morning, Ben intercepted me as I came around the side of the barn. "Took care of your mare for you last night. Seems like you forgot to unsaddle the poor thing. Stood right there at the hitching post, unbridled but still tacked up. Don't believe I've ever seen you do something like that before. You in a big hurry about something yesterday evening?"

"Are you finished?" I made a move to go around him.

He blocked me. "No appreciation for taking care of your horse?"

"Why, of course. I'm sorry." I patted his arm. "Thank you. I guess I was tired."

"You sick? Saw your note. Not too sick, judging by the chunk of cornbread you cut for yourself. And never mind, didn't leave me nuthin' but a sup of buttermilk."

"All right! Tired and *hungry*. I guess I just forgot to thank you."

"That the new skirt Mama had made for you? Split so you can ride? Sure does wrinkle though. What'd you do—sleep in it?"

"It's called a bifurcated skirt, Ben, and yes, as a matter of fact, I did sleep in it." I had to look away from his eyes. "I told you I was tired."

"So you gonna help me here at the house or are you headed off to see Jesse? Look at me when you answer."

Although it unnerved me, I stared straight into his eyes and said, "I haven't decided exactly what I might do. What will *you* do when I'm gone off to school and you can't manage my time?"

"Hey there." He took me by the shoulders. "It's part teasin' and part lovin' my little sister. It's okay with me if you go off to see Jesse." He gave my shoulders a little shake. "Just be careful. You know what I mean? I figure he's a pretty good-looking Indian and I like him fine, but you don't want to get yourself talked about. And I don't want you to get in any kind of trouble I'll have to kill somebody over." He kissed my forehead before I could object. "Now, go on but when y'all are visitin', remember to leave room for Jesus."

When I approached Belle's stall with a sugar cube in my hand, the mare turned her back on me and went to the far side. "Forgive me, Belle. I was in a state last night." I stroked her haunches and slid my hand around to her nose. "Peace offering?"

With only a momentary hesitation, the muzzle quivered in my palm and accepted the sugar before turning to search my pockets for more. "You little piglet." I ran my hands down the mare's neck and led her out to be brushed and made over. "We won't let a man come between us again, will we?" But even as I said it, I knew it might be a lie. Forgiveness bought with a sugar cube. More than anything though, Ben had made me feel guilty. My family loved me, and I was willing to throw away their affection and respect. For a boy. Gone the mood that was illicit and daring and euphoric. Self-reproach took over. It weighed heavy.

What would I tell him? That I had made a mistake? An error in judgment? I had thought I loved him, but maybe it was the thrill of the moment that got away from me. Maybe I'd know when I saw him again. I tightened the girth a second time, mounted and rode out. I glanced back only once to see Ben wiping his hands on that old red rag and watching me ride away. Too far away to read his expression, I still imagined his brow creased, his mouth drawn into a tense line. And I felt his eyes still on me until I rounded the curve that led to the hill above Jesse's place.

—ↀ—

The place was silent with only the chatter of an enraged squirrel and the repetitive call of a red bird. The breeze had gone and the heat of late morning bored into my shoulders. He stood with a colt, speaking in some quiet language I wouldn't understand even if I could hear it well.

"Jesse." I dismounted and walked to him. Although I knew he was fully aware of my presence, he continued his soft dialogue.

Without looking up, he said, "I've worried about yesterday, that it was wrong for you and me. Passion they call it? Yes, that, but you and I have different roads to travel." He led the colt through the corral gate. Away from me.

What had I expected? Certainly not this. If anybody was going to do the leaving it would be me. "What if I loved you? I do, you know. I think ever since I first watched you from the old pecan tree. Just something about you, I guess." I took one step toward him.

He turned to face me. "I think it more daring than love. You thought the chase would be challenging. You *are* very daring, Cora."

Where had I heard those words before? "Cora, you are very daring." I stood there, stunned a little bit. Then I remembered Mildred. That little girl on the wagon train who had been so impressed with my story about "handling the Indians." Instead, they had handled my life.

This hadn't turned out anything like I thought it would. I had planned to be slightly aloof, daring him to pursue *me*. Of course, he would. Wouldn't he?

Except I was the one in pursuit.

"Please, Jesse. Don't be sorry. I'm not sorry. Not one bit." I watched his mouth, his eyes for some sign that he didn't mean what he had said.

"Cora, it was a mistake. I should have never let myself lo— I should have never let myself treat you like that."

"You started to say 'love,' didn't you? You couldn't let yourself admit it? You coward!" I wanted to strike him and raised my arm.

Jesse caught my hand and entwined his fingers in mine. "Don't call me a coward." He spoke very quietly. The same way he had spoken against the ear of the colt. "What I am doing is anything but cowardice." He still held my hand clasped near his face. "You left your acceptance letters here, and I read them again last night. That's where your future lies." Turning my hand to his lips, he kissed my fingers. "You go on now."

"No, Jesse, I—"

"Go on. It's the way it should be."

Chapter Forty-six

Even though it was walking distance, we rode in Nathan's Buick to the depot. Past the garbage wagon and old Jim sweeping the street. Past the ice cream parlor and the skating rink. The early morning steamed still and hot. The humidity gave Ladonia an impressionistic look, as though Monet had contrived the light of this common little East Texas town and made it memorable despite the smell of exhaust and the rumbling vroom of the train's engine as it sat waiting on the tracks.

The train heaved on the shining rails like a breathing animal. Fed on steam, it would take me away on enormous wheels, the driving rods with their brass flashing in the sunlight of an early fall day. Their faces smeared with coal dust, the engineer and fireman stood talking about their next run. The fireman, his hat perched jauntily on his head, smiled a gap-toothed grin, and the conductor in his bright-buttoned suit punched my ticket and welcomed me aboard.

Goodbyes were easier than I feared. From the train window I watched them, solemn despite the confidence they tried to paste on their faces. Mama's pride and fear lay transparent on hers. There in the dab of hanky and the clinging to Nathan's arm was also a fragment of relief. I recognized it, for all of those emotions were ricocheting around in my own head—pride, fear and relief. The relief all having to do with knowing Jesse would be too far away to be attainable. Unattainable and near were more than I could take.

There were no tears since I'd been angry with everyone around me for the last month. I had eaten my meals, nodded respectfully in conversations and participated in the planning of going off to college, but all the while I felt a deep sense of loss. How could he love me one moment, and the next, send me away with some holier-than-thou words about what he thought right? He didn't know what was right. How could he know?

I choked when I tried to speak to Ben. "Take care of Belle for me. And Pepper. They'll want to stay with you and Blackjack." Unable to speak, he had kissed my forehead and nodded.

As witnesses to my future, Joe and his wife would meet me in Dallas. My future—so well planned and as confining as my skirt.

"Think about it as a great adventure like our trip from Missouri to Texas," Mama had said in the weeks before. "Remember? Such a challenge! And look how well it has all turned out."

"I remember, Mama. I remember it well."

She stopped talking then, stopped trying to encourage and excite me.

With a grim little smile on my face, I sat on the train in my russet-colored traveling dress with gray braided frog closures on the jacket that Mama had tailored for me. Like a wraith, my image wavered in the reflection of the train window. Fitting, I thought, for I was neither here nor there, but transported a little out of time and space.

—◊◊◊—

Two miles from Georgetown, I saw the new courthouse as it rose under construction above the town square. Though distorted by waves of heat from the steam engine, it promised to be an impressive building when finished.

Lucy Gates, the sorority president of Tri Delta would meet me. Letters had come in the mail from several sororities, but only Tri Delta at Southwestern University offered to meet me at the train depot. Lucy identified herself as a tall blond girl who would be carrying a sign with my name printed in large letters. "Don't worry about finding me," wrote Lucy. "I'll find *you*."

"Miss Allen, Miss Allen! Over here!" Lucy Gates called in an accent clearly not Texan. I suspected somewhere north of the Mason-Dixon Line. She sounded very similar to Charles Ingram. She gathered my valise, attached herself to my elbow and steered me to the buckboard waiting by the station where a young man held the reins of two horses.

"Allow me to introduce you to Mr. Edgar McClendon. He so kindly offered to assist us in your arrival."

I gazed up at him. Genteel-looking with his fashionably slicked back hair and a modified handlebar mustache, he stood slim and tall. His eyes swam slightly behind eyeglasses.

Lucy moved on to the gentleman's history before I could acknowledge the introduction. "Mr. McClendon is a civil engineering major who promises to make a notable career in the field. Isn't that right, Mr. McClendon?

Before he could answer, she began with my resume. "Miss Allen was valedictorian of her class up there in East Texas. Ladonia? She has an interest in a business degree. Forget school teaching, isn't that right, Miss Allen?"

I opened my mouth to answer, but Lucy continued nonstop.

"I told Miss Allen she was coming to the right place and that I wanted her right here with us in Tri Delta. You should have seen that copy of her valedictory address. What a dilly. Really called all those stuffed shirts out on the carpet. All about treating Negroes and Indians right.

Mr. McClendon tipped his hat. "My pleasure, Miss Allen. If you'll give me your luggage checks, I'll secure them for you."

It occurred to me that Jesse would have never thought to ask for my luggage checks.

"Isn't he the nicest man? Quite the catch." Lucy leaned in and spoke into my ear. "That's why I thought he might be just the ticket to help us with your things. I'm spoken for, but I think we might as well get you off on the right foot."

I studied the young man as he returned with my things. His smile was self-effacing, but he exuded confidence borne of the well-to-do. I noted the mustache was appropriately waxed, and then immediately wondered what it would be like to kiss him. So different from Jesse. Far more sophisticated than poor Mr. Ingram.

I gripped the crown of my hat and looked up at Mr. McClendon. "Thank you so much, sir," I said, as he lifted my trunks into the buckboard. He gazed briefly into my eyes and then looked away as if burned. Once again, I became aware of the power I held over some men.

Some men. But not Jesse Birdsong. Still, this one might do. He might do fine.

After a week, he finally came calling. I had begun to think I had less of an impact than I'd imagined. He arranged the surprise meeting with Lucy and her beau at the ice cream parlor. Instead of sitting at the counter with our friends, he ushered me to a small table near the front where we could comment on the passersby. I watched as he spooned the ice cream between his lips. I was so engrossed that it took me aback when he said, "Have I got chocolate all over my mustache?" Caught, I laughed and decided to be thoroughly brazen by leaning forward and dabbing at his upper lip with my paper napkin—an intimate gesture that both embarrassed him and charmed him.

It took him until New Year's Eve of that first school year and the excuse of the midnight countdown to kiss me—a chaste kiss, but it lingered. And the man could waltz. He gave me a private lesson on the veranda of the Tri Delta's sorority house before taking me to the dance floor.

"Look into my eyes, sweetheart, instead of your feet." He tilted my chin upwards.

"I *have* to see my feet so I'll know where to step! Count it out for me, Edgar. I think I can get it if you count."

He kissed the top of my head. "One two three, one two three."

Failing to step forward when he stepped back, I fell into him and he blushed so violently that I got the giggles and couldn't stop. "You know I spent half my life in a tree."

"You did not!" Edgar put mock horror on his face.

"Oh, yes, I did. First it was a mulberry tree and then a pecan. My voice trailed off with the memory of watching a dark-haired boy with a fishing pole walk down to the creek.

"Cora?"

"What?"

"You're looking over my shoulder like you've seen someone you know." He glanced behind him and looked back at me. "Did you?"

"No, no. I was just thinking about that silly old tree." I looked down at my feet again. "Give me another chance at this dance."

"All right, but look in my eyes." He took my face in his hands and moved in a simple box step version, but when he began to hum "The Blue Danube Waltz," I looked at his mouth instead. I forgot about Jesse, I forgot about my feet and was lost to the music of his baritone voice.

—⊸⋙⊶—

The school years were a blur with short, infrequent trips home. I never asked about Jesse and no one else mentioned his name.

When Edgar proposed, it broke my heart a little. He took me west out of town across the San Gabriel River in his new shiny black surrey with striped cushions. The horses' manes were braided, the harness buffed and the brass shone. It was the fall of the year, when red oaks had gone crimson and the sunset burned with the same hot-coal color.

"Cora, I want you to be whoever you want to be, if a part of who you are will be my wife." He took my hand. "I'll move wherever you like. I want to spend my life learning who you are." His face was backlit in the sunset, so if I wanted, I could imagine someone else saying those very words.

I said yes but made him promise not to make it known at school until I graduated. Edgar would make a nice compromise. Fair in his way of thinking and kind. Doting almost with regard to me. I wrote Lucy Gates who had returned to her home state of Illinois. Wouldn't she be filled with pride at the fruition of her instigating.

Shortly after that, I wrote to Mama, asking if Edgar might accompany me for a short trip home during Christmas break. It created the flurry of questions and preparations that I expected, but for the first time, I was conscious of pleasing her. I did not fail to mention his credits—his family's financial and social standing, although one look at him would reveal the humbleness underneath his sophistication.

—⊸⋙⊶—

When Edgar and I got off the train, Mama, Ben, and of course Nathan were there to meet us. Mama made every effort not to be gushing. She showed restraint with a smile and offer of a gloved hand, but I read acceptance on her face. Even enthusiasm—cloaked, but there.

Nathan watched Mama for his cues and followed them with the casual judgment worthy of a father.

After dinner on the night before we were to leave, Edgar took my hand in his and stood. "I've stalled," he said. "Nerves, I guess." He blushed, and I found it endearing.

"What he means to say is that I've—"

He put a finger to my lips and whispered, "This is my line, remember?"

It was my turn to blush.

"Mr. and Mrs. Cage, and Ben, I ask your permission to marry Cora. I'm afraid I'm smitten." He lifted my hand and kissed it before turning back to them. "I'd be honored. I would."

Mama glanced briefly at Nathan as if to seek his approval, but it was her call. I also knew that she had to be thrilled with the arrangement. I saw it written all over her.

Ben paid minimal attention to Edgar but watched me instead. He read every nuance, every gesture of true love I might reveal. I could fool Ben. He had never seen me with Jesse, so there would be no comparison. I felt truly fond of Edgar. Truly. I looked at Ben, defied him with my eyes and announced I had accepted Edgar's proposal of marriage.

—⁓—

We would be married in late August 1914 in the Ladonia First Christian Church, and Ben planned to give me away. Aware he had studied my face very carefully in the weeks before the wedding, I knew he looked for some change of heart, second thoughts that might send me flying back to the Birdsong place.

"I'm over it, Ben," I said. He frowned slightly as he watched me across the dinner table a week before the wedding. Mama looked between us but didn't say a word. Nathan glanced up from his ham and seemed to immediately intuit the meaning behind the words. He looked down even more quickly.

"Ben's got a lovely lady friend," Mama said brightly as she gathered up some of the dishes and stood above us. "Perhaps you'll invite her to the wedding."

"Ben's had that 'lovely lady friend' for years. I'll wager he'll give church a wide berth where she's concerned." I patted my lips with a napkin and collected the serving bowls to help Mama. "Isn't that right, Ben?"

"I figure I better stay single a while longer. In case you haven't noticed, Great Britain has declared war on the Germans after they marched themselves right into Belgium. President Wilson says we'll stay out of it, but we'll see."

"And that accounts for the last five years?" I turned to go to the kitchen.

Ben countered. "She could marry Mr. Ingram if she wanted to. A schoolteacher's wife might be more appealing than a farmer's."

"I guess it's your debonair charm that keeps her flashing those brown eyes at you. Mr. Ingram's short on debonair."

"Long on poetry, though. You have to give him that." Ben sat back with a wide grin. "Cut me a slice of that cake, please, Mama."

"Plus, you've got something he'll never have." I sat down, flourished my napkin, put it in my lap and fought to hide the smile that would only encourage Ben.

"What's that?"

"Land. You know you've done very well with the farm. Quit making excuses."

"It's a shame your brother Joe can't make it from Dallas to the wedding with that pretty little wife of his nearing her time," said Mama. "I hope it'll be a boy this time. Two daughters are a lot to handle."

"Really? As I recall you 'handled' three." I put a fierce little smile on my face and stared at her.

"Let's talk about roses, children."

"Let's do, Mama." I gathered my plate and silverware.

But she kept going. "Shall I cut you a bouquet for your wedding? The bush is full of buds. They'll be beautiful."

She never used to be so anxious to please. Hadn't she insisted we move that piano from Missouri? Hadn't she dragged us against our will across 450 miles to start a completely new life? Even if it had been successful, Mama dug us all up and replanted us and didn't care what hell she had to raise to get it done.

I modulated my voice to imitate her. "No, but thank you. That's kind of you to offer." My thoughts went back to overhearing her confession of her miscarriage to Nathan. First Love roses? It wouldn't fit, would it, for me and Edgar? Suddenly I wanted to whack at that rose bush again. First love? How laughable. Except that my eyes blurred with tears and I stood and stepped briskly into the kitchen.

I had not been back to our farm—Ben's farm—in the years since I left for school. There had been so little time. But in reality, I didn't think I could bear to see Jesse. Had Mama ever gone out? She never mentioned the mutilation of the climbing roses so perhaps she hadn't. Still it seemed odd that she had never wanted to go, even to visit. But then she had never been one for looking back. I was. But fear or pride, I didn't know which, kept me away. I still hadn't asked about Jesse, and Ben said nothing. Not one word.

—⁂—

Edgar's parents drove down from Arkansas for the wedding, and he presented me to them. Having rehearsed my response to the introductions, I said, "Ma'am, it is such a pleasure to meet you at last. Edgar has spoken of his fondness for you so many times. And, sir, what respect your son has for you. I think fondness and respect for one's family is the best recipe I know of for a happy marriage." I hoped I hadn't overdone it. Edgar didn't seem to mind one bit, I noted as I glanced his way, but Ben cleared his throat and went to stand at the window. Mama might have raised her eyebrows with the words, "fondness and respect," but I never looked her way.

On an August morning in the First Christian Church, I waited next to Ben and looked for my cue to move down the aisle toward Edgar who stood with the preacher at the pulpit. His smile was so guileless and open, I couldn't help smiling back at him. I thought of Mama's wedding to Nathan and felt relieved that no stained-glass would discolor my white dress. Although there were other things I had done that might discredit it. I did swear to love Edgar and honor him and obey him, and when the preacher asked if he would like to kiss the bride, he leaned down to me and smiled the most tender smile. There were tears in his eyes, and so I reached up and removed his glasses and kissed him back with almost all my heart. He *was* everything everyone wanted for me. He *would* make a good living and be a good father to our children and a good husband to me. On the sheet of logical reasons, I had made the right decision. I never felt fonder of him than at that moment. Love him I should, and so I would. But I never promised to forget that summer afternoon that seemed like a lifetime ago or the creek clear and shimmering, or the heat of Jesse's body that filled me despite the cool water that covered us from everyone's eyes but God's. That, I would never forget. The memory, still clear, nearly photographic despite the overuse, swam before me as I promised to be true to another man.

A Buick touring car waited outside the church. "Oh, Edgar! Is that ours?"

"My surprise for you!"

"But you gave me these last night." My fingers toyed with the string of pearls at my neck. "You spoil me, you know."

"Well, just you wait. After the reception, I have one more surprise for you."

He had always been fond of little surprises—a picnic by the San Gabriel River, a small gift of chocolates, but I never expected all this. "Oh, you mustn't make me wait! Tell me now."

"Really, it's a surprise." He pressed me against him and kissed me one more time with enough fervor to make me wonder what the wedding night might be like.

Mama held the reception at her house on Paris Road, and I didn't think I'd ever seen her glow with more pride than even at her own wedding. Of course, it had been her second, so maybe that was it. And, oh of course, it had already been consummated. I admonished myself to stop. Water under the bridge. Instead, I walked straight over to her and kissed her on the cheek. "Thank you, Mama. This has been beautiful, and I owe it all to you."

She looked genuinely taken aback, but so pleased. "I couldn't be happier for you, darling. I think this is meant to be."

"Why, yes, isn't it," I said as I moved toward my brother.

"Ben?" But I couldn't say more for fear of crying. He had been my first hero and perhaps always would be. Then I tried to make light. "It's your turn next. How is that pretty little brunette, Becky?"

"I expect it'll be a while before I take that step. You can let me know if you recommend the state." He kissed me quickly and walked away.

Oh, you old bear, I thought, you wanted to cry.

So. I was a married woman—lady. To Edgar. Not Eddie. Not Ed. Edgar. I had become Mrs. McClendon. Not Cora. Not Miss Allen. Mrs. McClendon.

—⟋⟍—

Even with the wind blowing, the afternoon was stifling. Mama had been in on the surprise of the car and had bought me a broad-brimmed touring hat with a scarf. The grit from the road made my eyes water but I refused the goggles like Edgar wore. The ride from Ladonia to Dallas took well over two hours, but when he pulled up at the entrance to the Adolphus Hotel, I cried out, "Oh Edgar, you didn't! A doorman helped me from the car, and as we strolled into the lobby, I pressed my lips together to keep my mouth from dropping open and smiled as though this were a common place outing.

At the door to our room, Edgar lifted me despite my objections and carried me through. I turned away to look out the window and waited until Edgar stood behind me. The lights of the city were coming on. "It's so beautiful, Edgar. I'm simply at a loss for words. I bet Lucy never dreamed of this when she first introduced us, but then she never did have much of an imagination."

"Cora! After all that girl did for us!"

I collapsed into giggles. "I am wicked, aren't I? But you know I thought the world of Lucy." Turning to the dressing table mirror, I said, "Oh my, let me get this contraption off my head. Look, I'm sunburned. Mama would kill me."

He leaned over me and kissed my nose. "Where the sun kisses, I shall too."

I wondered if this was his first overture of the evening, but he straightened and with his hands around my waist, watched me undo the hat. "I love you, Cora McClendon." And before I could respond, he grabbed my hand. "Let's dress and go downstairs to dinner. Put on one of your new gowns. We'll go early so we can have the evening to ourselves and miss the upper crust crowd."

Only mildly disappointed, I brushed away the imagined scene of being swooped into his arms and thrust onto the sumptuous bed. He had always been proper to a fault, but since I was starving, I made quick work of my toiletries and dress and accompanied my new husband down to the French Room.

The room dazzled in gold leaf and chandeliers. I could hardly keep my chin down for studying the magnificent muraled ceiling. Champagne and candles and silver and crystal graced the table, an opulence I thought never to see again.

I reached across the table and pressed my hands into his. "Thank you for this lovely, lovely surprise, Edgar. I have one for you, although it's not nearly so romantic. Okay, it's businesslike, not to put too fine a point on it. Neiman Marcus has offered me a job! As apprentice buyer. What do you think of that? And with your career in civil engineering, we should be in high cotton."

A wave of nostalgia swept over me. Years ago, Ben and I had been standing in front of the icebox at the old farm place. The land and hard work had produced a bumper crop, and for the first time, our heads were above water. Ben was so pleased, he'd even alluded to buying me a pony. Our days of "high cotton," full of calluses and sweat as they were when we were all together, held such sweet memories. For a moment, all this glitz and glamour felt lacquered and false. But I shook off the reverie with another glass of champagne and gazed again at the lights glancing off the crystal.

When we returned to our room, I took a long bath and almost fell asleep there in the tub. When I emerged in the silk nightgown Mama had bought me, he stood and held out his arms and I walked into them. Gentle, kind and only mildly unsure of himself, he proved to be a generous lover, but it might have been the result of careful research. The years of being an engineering student had made Edgar's arms softer, and no intense passion heated up the night. Instead, he was solicitous and thoughtful, like the man himself had always been. Lovemaking was satisfactory and comforting, and I felt relief that he didn't note the lack of blood on the sheet the next morning.

PART THREE

Chapter Forty-seven

Three years later in 1917, Edgar and I went out to Ladonia on Good Friday to visit family for Easter. We all sat at the table talking when Nathan came in with the newspaper and said, "I guess Wilson couldn't keep us out of it." It lay on the kitchen table, a vulgar testament to what we had all feared. I looked at the headline, turned the paper face down and pressed both palms to the table to steady myself.

Edgar turned the paper right side up and sat to read aloud all the details. "The United States has joined the Allies in their war against the Kaiser."

"You know what this means." Mama stood and paced between the dining room and kitchen.

Nathan went to her and held her against him. "It was only a matter of time. We knew it would come. We couldn't stay out of it any longer."

"It's *their* war. Not ours!" She beat her fists against his chest. She stopped and drew herself up. "Ben will be down at the recruiting office before lunch. He could get out of it, being a cotton farmer. But he won't. They've been trying to get his horses for two years. He won't let them take Blackjack's colt unless he goes with him. And he will, I know that boy. He will!"

"Lucretia, sit. Take a breath. Here's your coffee." Nathan went to the cabinet, returned with a bottle of Old Grand-Dad bourbon and held up the bottle to offer it to Edgar and me before pouring a small amount into Mama's cup. He hesitated and poured another splash.

She covered the cup with her hand and shook her head. "Absolutely not." But after silently staring at it for a few minutes, she closed her eyes and downed half the cup.

"Glad you let it cool some first." Nathan sat` beside her and took her hand. "I'm sorry. I know how against this war you are—against Ben

238   Mary Bryan Stafford

going. But he's a grown man, Lucretia. Has been for some time. You have to respect his decision. Even if you don't agree."

"And who will run the cotton farm if he's gone? He's already planted." Mama looked at me. "Ben used to say, 'We're in high cotton.'" She tried to make light but covered her mouth to hide the dismay we all knew was there. "We're in high cotton all right. Thanks to the war. And it will cost us the lives of our young men." She sat back down again and banged her fist on the table. Looking up at Nathan, she said, "Don't you see?"

"I see." Nathan stood to massage her shoulders. "I do see." He bent down and pressed her head against him.

Their intimacy still embarrassed me.

Finishing off the cup, Mama lay her head on her arms and spoke into the crook of her elbow. "Tell me you won't rush into this, Edgar. Cora needs you here at home. Isn't marriage a deferment?"

Until that point I had not even considered that Edgar might go, but then I realized that with his civil engineering degree, the army would want to recruit him. At least, with his education he'd make an officer. "No, of course, he won't!"

"Of course, I *will*, Cora. I've been thinking about it for some time. After the Lusitania, I knew our involvement wouldn't be far behind. Of course, I'll go." He went to me and took me in his arms. "Maybe we *will* have that snort now, Mr. Cage."

I stood looking at him in disbelief. For once, Mama and I completely agreed. Ben and Edgar should stay out of this until they were made to go. Why on earth would a man volunteer to go across an ocean and fight in somebody else's bloody fiasco?

—⁂—

I called Mama within the week to say that Edgar had signed up and that he would be leaving for a three-month training camp down in Leon Springs near San Antonio. He'd be back in July for a brief leave before shipping over to France.

My work at Neiman's had been demanding, and so the time went more quickly than I thought possible. That July morning, I met him at the station and flew into his arms. He looked suntanned and toughened.

The smell of his rough wool uniform and the cool brass of the U.S. insignia that pressed into my cheek made him excitingly different.

On the ride home, I insisted that he drive so I didn't have to take my eyes off him. I laughed and cried a little, sat as close to him as I could and laid my hand on his thigh. When we drove into our driveway, he left his bags in the back seat, carried me into the house, thrust me onto the bed and made love to me with a passion I had missed on our wedding night.

"Absence *does* make the heart grow fonder," I said afterward. "I can hardly catch my breath."

"Absence nearly killed me!" He laughed and fell back on the pillows.

I kissed his cheek and started to wrap the sheet around me. "Let me fix your supper. You must be—"

"Starved." Edgar pulled me back over on him. "And you aren't going anywhere."

I made a false struggle and then whispered against his neck. "The Army has given you some new ideas."

"The way those boys talk, they'd have given Casanova some lessons."

"Ah, but it's all in the delivery."

—※—

Edgar's orders had him scheduled to leave very early that summer morning, and I sat on the bed watching him adjust the Sam Browne belt and strap across his shoulder. "We're supposed to call them 'Liberty Belts,' so they sound more American," he said. His boots were soft leather and polished, his eyes determined. He was more masculine than I ever remembered him being.

Despite the night before, I thought about making one last seduction before he left, but he gently removed my arms from around his neck and whispered, "They'll need me to have enough strength left to climb the train steps." He kissed my nose.

"Oh, all right. Here, let me," I said, and I buttoned the two top buttons of his high-necked uniform.

He tried to talk me out of going with him to the train station, but I would not be dissuaded. We rode in silence, but he drove with one hand and held mine with the other. Before he boarded, he took me in his arms and kissed me.

I sensed the desperation in his kiss as though he believed these few days could be our last. "You remember our week together while you're gone," I said. "And come home. Come home as quick as you can."

"Behave yourself, darling." His voice broke and he cleared his throat to disguise it. I took off his cap, put it on my own head, and saluted him, before putting it back on his, gently and carefully.

I drove back alone, the hot Texas wind blowing across my tears. I hated everything about this war. It changed all our lives and would tear so many lives apart. Women rolled bandages and knitted for soldiers and volunteered for the Red Cross. We Americans were asked to supply food to our allies in Europe where there were desperate food shortages, and any extra from our own gardens was sent to soldiers and starving civilians. Windows displayed Red Cross service flags and posters in markets promoted "Meatless Tuesdays and "Wheatless Wednesdays."

I knew I should let Mama know Edgar had left, but I chose to wait until the next day. I found it hard to realize that he had gone and would see things I would never see, horrible things and beautiful things, and I wanted to have time to compose myself. Finally, I picked up the phone. "He'll be in the 21st Engineers in a Special Regiment constructing and operating light railway from railheads to the trenches. He reports to 1st Division headquarters, Menil La Tour, France, or however you say it." I tried to keep the emotion out of my voice, all the while thinking I really didn't know what to do.

I had made senior buyer for Neiman Marcus, but even if my salary provided enough to live on with Edgar's military allotment, I didn't want to stay in Dallas. The city had never suited me. It was like wearing shoes that were too small. The buildings confined my view and even sitting on my front porch, I had nothing to see but other houses. The noise never stopped. Working challenged me, but I never quite saw the direct result of my job, its value diffused by the work of so many others. Mama's home would drive me crazy, of course, but the farm needed tending. And who would run it with Ben gone? Although highly lucrative, Nathan's cotton gin machine business gave him very little time for anything else. And then a plan lodged in my imagination and began to take on form and color.

—∾—

How could life change so radically and irrevocably? Perhaps I *was* in shock. Ben and Edgar were both gone to war, and I intended to leave my nice, pat life that promised a lovely home in Dallas and a career at Neiman Marcus. The cotton farm—hardly what I went to college for— would leave me sunburned with dirt under my fingernails and sweat rings on my dresses. But something about it had wormed its way into my heart. Perhaps I wanted to go back to those long ago days. I drove out to Mama's house in Ladonia.

"You absolutely will not, Cora Allen!" Mama caught herself. "McClendon." She turned to Nathan. "Talk to her!"

"Now, Lucretia, it's not my—"

"Oh, never mind." She threw up her hands and turned to the window.

"Mother—"

"When did you start calling me 'mother'? Wasn't it always 'Mama?'"

"Mama, then. I *want* to do this. Until the war is over. It can't last long. I can go back to my job when Edgar and Ben come back home. Ben's already planted, and I bet the weeds are coming up faster than the plants. I can be there every day. Cotton needs constant overseeing. And frankly, I guess I miss the old place. You know I never wanted to move to town."

"You never had to do the real work on the place either. The boys and I did most of that. You have no idea what we went through to make it a good cotton farm."

"And that's my whole point, Mothe—Mama. We don't want to lose it now. Cotton prices are high. Just a year. Until Ben gets back."

"Nathan is overseeing it, himself, and is looking to hire a manager."

"Well, now he won't have to, will he." It was not a question. I had my hand on the doorknob. "I'm going out to the farm for the night, but I'll come back for a few groceries tomorrow. I want to be settled in by Sunday. Wish me well." I took Mama's hands. "Remember when you were hell-bent to travel over 450 miles to get to that place?"

Her eyes filled with tears.

"Well, Mama, I'm hell-bent to travel 80 miles to come back home." I softened my voice. "Seems like I've been gone so long."

Chapter Forty-eight

Spindrift dust from the road sifted under my scarf and needled its way into my skin. The Buick roadster made the trip so much quicker from Ladonia to the farm, but I longed for the slower pace of Belle's nice little trot without the pulverized grime, the sun in my eyes or the roar of the engine. Summer was in the air, but I couldn't smell it and couldn't hear it. I thought of Jesse. I didn't mean to, but like the spindrift dust, he crowded his way back into my thoughts to make me remember how I felt with him.

The first night I sat at the table and made a list. I put "Get a puppy" at the top. I missed having a companion. I felt lonely without Pepper who had died a few years before. It was a little lonely, period. I forced myself to write practical things like tack notices for workers at the feed store and in the church bulletins and check the barn for supplies. Ben would have stocked up, but I had the critical and immediate task of getting the weeds out that had grown in his absence. God, what had I got myself into?

Despite details buzzing around in my head, I made myself go to bed. I lay up there in my old bedroom with age-stained wallpaper and looked out into the night. After the city noises, the quiet of the country became a swallowing silence broken only by the occasional far-off call of whippoorwills. The sky came alive with starlight, and a deep peace I had not felt in the years I'd been gone slowed my heart. I breathed in the heady lemon perfume of the magnolias, their white, fragile blossoms punctuating the dark.

Home. I was home.

—◊◊◊—

The remaining summer reigned hot and humid, and my days were filled with sweat and dirt. My hands blistered and my nose sunburned despite the hat I wore. My hair braided and pulled back into a tight coil, I refused to look into the mirror. Quite a change from days at Neiman Marcus when I wore dainty shoes and the new linen ankle-length fashion that made me something foreign even to myself. It had been a lovely masquerade.

But I made progress on the farm. I could see it, and it satisfied some basic need in me. For the first time in years, I felt honestly happy being a little grubby with no one looking over my shoulder at the department store or checking the seams in my stockings. What freedom to go to bed in an old cotton shirt if I wanted instead of the expected silk nightgown, and after a day overseeing the fields, I wanted the comfort of worn cotton. Of an evening, I sat on my porch eating a ham sandwich and gazing at the burnt sunset blurred by dust and heat.

A month later, wearing my overalls and the floppy hat, I rode Belle bareback at a slow walk over to Jesse's place. Having made no effort to appear attractive, I felt sure whatever desire he used to have for me would be quelled. What if he had found himself a woman? No, Ben probably would have said. Anyway, we could be friends. After all, I had a husband. It would be nice to know I had a neighbor nearby in case of an emergency. But something in the back of my mind told me that I trod on quicksand. Well, I didn't care, I told myself. I could handle this.

From the hill, I could see the house he'd built years before and it had a well-cared-for look. All that log planing paid off. His uncle would have been pleased. Jesse, already out with the horses, worked with them one at a time. He hadn't seen me yet and the horses had not whinnied. Maybe this *was* wrong. Maybe I should turn back, maybe I should—

But then he looked up. His hands dropped to his sides, and he turned full around to face me. I couldn't read his expression, but his body seemed to lose its energy. I slid off Belle and walked to greet him, extending my hand and smiling. "It's been a long time, Jesse. I'm back at the old home place and thought I'd—"

"What can I help you with?" He watched me intently, his dark eyes keen and wounded.

"Absolutely nothing." I withdrew my hand that he had not taken. "I wanted to let you know. Be neighborly."

He scanned my face seeming to search out lies. But he said nothing.

"So." I wiped my palms on my pants leg. "You're training more horses. These don't look like the ones your uncle used to have." Why had I mentioned his uncle? I hadn't planned this conversation well enough. I'd hoped it would go differently after such a long time. But he was so cold.

"Getting these mustangs halter broke and manageable enough to lead onboard ship. The army needs horses, and if any animal can take the punishment, these can."

"They're going to war?"

Jesse nodded. "I don't think about it or get too close to them. They're probably the only things standing between me and the draft."

"The house is nice." I knew my smile must be ingratiating, but I wanted to speak the truth. His home was far bigger than he needed, but perhaps he planned to marry one day. Of course, he did. He'd even painted it white, trimmed the windows out nicely and added a shingled roof, instead of a tin one. Although it lacked the attention a woman would have given it, it *was* nice. Didn't quite look like a house an Indian would live in. The thought amused me, and I chastised myself mildly.

He looked back at the house and shrugged.

"Would you like to show me the inside?" I asked.

"Busy," his only response.

"What?"

"I'm busy."

"Oh, of course. I'm taking your time." But I couldn't stop myself. I kept blathering on. "I'm doing the cotton farming while Ben's gone. I guess he's told you." I stopped. That I had married? It had been in the papers. Maybe they didn't talk about me at all. Why would they?

Jesse looked up at the sun.

"Well, I thought I'd say hello. It's been a long—"

"Yep." He turned away, and I couldn't bear it.

I searched for some trite phrase to show none of this meant much to me, but flashes came over me of another summer's heat and his skin, his mouth. "Don't be a stranger," I said. I wanted to touch him, but that would never, never do. I led Belle to the upping block and grabbed her mane to mount. Jesse made no move to help me. He walked back to the horses.

"If you hear of anyone with a nice litter of puppies, pass it along. Pepper died sometime back. She was getting up in age, you know."

He stopped but didn't turn to face me. Like he was waiting for me to finish—to shut up so he could get back to work.

"Well, then." My voice faltered. I should have never come. Never. But part of the child I used to be let resentment bubble up in my chest. *I could. I could if I wanted to.*

Chapter Forty-nine

By late September, it was done—a bumper year—with cotton selling at unheard of heights. Nathan's expertise had gotten me through, but I took as much credit for it as I could. I had been the one to stay there throughout the summer, had supervised the fertilizing and the weed hoeing. And it had nearly killed me. Letters came from Ben and Edgar filled with bravado, I felt sure, and I dutifully wrote them back, careful not to seem too prideful of my accomplishments. I told Ben it was harder than I'd ever imagined. And it had been. Edgar had thought me ridiculous for taking on the farm. "You're an educated woman, Cora! With a promising career." But he still signed the letter with love and begged me to care for my hands. "You've always had such lovely hands."

I studied my hands—callused, the nails broken. I had taken off my wedding ring to protect it.

I had not seen Jesse. He was like a memory that lingered too close and took up too many of my thoughts. I should have been thinking of Edgar, at least more often than I did. It wasn't that I didn't love him, but it was a different kind of love—a practical kind of love, the respectable kind, the logical kind. Still, with Edgar's furlough home, I had enjoyed the not so respectable, not so logical moments.

The crop came in, and Mama asked me to come stay with her and Nathan until Edgar got home, even though she knew work still had to be done. It seemed never done. I refused, promising to visit more often.

—⁂—

October was a lovely time of year, and toward the end of the second week, the rain began—a godsend at first, a steady light rain that soaked into the soil and replenished the groundwater after an especially dry summer. But it rained on, well after the soil became saturated and run-off filled the creeks. I sat on the porch and watched it, thankful we got the cotton crop in.

Although the farm sat on high ground, roads had become impassable. Boredom affected me more than any consternation about the weather, so I sat on the porch and tried in vain to read. Instead, I watched the rain come down, the rose bush sag with autumn's burst of flowers hanging like spent hopes on the trellised limbs. Maybe the rain would drown the damn bush.

At night, I lay sleepless, listening to the rain. It had ceased to be that comforting background that lulled you to sleep like I'd heard the sea could do or a soft breeze through leaves of trees. It became a distant beat of a kettledrum, ominous and perpetual. The thunder resounded in my belly and rose to my throat.

At the beginning of it all, I set out the copper rain gauge that held five inches and had already emptied it once. Creeks could flood quickly from upstream rains, and Jesse was not 200 yards from the creek. The townspeople still told stories about a deluge back in the 1800's. How much had it rained then? I made up my mind to ride to the hill in the morning to see exactly how far it *had* risen.

Morning came dark, the rain relentless. I threw on a slicker, saddled Belle and tried to stick to high ground. The gumbo soil that produced such good cotton became a mire in heavy rain, and I dismounted several times to keep Belle from sinking hock deep. The view from the hill above Jesse's place revealed a sea of water encroaching on an island of one house and one barn. He was going to have to move the horses out, but he would be too proud to move them to my land.

I rode down.

He was in the loft of the barn restacking grain sacks higher. The pounding of rain on the barn's tin roof drowned out the sound of my footsteps as I led Belle into the barn. It killed me to watch him—his determination. Bullheadedness might be a better word for it. "Hey!" I called. "Hey!"

He didn't look down at me but paused as though I were some memory that passed through his mind and not the reality that stood near him. When he turned and jumped to the floor, his torso flexed and his chest heaved with the exertion. I looked away but yelled. "Move your horses up to my land. I'll help. Belle and I will."

"What?" He pointed at the tin roof. "What?"

I had to move closer. I took off the slicker, shook it and held it before me like a shield as if to ward off the feelings I feared would show.

"We'll move your horses." I pointed toward the hill. "To my land." Closer to him than I had been in years, I wanted to lift the swatch of black hair that stuck to his forehead and smooth it back. "C'mon."

Had there been any other alternative to save his herd, he would've taken it. I saw it in his face. He nodded and moved to saddle his own mount.

The horses huddled and surged and at first refused to move. Stamping their feet and snorting, they finally burst through the gate. The lead mare was a silver grullo that shaded black in the rain, the stripe down her back barely visible and the leg bars obscured by mud. She headed instinctively toward high ground and the others followed. Despite their enthusiasm for freedom, the progress was slow in the mud. Jesse rode alongside to steer them to the elevation of the sandstone-capped hill on our land, and I brought up the rear.

Belle's hind legs sank with each lunge as she tried to keep up with the herd. I considered dismounting but knew I'd be left behind. I stood in the stirrups and lifted myself off her back, but it only seemed to throw her off balance. As I decided to get off and lead her the rest of the way, Belle faltered. Her haunches sank, and I was thrown backward. We were down.

"Oh, God no! Belle! Get up. Get up!" I looked for Jesse, but he had ridden well ahead of me somewhere behind the curtain of rain. "Jesse," I called, but my voice was hardly audible in the downpour. I scrambled to the mare's head and tried to stroke her, but she thrashed in her effort to free herself and became as dangerous as the flood waters.

The rain broke for a moment, and I scanned the hill above me for Jesse. They must have topped the hill to my farm. Slipping and sinking in the mud, I pulled myself to a point where if he were looking, he could see me. He turned back as though he heard me call his name. Scrambling back down to where Belle struggled, I tried to comfort her. "He's coming. He's coming. Shh, be still. Wait for Jesse." I had begun to cry in relief that he would know what to do, but as he reached us, I read something like disapproval on his face.

Belle saw Jesse and ceased her frantic struggle. He approached her from the side and laid his hand on her neck.

"She's glad to know you're here," I said.

"She's exhausted, not glad. It's not as bad as it looks. Her front feet are good. Take off the bridle. We don't want her to get tangled in it. Quick while she's too tired to fight."

I tried to wipe my hands, but I had no clean place left on me. My fingers slid against the mud and the leather, but I finally got the bridle and reins off.

Jesse slipped a rope around the mare's neck and dallied it around the horn of his saddle. He mounted and waited. Moments later, when Belle began to struggle again, Jesse's horse backed, pulling the rope taut.

"C'mon, you got to c'mon!" I smeared my arm across my face to wipe away the rain and tears. "Belle! Please, Belle." But the horse needed no encouragement. She writhed and struggled to pull herself along with the help of the rope, her front feet finding purchase at last. With one great heave, she struggled up onto shallow mud. I buried my face in the muck on her neck and tried to find words to thank Jesse.

"Get your bridle and come on. We'll pony her back, but you'll have to keep from getting stuck yourself. My horse is plumb worn out. Don't think he'd like to rescue another critter today."

The rain began again, streaking the mud down my cheeks and for a moment, Jesse looked down at me with a brief smile—fondness or pity, I couldn't tell which. When we reached the top of the hill, I said, "Stay at my place. It's not safe at yours."

He made an almost indiscernible shake of his head and turned to leave.

"Wait!" I blocked him. "Stay. If it gets any worse, then stay in my barn. Don't be a fool."

He shrugged and rode on.

The next morning, I checked to see if he had come to the barn after all. The horse blankets were hung far more neatly than I had left them. Belle was already eating her hay.

By noon the rain had stopped, the skies gone blue with a shift of the wind from the north.

His horses were gone before sunset the next day.

—⟋⟍—

At dawn a week later, whimpering or some louder sound woke me. I lay there listening. It *was* whimpering from the porch. From my window, I saw nothing. Stumbling down the stairs, I hesitated before opening the door. The puppy, another border collie, wandered about, probably searching for her mama or littermates, but when I stooped to pick her up, she behaved as though I were the only one that mattered. It broke my heart a little, remembering Amazing Grace and Pepper.

With the pup nestled under my chin, I scanned the road, the barn. Nothing. But it had to have been Jesse. I remembered the day when I was a child. Ben and I had gone to town. I had screamed at the Indian with the puppies and cried and accused him of the atrocities of the Choctaw renegades. But I came away with Pepper, my best friend for so many years. The feeling for Jesse that swept over me felt like part gratitude, part heartbreak.

Chapter Fifty

I stood in the post office and read Edgar's letter.

We were bombarded by German aviators six weeks ago, but they missed me. Ha ha. Can't say the same for the flu. But I believe I've got it whipped now. Just a cough hanging on. Good news is I'll be home soon. Seems they don't want me around anymore. Will telegram when I'm stateside.

Your loving husband,

Edgar

I held the letter against my breast. *He's safe. He's coming home.* And Ben will be home someday to take over the farm. Life would get back to normal. Normal. Wasn't that good? Wasn't that what we all wanted?

I walked back to the car and sat there to re-read it. He didn't say when exactly. A month? Six weeks? Our life would go back to its nice little cube—all sides riveted and moored. Back to promising careers in Dallas—or children. City people. I'd join ladies' auxiliaries or the suffragettes. When the war was over. When life went back to its nice little cube.

—∭—

A Model T turned down our road while the pup and I watched from the porch swing. Molly barked as I stood holding her in the crook of my arm and accepted the telegram. Edgar would be home in a week or less it said, depending on the trains. No mention of his health, but surely, the army had cured him. So many had died.

What would it be like to see him again? I did love him and I'd missed him, but I'd heard about how some of the men struggled with memories of the war. Shellshock they called it. He'd need to take it easy for a while and not get straight back to work in Dallas. And the cotton needed to be planted soon. Between Nathan and me, we could supervise the work until Ben got back. Perhaps Edgar would consent to stay at Mama's. She had more than enough room. Yes. That's what I'd suggest. Mama would back me up. I began to feel better. I wouldn't have to leave the farm quite yet.

I'd need to do the best I could with my hair, my skin, *my hands*. Maybe I'd make one quick trip to Dallas for a new dress. Try to look more like the picture I had given Edgar to take with him. In it, I was coiffured, dressed in silk, my skin pale against my black hair and blue eyes. But my hands. Oh, my hands.

—⁂—

We all met the train—Mama, Nathan and I. We stood at the depot and watched it pull up in smoke and steam and clatter. Scanning the passengers, we waited while one after another disembarked. We had almost given up hope when Edgar came into view. Holding tightly to the handrail, he lowered himself onto the platform. He worked at a smile and opened his arms, but I was the one to hold him steady.

When he left for the war he had been so tall and trim, his chin firm and determined. Now the word that came to my mind was *diminished*. The circles under his eyes were like bruises. His chin quivered. Perhaps the stress of the long journey home and his response to seeing me again had undone him.

"Edgar, darling." I tried to keep the distress out of my reaction; I hoped the emotion could be mistaken for joy. "You're home!" The over-brightness of my voice sounded transparent even to me. "Look, Mama! Edgar's finally here. Doesn't he look handsome?"

Nathan stepped to the other side of Edgar and took his arm. "Lucretia's got a home-cooked dinner waiting for you. Thought you'd never get here."

"Nor I, Mr. Cage. Nor I."

I watched him all through dinner, my eyes almost never leaving his face, except when he glanced up and took my hand. I kept a smile on my lips but could hardly bear to look into his eyes. The hard glaze about them seemed to mask some weakness he feared might be exposed.

He coughed only once during the meal, but the tortured bout made Mama gasp at the intensity as if it were a memory she had tried to forget. It was more than either of us wanted to think about.

Edgar and I walked up the stairs together. Halfway to the top, he stopped and gazed up as though the steps might never end, but then he turned to me and smiled in a tepid effort, and we resumed our way. In the room Mama prepared for us, I slid his jacket from him and felt the bones of his shoulders beneath my fingers.

"Oh, Edgar. What have they done to you?" I unbuttoned his shirt and wanted to weep at the sight of his reduced frame. "We'll get you fixed up though." I kissed his throat and helped him with his pajamas, a new pair I'd bought for him at Neiman's. I lay down beside him and waited for sleep to overtake him. He was so exhausted it should have only taken moments, but I slept first, only to be awakened much later at the sound of his cough and the sight of him sitting on the edge of the bed, his pillow stained with sweat.

—⚹—

Edgar and I sat in the wicker chairs on the veranda as Mama had instructed. "I'll bring some tea out. This warm spring air will be good for you, Edgar."

"It *is* pleasant. Seemed like it rained every day over there." He took a deep breath but collapsed into a round of coughing. "Damn cough." He patted my hand and said, "I don't mind a bit if you need to see to the farm. Your mother dotes on me. I think she pretends I'm Ben here at home. Besides, I see how all this bloody farm work suits you."

"Bloody?"

"An endearing little term I picked up from the Brits. You mind?"

"It seems like you've picked up a bit of their accent, too." I mimicked him and laughed. "I don't mind a little Brit if you don't mind a farm girl."

"You won't be a farm girl much longer. Soon as I get better, we'll get back to our lives."

I forced a smile and hoped he wouldn't see the slight twist of bitterness. I could think of no response that would please him, so I sat silently, lulled by the warmth and lethargy of the afternoon. When I looked up again, his chin had sunk down to his chest. I rose quietly and stepped inside.

When Mama saw me with my finger to my lips, she set the teacups down and motioned for me to follow her to her room. "I want to talk to you about Edgar," she said. "Now, I don't want to scare you, but I don't like the sound of his cough. It sounds like, well, it sounds like your father's did, and when I picked up the napkins. . . ." She held out the cloth. It wasn't much, but a red spray scattered across the fabric.

"It can't be." Searching for some trace of doubt, I stared hard into Mama's eyes.

She blinked and looked down for a moment before locking her eyes on mine. "We'll need to see." She straightened, and I saw once again that determination I remembered so well. "Go wash your hands and I'll set you up in the bedroom next to Edgar's. For now, at least, until we get a diagnosis. I'll call Dr. Rogers and see if he can't see Edgar tomorrow."

—⁂—

Edgar begged off the follow-up visit. "He'll tell you, and you can tell me. No use in all of us sitting up there." I accepted his decision, thinking it was exhaustion that made him appear unconcerned. So Mama and I sat very still in the doctor's office, our hands in our laps as he explained in his quiet voice.

"He survived the flu, but it set him up for pulmonary tuberculosis. I'm afraid he's not well prepared to fight it. I recommend a sanatorium. They are better equipped to handle all his needs, and you need to think of yourselves as well. The nearest is in San Angelo, and I can arrange—"

"Not yet." I stood and faced the wall of framed credentials. "I'll need to consult with Edgar. It's not fair to make decisions that he's not a part of." I turned back to Mama. "Besides, my mother here took excellent care of—" I said, nodding toward her as if the doctor didn't know our relationship.

"I've quite a lot of experience at caring for the consumptive patient," she said. "My husband, my late husband, managed several years before he succumbed." She wrung her gloved hands and looked away. "I know the degree of precautions to take."

"We'll talk. We'll let you know," I said. The sudden memory of sitting by Papa's side and singing to him the song he no longer had the breath to sing—*Low, low, breathe and blow, wind of the western sea.* I had willed him to breathe. "Breathe, Papa." Until, of course, he no longer could. "I need to think." I twisted my wedding ring. "I just need—"

Mama stood and embraced me. "Come along, Cora. We'll think of something." And to the doctor, "Thank you. I'm sure Cora and Edgar will reach the right decision."

Chapter Fifty-one

Mama took on most of Edgar's care. She insisted on saying, with some logic, that she'd been exposed to tuberculosis before and never fallen ill, although I knew she was really trying to protect me.

"Go on," she said. "You're needed at the farm. Nathan has to be at the gin nearly all the time. You know I'll take good care of that man of yours. We'll get him through this, but meanwhile, any time you go in that room, I want you wearing these." Handing me a gauze mask and bleached white gloves, she patted my hand and sent me out the door.

Even when I came back in the evenings, I watched as Mama made trip after trip upstairs to see to Edgar. She cooked and carried and cajoled and turned over very few things to me until Nathan said, only partly in jest, that maybe if he himself were sick, he'd get more of her attention.

Despite her efforts and my daily visits, Edgar still immersed himself in the war. He became compulsive about the newspaper reports and insisted that I bring him the Dallas Morning News every day. He pored over the horror stories of the Spanish flu pandemic that had reached the United States and new German offensives to break the Allied deadlock. "Listen, listen to this," he said. "'The German front moved to within 75 miles of Paris. Three heavy Krupp railway guns fired 183 shells on the capital, causing many Parisians to flee.'" He broke into a coughing spell. "Look!" He held the paper up for me to see. "'The initial offensive was so successful that Kaiser Wilhelm II declared March 24th a national holiday.' A damn holiday! Why, if I could get back on my feet—"

"It's poisoning you, Edgar," I said. "Let me read something else to you. I've brought you Robert Barr's book of mysteries. You should love—"

"No, thank you."

"Well then, what about *20,000 Leagues under the Sea?* I've never read it, but I hear—"

"It's not that I don't appreciate what you're doing, Cora. Please believe that." His voice became measured and low as though it were taking everything he had to be civil. "I want to read the paper. That's all I want to read. Stop needling me with your suggestions. I'll let you know when I want to read fiction." He said the word "fiction" as though it were a cartoon, a Pollyanna for real life.

I picked up the books and turned to leave. "I understand."

"It's all right if you don't, you know."

"Yes, Edgar." I shut the door quietly behind me.

—⚜—

The next morning, I found Mama preparing Edgar's breakfast. "Here, Mama, let me do it. I should be the one."

"No, I want to. Besides, you don't know all the preparations for it." She turned and cracked four eggs and began scrambling them.

"I can certainly learn. What in the world is this nasty looking stuff?" I picked up a bottle and stared at the label. "Creosote?"

Mama took it away from me. "This is the pure double-distilled tar of beechwood. If you mix it with whiskey, it's not quite so bad. He's got to have a dram of it three times a day, and he doesn't like it. He probably wouldn't take it from you."

"But he will from you. Is that what you're saying?"

"Well, I just know how to—"

"Let me ask you something. Do you wear a mask and gloves when you go upstairs?"

"Well, no. I think he needs to see a human face, and I never fell victim to the disease all those years with your father so ill. I must be immune."

"But you want me to hide from him—behind the mask and the gloves. You send me out to the farm nearly every day. It's almost as though you couldn't save Papa so you're going to become responsible for curing *my* husband."

"So, am I supposed to let you take the chance of dying too?" She stopped herself. "Maybe he's *not* dying. Maybe we *can* save him. But I am not willing to sacrifice you. You're my child."

"I am not a child, Mama. Despite your very best intentions, you are stripping me of adult responsibility. I'm sorry. I appreciate all you've done. I do, but now let me take care of him. Teach me how." I took the spatula from her and poured the eggs in the skillet. "What else?"

"You're right, you're right."

Softening my voice, I said, "Go get one of your roses. We'll take it up with his breakfast."

When she came back with the rose, she said, "He needs as many eggs as you can get down him a day and at least eight glasses of milk. Steaks. Steaks are good and butter and anything you can think of to put weight on him. He can't fight this as poorly as he is."

I remembered how thin Papa became. I hardly recognized him toward the end.

But Edgar fought the creosote in whiskey. He fought the eggs and milk and steak. He fought me. And then he collapsed in my arms, sobbing. "I'm sorry. I'm sorry."

One evening, I sat with him playing gin rummy. I wore the white cotton gloves Mama gave me for protection, but cards slipped through my fingers and sprayed on the bedside table when I tried to shuffle. After the second game, I put down the cards. "Your parents asked to come down. They are so worried about you."

"Keep them away from here. I can't stand for my mother to see me like this. Tell her I'm getting better. Tell her we'll come visit soon. Oh hell, tell her anything." Slamming the cards to the floor, he tried to catch his breath, and I almost didn't hear him say, "I'd rather have died on the battlefield than like this."

"No, Edgar. You've come home to me. We'll get you well. Mama and me. We'll—"

He was thrust forward as a storm of coughing overtook him. Until he could do it no more. Whatever lodged in his throat stayed there, and I thought he might never breathe again. But at last, with a shuddering attempt, the breath came, leaving him spent and sunken. "You see, darling?" He looked up at me, his eyes bitter and bloodshot.

I shook my head no. Tears fell onto the sheet, and I tried to scrub them out with my glove. "No, I don't see. I don't want to see. I don't have to."

"Imagine instead that you'd received that telegram saying I'd died a war hero, saving my command from utter devastation. That I single-handedly stormed the Krauts before they brought me down. That's the way I wish I had died."

"Was it like this with Papa?" I asked my mother later. "Did he just give up hope?"

"No, I think he believed he'd get better every day. He had you children, at least, to put up a front for."

I felt like I'd been stung. We'd tried hard to avoid having children. At least I had. Searching perhaps for some understanding of myself, I asked, "And you? How did you survive it?" Although I knew. I *knew*.

She turned away quickly to fold the linens, then excused herself and stood briefly in the pantry. "I forgot what I went in there for," she said, laughing a little when she returned empty-handed.

Not waiting for her to think of something to say, I opened the icebox and said, "I'll take him some lemonade."

"Maybe he'll drink it for you. I've had no luck with it. I guess things don't taste the same to him."

But he refused. "Get that maid your mother hired to change these sheets. It's so damn hot, they're soaked through." Then came the remorse. "I'm sorry. It's—"

"It's all right, Edgar. I know—"

"But it's not all right." His voice became a harsh whisper. "And no, you don't know. I hope you never do." He crushed the newspaper in his fist and sank back onto the pillow, his fingers ink-stained, his face sheened with sweat.

"Don't give up like this! You've got to believe you'll get well. Let me help you. Let me get you back on your feet. We'll go back to Dallas. You can go back to work, and we'll buy that lot in Oak Cliff that we looked at. Remember, darling? Neiman's said I could come back to work as soon as Ben got back from the war. We can—"

"Stop it, Cora." He sat up a little straighter. "Hand me a cigarette."

"You can only hold it. I am not lighting it for you. I'm only trying—"

He turned away, but not before I saw tears in his eyes. When he turned back, the tears were gone, but anger reddened his face and for a brief moment, he even looked healthier.

"You want to know the truth, Cora?"

"Of course," I lied. Truth had become such an ugly thing. No. I didn't want to know the truth. Although I couldn't explain it, it seemed my health annoyed him, my energy some deep criticism of his lethargy.

"I don't want you sitting next to me making pathetic attempts at encouragement and sympathy when all I see is pity."

"Why, Edgar. That's not—"

"Yes, it is. If you could only see your face." He put the unlit Camel between his lips. He grimaced—the caricature of dying man. Van Gogh's *Skull of a Skeleton with a Burning Cigarette* flashed in my mind. It had terrified me in an art history book back in college. I tried to block it from my mind.

—⁓—

I trudged up the stairs and tapped on his door. "You awake, Edgar?" And I waited until I heard the rustling of the newspaper. I opened the door and smiled at him.

"Stay there," he said. "You don't need to be here with or without a mask."

"But I want to see you. Speak with you a moment before Mama sends me out to the farm again. She keeps making excuses why Nathan can't do it," I said. "I think she wants you all to herself." I started to step into the room.

"That's not it at all, and you know it. She doesn't want you dying from this any more than I do."

It was the truth, and so I remained silent.

"From now on, please stand at the door," he said. "We can talk well enough from there. I don't need you to see what's become of me. I'm nothing like I used to be. I don't even feel like the same man."

"Edgar—"

"Let me finish. Please respect this one last thing I ask of you—this last kindness." He paused to catch his breath. "Don't look at me. Talk through the door. I'll turn away if you try to come in. Please, Cora. Give me one last dignity."

"But I love you. I want to—"

"You may have loved the man I used to be. Come by and tell me good morning through the door, but let your mother take over the grim details of my care. It won't be long. Please, Cora. This is how I want it. Close the door. If you love me, close the door."

I stood at the door and looked at him. I knew he must feel trapped. There seemed some accusation in his eyes, but maybe it was the fever. If it were I who lay in bed trying to breathe, the air thick, almost congealed and choking, I would want to accuse someone, too. I breathed deeply through my nose and fought off the panic I imagined would result if I could not.

Chapter Fifty-two

The summer wore on—the heat and the cotton fields and the exhaustion. Right and wrong seemed entangled those days. I needed someone I could lean on who would not question my motives. Someone who wasn't dying.

I rode out at dusk, the evening filled with the pulsing of crickets and the soft fall of my mare's hooves on the path I'd worn over the years. Jesse stood in the doorway, watching me as I slipped down from the saddle. Not waiting for him to reject me or ask questions, I walked to him and lay my head on his shoulder. "Please," is all I said.

This time I was thankful for his silence. He didn't speak but lifted me and took me to his bed. When he tried to step away, I pulled him to me. "Just this once." But I knew it would not be just once.

He lay down beside me and held his breath while I unbuttoned his shirt and slipped it off his shoulders. I felt his heartbeat and breathed in the smell of him—the scent reminiscent of horse and hard work. It had been so long since I'd felt this way, since strong arms demanded me. I wanted to tell him that I'd imagined how our life would have been together if I'd chosen differently. If I'd refused Edgar, but Edgar's name never came to my lips. Only *Jesse*.

Nothing else mattered to me. I would take this chance to know again what I only remembered. He pushed back the bodice of my dress until he found my shoulder, my throat. I was lost to it. A window was open, and a night bird called—a whippoorwill. In my mind, for what I was about to do, it became some kind of blessing—absolution.

I woke in the early hours before daylight. I rose quietly and stood at the open window. The only sounds were the twitterings of birds and the barest beginning of a breeze as the eastern sky lightened. Then I felt him behind me—the warmth of him. "You must think me a Jezebel."

"No."

I turned and leaned into him. "He's dying, and I can't save him. He's been a good man. I should have never, never have—"

"What? Come here?"

I nodded against his chest.

"It's not so wrong to ask for comfort."

"I've asked for more than that, Jesse. You know I have. I shouldn't have married him. It was always you. Always."

I stayed through the dawn and returned the next evening. There was no pretense anymore. No one to see. No one to judge. Not yet.

—⁂—

August required me to stay at the farm for longer hours. Harvesting was almost upon us, and workers had to be engaged for dawn-to-dusk hoeing and weeding. Nathan drove out often to make suggestions for the work to be done. But I fantasized about the nights. The nights were filled with Jesse. Despite the heat, I longed for his body. I remembered the first time with him in those cool depths of the creek and yearned for the end of each day when we could go there again. Mornings I spent visiting Edgar at Mama's, although he hardly seemed to want me there. Did he use the pretext of protecting me from his illness or did he really just want to be left alone except for her?

—⁂—

On the last day of August, I freshened up as best I could and came to visit Edgar. Guilt or fear had kept me away for several days. Mama rose quickly when she saw me come through the door and embraced me. She stepped back and clasped my hands in front of her. "He's delirious at times, Cora. He calls me mother and begs me to stay at his bedside. I'm doing what I can to keep the fever down, but. . . ." She shook her head. "The doctor is afraid this is the last of it. Edgar's been coughing up pulmonary tissue. And there are signs of kidney failure. You may want to stay here at night. When the time comes, he will need you near, I'm sure."

"Why on earth would you think that? He turns his head away, so I can barely hear what he's saying, if anything. He doesn't want me to open the door more than a crack when I speak to him." I picked up a cup and slammed it into the kitchen sink. "We are husband and wife and should be going through this together. But he thinks you're the only one who will understand enough to take care of him. He's shut me out."

"It may seem that way. But he's trying to protect you from the contagion and the ugliness. This may be the only way he's able." She paused. "And do you know what he told me?"

"No, Mama, I *don't* know what he told you. How *would* I know?"

"He wanted you to remember how he used to be. Before the war. He wanted to remember you like you were when you first met. Surely, you understand."

"I do, Mama. I feel the same way, but that's not our reality, is it?"

"Sometimes our men need delusion to hang on. And it's up to us to supply it when life gets too hard." Mama's face crumpled suddenly, and all her bravery and stoicism collapsed into old griefs. She seemed suddenly fragile.

"You thought you could save him, didn't you?" I took her face in my hands and kissed her on each cheek. "Bless you. You couldn't save Papa, but you thought you'd found a second chance."

She stood and held onto the back of the chair. "No. He's just a boy who shouldn't have to pay this price for serving his country. Go on up. He wants to see you."

"You mean, talk through the door, don't you?"

"Cora."

"All right, I'm going, but I'm tired of this through-the-door relationship. I'm going in whether he likes it or not."

Mama handed me white gloves and a surgical mask. "Good. I'm proud of you."

When I got to the top of the stairs, I could hardly breathe. Not from exertion but anxiety. What if this was the wrong thing to do? Maybe I *should* protect his delusions even if he had almost no chance of escape from his fate. So wrong to face death as a young man who had his future before him. Surely, he could find someone to blame. And I was as good a choice as anyone. I deserved the wrath.

"Edgar?" I heard the brief shuffle of sheets and then his gravelly voice.

"Yes. Want to talk."

I almost couldn't understand him. He paused for a long time, and I waited. "I want to talk to you, too," I said, "and I'm coming in. I promise to close my eyes if that makes you feel better."

"No!" But the effort in speaking caused an onslaught of coughing.

"Hush, darling." I stepped into the room, felt for the chair near his bed and sat down. "Now, that's better." I kept my eyes lowered but took in the room.

Silent except for the breath that rumbled in his lungs, Edgar lay still. I could barely discern the rise and fall of the covers. He no longer coughed, but the sheet and the wallpaper nearest the bed were blood-sprayed. "I remember how you were on our wedding day or perhaps even more so on our wedding night," I said. "You were so gentle and loving. I'll never forget that night. And the next night and the one after that. What do *you* remember? Was I divine?" I laughed gently. "Not sunburned with callused hands like I have now?" I opened my eyes a little more. Just enough to see in case he did look toward me. But even though he kept his face turned away, I saw a tear slide down the emaciated cheekbone as he nodded. "I remember the first time I saw you when you and Lucy came to meet me at the train," I said. "And how Lucy wouldn't shut up. And how I couldn't think of a thing to say. You were so tall and handsome and—"

He reached for my hand, and I put it where he could find it. "Good times." He tried to clear his throat but strangled with the effort.

"Oh, yes, Edgar, there were lots of—"

"Shh. Let me hold your hand."

I watched his face. It relaxed as though he was reliving the memories. I leaned forward and laid my cheek on our still clasped hands. His breathing was so shallow, I hardly noticed when it ceased.

Chapter Fifty-three

In the picture I kept on my dresser, Ben's summer uniform was pressed and sharp with starch, the high collar emblazoned with US discs, his chest puffed out proudly. That self-assured smile on his face I remembered so well. He had the photograph taken and mailed to the family. It was all we would have of him for the rest of our lives. He died at the battle of Argonne Forest on the fields of France, October, 1918.

Both headstones stood in the Ladonia cemetery, but only one body was laid to rest. Ben's was never recovered. I knew his body lay somewhere in France and I prayed marked with the plain white cross of an unknown soldier, and not torn and twisted in some unimaginable grave. Mama and I returned to the cemetery each week to stand before the marker that stood above Edgar's grave and Ben's empty one. Empty described what we felt more than anything.

Work would have been my salvation, but I could not leave Mama. In 1918, on the eleventh hour of the eleventh day of the eleventh month, a ceasefire came into effect. Even with the war over at last, so many of our men—the youngest and best—never returned, victims of warfare or influenza. Many of those who did come home, appeared vacant and lost even if their bodies were whole. Then there was Edgar. Edgar with his analytical mind, his gentleness. The sting of guilt made his dying even more painful. He trusted me, and I had gone to another man for comfort.

While it seemed impossible that we would never see Ben again, never hear his voice, Mama and I went through the motions of daily life. In the spring when we tried to set out the vegetables and a few annuals, Mama sat staring at the seed packets as if she'd never seen the result of planting. "I feel poisoned," she said, and began to prune the crepe myrtle until only a few branches remained.

I stilled her hands. "I know, Mama. I know."

I controlled my own feelings so tightly that the slightest letdown of my guard loosed all my emotions. A smile became a grimace. A laugh, a sob. And the guilt, oh, the guilt.

Chapter Fifty-four

It had been six months since I'd been with Jesse. I thought maybe I could do without him since my mind and body seemed shut down. I only wanted to work in the farmhouse. I had gathered Ben's clothes and packed them neatly into the trunk upstairs where we kept Annie Laurie's things—the hope chest she'd started when she became engaged. In it were lace camisoles and handkerchiefs wrapped in tissue paper, bed linens, an unfinished quilt and a locket that held a long curl that I had scissored from my hair those many years before. Why would Annie Laurie have kept that? I remembered Mama's words. *Self-mutilation won't assuage grief.* She couldn't have been more right. I could think of nothing that would remedy the heartbreak we all felt, even if I pulled every strand from my head.

I refused to launder Ben's garments before I packed them. I could not bear to wash away the shave-cream smell of him on his white shirt. I pressed it to my face and breathed in, almost believing he could somehow still be there. Not in physical form perhaps, but as some presence I couldn't deny. Annie Laurie had always worn a lavender fragrance, and particularly on early evenings when the mountain laurel bloomed, I could sense both Ben and her. I'd sit on the front porch swing, close my eyes and believe them there in the gentle nudge of the breeze.

Molly was my only company. I never had to explain or pretend to her. With a sympathetic whine, the dog would sit near me and wait for the grief to subside.

—⁂—

April, and the world had come alive again before I admitted I needed Jesse. At least, he would not require anything of me. And that drew me. I walked instead of taking Belle. The last night's shower had stilled the air and softened the dirt road, and morning occupied itself with the business of new life.

Entering his house, his white painted house, I waited for him as he climbed down from the barn loft. Although he didn't immediately come to meet me, I waited, knowing I could not keep from him as I had convinced myself I could in the past months. I watched him. More than appetite that could be satiated, my need in that brief moment heightened into something beyond the physical. I didn't analyze the feeling. It became instinct.

I stood in the dim recesses of his home and waited. He had set the grate with firewood, although it had been a month since he needed it. A massive chifforobe stood against the wall, and the windows were open to the early evening. I scanned the simple, handmade furniture and stacks of books that stood in the corner of the room. Running my hands over the leather-bound volumes—Shakespeare, Charles Dickens, Herodotus—I stared at the works I'd never noticed before. He'd shunned Indian schools pretending not to care about learning, but he'd elevated his own education with hidden endeavor. I sat in the rocker he had probably made and smiled. "You fake," I whispered as I perused the evidence of his determination. What else did I not know about him?

There was almost no sound as his shadow filled the doorway, and he stood there watching me. I thought to rise, but I didn't trust my legs to hold me.

"I heard," he said, his voice low and tender.

He'd said the same thing as he rode behind me on Blackjack when Annie Laurie died. I folded my hands and nodded. I wanted to be stoic, but the kindness in his words undid me. The tears, once they started, were a flood of remorse and despair. I had always tried to be saucy and bold, a façade he probably knew masked my weakest moments. He knelt by me, took my face in his hands and kissed my eyes and my salty cheeks and mouth and never said a word.

Chapter Fifty-five

Perhaps it was the shock of Ben and Edgar's death so close to each other, the strain of getting the cotton planted, but when the nausea began, the tenderness of my breasts and the second month came, but not the blood, I could pretend no longer. No one would believe Edgar could have fathered the child. It had been too long. In Dallas, war widows were abundant. I could go there with an easy enough story to believe, but of course, Mama would know.

God, I'd made the same mistakes she had, and I had condemned her, silently if not in open accusations. Mama ran away from her sin, but there had been no real choice. It wasn't the rocky soil of Douglas County, Missouri. It wasn't the search for good blackland. She had been with child—her sister's husband's.

At least once a week I made myself visit Mama, and each time she grew more dependent on the visits, plying me with pastries and tea, trying to put a pleasant face over her own grief. She'd begun to garden again, and that afternoon I knelt beside her and helped separate the hyacinth bulbs. As I silently troweled the dirt, she studied me from the corner of her eye. Finally, she laid her hand on mine and asked, "What is it? What's troubling you?" She sat back on her heels and waited. "It's something different, isn't it? Not Edgar, not Ben. Something else."

Stabbing furiously at the dirt, I felt the hot sting of tears behind my eyelids and could not answer. Once again, she stilled my hand.

I stumbled to my feet and faced the arbor that was overgrown with roses. "Remember after we crossed the Red River?" I didn't stop for an answer. Of course she remembered. "And you slipped off into the woods alone? I followed you. I worried that you were sick. I never put two and two together until I overheard you tell Nathan that you miscarried his child."

Mama did not stand. With her hands in her lap, she bowed her head and said nothing.

"I know why you toted that rose cutting all the way from Missouri. First Love roses. Not for Papa. For Nathan. That's why."

Without looking up, Mama nodded.

"I hated you for it. I never told your secret to anyone else. But I hated you for it." I drew a deep breath. "But you know what's funny?"

She came to her feet then, pushing up from her knees and brushing the soil from her skirt before she faced me.

"I find myself in exactly the same situation." I laughed at the irony and turned away from her to wait. Moments later I felt her hands on my shoulders. My eyes blurring with tears, I turned to face her and said, "But I rather imagine I won't have the advantage of a miscarriage."

She slapped me. A hard, striking blow that made me reel. "It was a terrible loss, Cora. You have no idea. No idea! How could you say such a thing to me?"

The horror of what I said dawned on me. I hadn't meant it. Why in God's name had I even thought of such a brutal thing to say? "Mama, I'm sorry, I'm so sorry. I don't know why I said it." I covered my cheek. "Please forgive me. You were trying to help, and I turned it into an attack." I staggered, almost collapsing.

She reached for my elbow to steady me but said nothing.

"I'm so scared. And angry. Angry that I let this happen, and I struck out at you."

She slipped her arm around my waist and nodded toward the settee in the garden. "Sit." Clasping my hands in both of hers, she said, "Does he know? This Jesse Birdsong?"

"How did you—?"

"Please, Cora. I've seen it for years. Even when you married Edgar, I knew your whole heart wasn't in it. You thought you were doing the respectable thing. You probably thought I wanted that for you."

"Didn't you, Mama? Didn't you? You've become a lady in the eyes of this town. You had to want me to marry well."

"I loved Nathan." She looked up at the grounds, the Victorian home on Paris Road. "He made all this possible, but he didn't do this for *me*." She laughed quietly. "He doubted himself as a farmer. Men and their egos, you know."

"I don't guess you'll ever tell me about your love affair with Nathan." Despite my own culpability, I couldn't help feeling it tawdry for asking.

"You said once that I married the first boy to come along. And that's not true. Nathan and I were childhood friends. We spent long summer afternoons riding double on his old mare. We swam in ponds, though I would never admit to it then. We used to sit on the porch, the moon and the mockingbird behind us, and talk about God and the heavens, our fears and plans. I sprained my ankle once and although he was barely taller than me, he carried me home. My mother thought we were getting too serious and sent me off to school. I think that's what made my father agree to let me go. I only stayed two years, met your father and came home to announce we were getting married. Best laid plans, and all that." She tried to laugh—a sound full of nostalgia and not much humor. "Oddly familiar behavior, wouldn't you say?"

My brothers' taunts came to mind when I complained about Mama. *You better hush up, you might turn out like her.* How that had infuriated me.

"So, have you and Jesse decided what to do?"

"He doesn't know yet."

"Well, you tell him then."

"You didn't tell Nathan."

"I couldn't. My sister was dying. I couldn't hurt her like that. I had to leave. I had that one chance to come here to East Texas, and I took it."

"But what will people say?" I stood abruptly. "Funny isn't it, how I hated Indians. How I clumped them all together and hated them? But Mr. Birdsong was the kindest man, and despite it all, Jesse Birdsong fascinated me. Ever since I was a child."

"Does he love you?"

"If actions show. He's never said."

"And you? Have you told *him*?"

"I think it's clear, though I've not said the words."

"Well, you and Jesse Birdsong have some talking to do. Times will change if that's what you're worried about. Not right away, but in years to come." She pulled me close. "Why with women's right to vote around the corner, imagine how things will change."

"Hah! Not here in this part of the South."

"Don't be a coward, Cora Allen." She didn't use my married name. "Don't you be too cowardly to stand up for someone you love. Even if it doesn't fit the mold the world carved out for you. I never raised you to be faint-hearted. I seem to recall a valedictory address: 'We must rid ourselves of prejudice toward other races, the Indian and the Negro'. . . something, something. . . . 'It is time to step out of our cocoons of habit and hatred to search our souls.' Sound familiar?"

"You memorized it?"

"From time to time, I looked at the copy you left." Mama smiled. She looked up. "Ah," she said, "here comes Nathan. You go on. And let me know what you all decide. You don't have to run away like I did. You love this young man and you can do whatever you set your mind to."

I pressed my hands in hers and turned away, but not before taking the shears and snipping a cutting from the rose bush. It would grow and it would flourish.

I started to walk past Nathan but stopped to look up at him. "Thank you, Nathan."

In confusion, he looked between Mama and me. "What? What for?"

"For loving my mother." I touched his shoulder. "I hope to be loved like that."

—※—

The days were hot, and the summer sunset washed the fields aglow as though by firelight. I watched him as the sun slid down among the trees. He was still with the horses, making his last check of the evening. Walking among them, he slicked his hands over each animal. If he was speaking to them, I couldn't hear. The sunlight glinted off his bare shoulders and showed them a burnished red. *A red Indian.* That thought made me smile. I wanted to touch him like he touched those horses. His connection with them was so pure and beautiful, his manhood so reassuring, that watching should be enough, but it wouldn't be. Late for the season, a night bird sent out its liquid call and from the darkness came the answer. I would not hear another whippoorwill until April. But I could wait. I gathered my skirt and began a slow walk toward him.

About the author

An award-winning author, Mary Bryan Stafford's first novel, *A Wasp in the Fig Tree,* was the 2015 winner of Best Historical Fiction by Texas Association of Authors. In addition, her credits include a memoir, "Blowout," published in *Women Write about the Southwest,* winner of the Willa Award, and memoir "Epiphany" in *The Noble Generation III.* Her poetry appears multiple times in *The Texas Poetry Calendar.* Seventh generation Daughter of the Republic of Texas, she makes her home in the Texas Hill Country with her husband.

www.marybryanstafford.com

www.ingramcontent.com/pod-product-compliance
Lightning Source LLC
Chambersburg PA
CBHW071550110726
47908CB00007B/2056